the

Teenager

with a

Chameleon
Soul

Cindy McElroy

the Teenager with a Chameleon Soul

Breezy Way Publishing
Thousand Oaks, California

This book is a work of fiction. The names, characters and events in this book are the products of the author's imagination or are used fictitiously. Any similarity to real persons living or dead is coincidental and not intended by the author.

The Teenager with a Chameleon Soul

Published by Breezy Way Publishing
Thousand Oaks, California

ISBN (paperback): 9781642373295
eISBN: 9781642373288

Printed in the United States of America

Contents

Chapter 1
   The Broken Chameleon 9
Chapter 2
   Glenlivet & Giggles.................................25
Chapter 3
   Shots And Shots 37
Chapter 4
   Below Average 46
Chapter 5
   Math Jokes, And, Miss Potential.................56
Chapter 6
   Grams And Jacuzzi Jabbing 69
Chapter 7
   Sup Boarding 79
Chapter 8
   Rummy Cube And Pb & J Sandwiches 92
Chapter 9
   Extra Credit 104

Chapter 10

    Swimming In Chardonnay And Lies 113

Chapter 11

    Treehouse Chatter And Big Fat Cushions 126

Chapter 12

    The Truth Revealed 132

Chapter 13

    Chrysalis And The Kiss From Death 144

Chapter 14

    Black 155

Chapter 15

    Floating..157

Chapter 16

    Dear Grams..161

Chapter 17

    First Day Of Senior Year..............................171

Chapter 18

    Meeting Gracie And Judgey People 181

Chapter 19

    Glenlivet, Rum And Coffee...........................195

Chapter 20

    My Pinky Pillows 210

Chapter 21

    Crazy Talk And Flier 223

Chapter 22

    Old Friends And New 233

Chapter 23

    Dolphins And Pumpkin Necklaces.................240

Chapter 24
    Percentage Against Us....................................247
Chapter 25
    Misunderstandings 262
Chapter 26
    Christmas Decorations 275
Chapter 27
    Christmas Break Catchup...............................291
Chapter 28
    The Nomination And Positive Talk 306
Chapter 29
    Men's Underwear...316
Chapter 30
    The Nomination 326
Chapter 31
    Mysterious Guy In The Baseball Cap 340
Chapter 32
    Future Talk..347
Chapter 33
    The Wrist Kiss...358
Chapter 34
    The Arch Of Love—Take 2 371
Chapter 35
    Everyone Makes Mistakes...............................379
Chapter 36
    Fridge Manuals, Encouragement And Gold....392

Tribute 399
About The Author..401

Chapter 1

THE BROKEN CHAMELEON

A chameleon changes colors according to its environment. It can . . . fit into any group it wants. It can be defensive, predatory, mostly indecisive and has no moral compass." Jay Felix known as Big Fat Mexican, or BFM, holds his sculpted chameleon like a Golden Globe. "But she's mine." It's lovely, a collage of colors: cobalt blue, olive green, canary yellow, scarlet red, hot pink and obsidian black. I imagine the olivegreen color surrounding me in a swirl like the smoke from a freshly lit cigarette.

"Each color represents a side of the chameleon," he adds, shoulders back. BFM has confidence that is unwavering for a guy that is oddly tall and rotund. I know I shouldn't call him Big Fat Mexican but everyone else in my class does. His eyes flash to mine. Boom! Sweat permeates in my Uggs, and my eyes drop to my watermelon-colored pink Kate Spade Summer Edition tote. 'Lipstick, cigarettes, lighter, wallet, cell phone, gum, house and car keys with Dad's fire truck keychain, gum wrappers, Nordstrom Rack receipt, empty travel size Malibu rum bottle, Ray Bans, check, check, check, check, check, check,' I feel for the items in my pink tote. I'm not sure why I'm panicking to find a distraction. It was a quick stare. Did he think I was a chameleon? Was he talking about me? Maybe he knows I'm being called in the office this afternoon to determine my future. Or maybe he's staring at Mr. Cooper's half-eaten bear claw on the desk behind me? My inner self rolls around with laughter at my joke, but my face on the outside is stone cold, in this case, the obsidian black side of the chameleon. Nevertheless, I set my tote down by my feet gripping my desk as I bring my eyes to the front of the room again.

CONCENTRATE SADIE!

The class puts their hands together clapping. I put my hands together, feeling arctic blue eyes on me. Tim watches me as he slips a folded piece of paper to Betsy Grimes sitting at the table behind us. Betsy Grimes is an average-height cute girl with short, yellow hair, pretty chocolate brown eyes and large cantaloupe-sized breasts. She is part of what we call the minions. I move my eyes at the rest of the Pop Crowd. Chase is still adjusting his

Nikon D4S camera lens. Nicolette types her daily food intake on the Macros app on her phone. My eyes rest on the silky ombred haired beauty queen sporting a new merlot-colored baby-doll dress and brown boots to her knees looking like she easily walked out of Maxim.

"What?" her caramel-colored eyes square me. "I'll clap when I'm impressed, Sades." She puts her hands around her mouth like she's holding a pretend megaphone. BFM's cheeks crimson and while I wait for him to stomp his big, fat Reef sandals over to our table, he manages to maintain.

My nose flares up in annoyance at her. I anxiously watch the door for someone to bring in a pass from the office. Tickling my nose allows it to go away for a second. Just like things in life . . . I suppose.

"Why are you itching your nose all the time?" Allison asks. "I'm itching my nose because I have allergies," I say in a matter of fact manner. My tone is not pleasant, but I feel like she deserves it. Last week she called me dumb four times.

"Well, it's getting on my nerves," she retorts. "You're getting on my nerves," Jay mumbles.

I feel my cheeks rise. I'm the closest in proximity to him and probably the only one who heard the joke. He glances in my direction, but I don't look up. Most Mariposa Beach High School groups worship the ground Allison Pratt walks on, but Jay isn't part of any Mariposa Beach High School groups.

Ceramics is the only class that I have with the Pop Crowd. Most days, we lounge in the corner at a rectangular metal table crusted with paint from the previous students. Mr. Cooper's art room encompasses vivid colors like lilac purple, lemon yellow, sky blue and parakeet green painted on each wall. We are up against the parakeet green wall with the obtuse-looking drawing of Albert Einstein with words falling out of his mouth, 'Creativity is the intelligent mind having fun.' The quote reappears in my head every single day and I think to myself I have nothing intelligent in my genetic makeup.

Nonetheless, every day in ceramics Chase's speaker plays music like Drake, Sia and Ed Sheeran as we chew sour Skittles while sharing about our new Alo yoga pants. Most foggy days, I sat next to the open window and breathe in the sharp, salty ocean air. It filters through my lungs and helps me realize I am still alive. And, other days, the ocean view reminds me that I am so small next to it and its entirety.

Today is Show and Tell (The Most Profound Piece and Intellectual Writing Piece) pre-qualifications for the seniors only in Ceramics. After, all the seniors present theirs, Mr. Cooper, an African American spirited hipster artist, allows the juniors to share their practicing pieces. This is the one of the many artsy academic things Mariposa Beach High School does. It's a writing contest accompanied with a ceramic piece. The categories are best essay, story and poem accompanied by a ceramic piece to represent the theme.

Once all is said and done, all the students vote on the best. The prize for each category is a small, gold trophy at graduation and sharing their writing piece with the graduating class. And, it's a good thing to have on college resume. The coolest thing is the winner each year gets their writing piece painted on the Self-Expression Wall near the quad. The Self-Expression Wall is about one hundred feet wide and twenty feet tall, made of wood and sits against Building B. It's full of the winning students' poems, stories and essays from 1973 on.

Public speaking has never been my favorite, and I really have nothing to do with our practicing piece so here I am hoping to be called out again to speak with my counselor about my SAT scores before it's my turn to share.

Mr. Cooper taps Allison's knee-high Hunter boots with his pencil. Allison gasps removing her legs from the table, "Coop, those are brand new Hunters."

Jay's hyper-focused on his rainbow-colored chameleon. However, his left cheek's dimple appears along with a half smile. My eyes shift in his general direction, but he doesn't look up this time.

"Nicolette, Allison, and Sadie," Mr. Cooper says, "you wanted to share yours together?"

Betsy pretends to drop her pencil and slips the paper back to Tim.

What are they writing about?

My sweaty hands grip the metal table again as I pull myself up. I pull my short jean shorts down feeling a sharp pinch on my left butt cheek. My head turns to find a very smokin' hot, very taken Tim Miller smiling broadly. Tim Miller is a tall, fit, dirty blond-haired, bronze skinned, white boy with a Crest commercial smile and piercing, see-through arctic blue eyes sporting his Mariposa Beach baseball jersey and snug Seven blue jeans.

He loves that his girlfriend didn't see that. I mouth 'stop' to him. My Ugg boots, with my feet and body and my lack of self-worth attached, shuffle to the front of the room.

"Sades, stand there, okay. Here we are, a best friend charm," Allison moves us where she wants in the front of the room like we are her little puppets. We carefully place our ceramic pieces together. I secretly roll my eyes. The sting from her mean words overtakes my thoughts.

Allison BE	Nicolette S	Sadie T
FRI	END	S

At cheerleading, Allison explained to me I had the least amount of letters because I was the last one to join the Pop Crowd. Inside, I was a little sad she didn't let me have more letters. Maybe if I had more letters, I'd feel less like taking less breaths of salty ocean air to feel alive.

"Uneven," Jay clears his throat.

My eyes flash to him, and I feel my forehead puckering. Yes, I agree it's 'uneven.' It's a friggin' cyclops. In response, I want to release a gutful of laughter that's been stuck in my belly since Christmas three years ago but hold my stomach to resist. I know my place. We don't laugh at jokes that Allison is the butt of and, besides, uneven or not, love or hate, we are BFFs. Just look at the big ceramic sign in bubbly pink, glittery letters.

"Respect," Tim Miller growls as he shoves the paper from Betsy in the pocket of his jeans.

Jay faces Tim and says louder and growlier than Tim, "I guess when I'm clapping, then you'll know I'm impressed."

Everyone heard that one!

I pop red, sour Skittles into my mouth to keep myself from expressing a noticeable smile. Allison's face is the color of the Skittles. Tim stands up.

"Calm down." Chase sets his phone down and grabs Tim's arm.

"Whoops," Allison swoops by Jay's desk, knocking his chameleon over onto the floor. It breaks into a few pieces.

What is her problem?

The entire room is silent except for Betsy's maniacal laugh. My teeth crack the rest of the Skittles as my heart cracks for Jay. Nicolette nudges me be quiet. I want to help him pick up the broken pieces and tell him 'it's okay,' but I just stand there in the front of the room wanting some sharp, salty ocean breeze and maybe a shot. Jay stands up and accordions his body down to the ground in order to pick up the broken pieces.

"So submit your votes to me for the most profound essay, poem and story," Mr. Cooper says, "And, I can help you remake that chameleon. Allison, detention."

Tim gives Allison a once-over like he wants to giggle. Allison tosses her Modge Pod glue to him. "Sorry Jay . . ." she shrugs. "It was an accident. I'll have my parents call you, Mr. Cooper."

MR. & MRS. DALE PRATT, ATTORNEY AT LAW, WE WILL PROTECT YOU! The words of their commercial appear in my brain.

"We will see about that," Principal Dow says. He's a short, stocky, chiseled man in his forties, with a full head of rust-colored hair and wearing a beige three-piece suit. He puts his hand on Allison's shoulder. His eyes look bloodshot, probably from all the high maintenance parents at this school.

"That's my girl, say sorry," Tim pats her back with one hand and focuses in on Chase's photos as he flips through them.

"Yes, you did say sorry, Al," Nicolette chimes in, picking up her cell phone again. Is she really doing the Macros Diet app again?

"Yep," Betsy mimics at the table behind. She is such a kiss ass.

"Thanks guys." She does her famous and annoying pouty lip. Allison wraps her arms around Tim and he kisses her cheek. Chunks from my protein shake rise into my throat. I count in my head how many steps to the trashcan. Principal Dow pairs off with Mr. Cooper, probably feeling chunks of whatever he had for breakfast, too.

Sophomore year, Al and Tim started dating because, hands down, he was the hottest guy at Mariposa Beach High School. They were a beautiful couple. If they had a baby it would have to be ugly, because their double beauty would cancel each other out. Regardless of the ugly baby, Allison has cheated on Tim several times. Two times that I know of for sure, because I was with her in San Diego with a bottle of Tito's Vodka in the hot tub with the cast from Sweet Valley High School and in Mammoth at Grumpy's Bar with the USC Water Polo team and a game of 'Not It'.

Nicolette and Allison became friends in elementary school. Nicolette is and will always be Allison's main girl. I sometimes think it's because they have the same intelligence level. Or maybe the fact that Nicolette will do whatever she says, even call her own mom a bitch several times on Twitter and eat nothing for ten days so she can fit into a sexy bikini. These are my two best friends, and being part of the Pop Crowd is the only thing I've ever known in Mariposa Beach. They took me in, and I am forever grateful.

"Hey Allegra, the bell rang," Allison waves her hand in my face.

Allegra, like the sinus medicine, now that's funny! At least she has some good jokes. Some for the books too: 'Sadie, you're too skinny; you look homeless in your Uggs.' 'Your mom is a bored housewife. Has she ever worked?' 'Those eyebrows really need shaping; my gardener has a weed whacker.' 'Maybe your dad can work some overtime so you can have clothes like me.' 'I love your boobs; they remind me of coin purses.' 'Do you think you'll marry a firefighter like mommy?' And, the two from last week . . . 'Do you know how to read multi-syllabic words?' 'Do you think you'll ever pass Geometry?'

My mouth moves, but words don't escape. Thoughts spin in my head like a twister, and I don't know what to spit out first.

"God Sades, your crap is everywhere," Nicolette says, as she slides my pink Roxy sweatshirt across the table. It causes my papers to catch wind and fly. "You should get organized."

If my friggin' counselor would call me in . . . She follows Allison out.

"Maybe we could get organized later?" Chase's eyes squint, as he tugs my ponytail.

I stand there speechless and alone, holding my sweatshirt as the twister of words is still spinning over my head. I want to pluck the right words out and put them in my mouth to use but my brain doesn't work that fast.

"Need help?" I feel a presence behind me.

My head tilts back looking at Jay, as he is at least a foot and a half taller. I don't reply. What is my problem with him? We were smiling at each other's jokes five minutes ago.

He sets his grey Billabong backpack down on the table and grabs the three white papers from the floor underneath. "Well, I'm going to help anyway."

I take them. Rather, I grab them.

He nods. "I could help you with that, too," he points to my graded math test.

My cheeks get hot and the heat permeates my entire body.

Friggin Uggs!

"STOP!" my voice octave rises.

"Sorry," he replies, frowning as he places the rest of my papers on the desk.

I watch him pull his backpack over his shoulder and maneuver his way through the desks mumbling some choice words.

There I'm left alone with a backpack, an organizer, a 45 percent on my math test, 55 percent on my English, 53 percent on my science and my self-esteem in the trash. I need a serious shot of something and it's not B12.

School has never been my jam. When I lived in Wisconsin, I attended a private, Christian school from preschool through eighth grade. They had smaller classes—like really small. Three years ago, my dad gave up his career with the Madison Fire Department in Wisconsin where I grew up. He was 35 at the time, the oldest man in the history of LAFD to start the drill tower, basically start over. My dad, Wyatt MacPhearson, basically gave up his career as fire chief to move to

Mariposa Beach to be next to my grandma. His father-in-law passed recently. And, his parents died in the last three years.

My grandma Annie Styles (who I call Grams), parents and I live in a (small for Mariposa Beach) beach bungalow, painted South Hampton blue. It's a perfect, one-story with 2,000 square feet, a modest, wrap-around front porch, lots of tropical greenery, and is a few streets over from the beach. For a while we were fishes out of water, by the ocean. But, it wasn't long until my mom and I started getting our hair and nails done to blend in. Grams bought us nice brand-name clothes. I think the pressure of keeping up with the really elite people of Mariposa Beach got to us. I guess we are all chameleons at some point in life.

But my dad Wyatt, he never caved. He is different from most of the fathers at Mariposa Beach. He is a blue-collar worker and sort of sticks to himself, working on his old Chevy Camaro, SUP boarding, gardening, and working at the fire station.

When I moved to Mariposa Beach, the public high school classes were a lot bigger. I got lost. As much as I tried to make school my jam before and when I met the Pop Crowd, I'd fail. I would take the best notes I could in class or borrow excellent notes from someone else. I made flashcards for every subject, studied like a rock star, and NADA. Freshman year, when I knew I had to have decent grades to be part of the Pop Crowd, I knew I had to figure out a way of passing.

I remember the day I figured out a plan. It was the first test I'd taken at Mariposa Beach High School. My freshman history teacher gave me a condescending look and said "History isn't your subject," as he handed me my history test with 5/20 circled in red pen at the top. It was really embarrassing. I had tears in my eyes and asked to be excused to the bathroom. Chase cornered me after class and said he would help. That evening I went over to his house and we made the first exchange. This was our secret. When I took the tests, I would deliberately get at least 10 percent or so wrong leaving B's in my corner so I wouldn't look so obviously like I was cheating. But, lately, Chase has violated some of the 'favor exchange' rules leaving me to my own wit.

The Pop Crowd doesn't know what happens in my bedroom at night when I try to do homework or study for tests on my own. They don't know the sick stomach feeling I get when graded tests or papers are handed back in class now. They just think I'm a B student.

The twister in my head spits me out to the quad on campus. The quad, the center, most elevated part of the school campus where the pop crowd flutters around like beautiful Monarch butterflies trying to get the nectar from the stamen of the flower. SUCKLE SUCKLE SUCKLE! Mariposa Beach High School is competitive. Every student is always moving towards something and striving for something: lettering in a competitive sport, participating in ASB, winning awards, getting high SAT scores, GPAs and into good colleges. I am just trying to pass.

I plop down; pulling out my homemade chicken, apple and Gorgonzola cheese salad and Diet Coke from the Lunch Box cooler my dad bought me. I graze the chicken and apples as my eyes wonder around at the various groups outside the quad. The buff female softball players drink their energy drinks and throw softball around. Are they really wanna-be models inside? The glasses-wearing Chinese mad scientists work on their extra credit Chemistry experiments. Do they secretly want to stay out past 10 p.m. one night and party like its 1999? My eyes shoot to Orange, a mute, plus size African American girl with horribly dyed orange hair sitting alone reading a book, *My Life In France,* by Julia Child. Sometimes I wish I could be a loner. Does she need a friend? Who is really happy in high school?

"You okay?" My thoughts are interrupted with Tim pulling Al onto his embrace. I look down seeing if my eyes rolled out of their sockets and onto the cement.

"Yeah baby, some people can be bullies." She nestles her head in his neck.

"I gotta get these damn Uggs off," my lips mumble.

"Well it is almost 80 degrees out, Sades." Allison runs her hand across Tim's chest.

I let my mouth open, putting my teeth on display. "True."

Tim locks eyes with mine, smiling back as he runs his nose through Allison's newly ombre'd hair. "Coconut Shampoo, Al."

This was a little sickening—this game between Tim and I.

But, it is the first real smile and eye contact I'd gotten from him in weeks. A smile and eyes locked, I'd prefer. I am not sure why things were so right on with Tim and Al. Just this morning, they were screaming at each other in the parking lot over Tim looking at Betsy Grimes' short skirt. Something within the last hour caused them to be united and it continues to give me a squeezy feeling.

"So, I'm elated to announce that I got a 1500 on my SATs," Allison barks out as we sit there, hands above waist in front of the campus supervisors. "My house-keeper called my mom this morning with the results."

My heart falls to my stomach as I rip off my Uggs. My eyes shoot to Chase. He is relaxed, adjusting the lens on his Nikon D4S.

"It beats mine," Nicolette says, "1444."

"Mine too," Chase says, pointing his camera to her, "1390."

Nicolette pulls her long, black hair over her shoulders, pulls her new white Kate Spade sunglasses onto her head and strikes a pose in her new black romper.

Al pulls the camera, "let me see," and looks at the picture at a closer angle. I pray to God she doesn't flip through to the other pictures.

"Cute, right?" Chase shows Al as Nicolette dwells in the house of compliments.

"Doesn't beat mine," Tim says. "I got a 1510."

Allison hands the camera back to him and lies on Tim's chest. "It's because you are a smartie, hun."

I imagine four sets of eyes rolling on the cement now. "What about you, Sades?" Al asks in her high-pitched, sweet voice as Tim caresses her. With clammy hands, and my heart weighing on my now bare toes, words cannot leave my mouth. "Huh?" Al takes off her sunglasses and kicks my ankle like it's an annoying, barking puppy.

"Ouch." My cheeks are hot. "I . . . I . . . actually never took them."

"Oh that's weird, because you were actually there with Nic and I," Al's goofy grin reveals her pleasure.

Chase looks at me, "Yeah, I do remember your mom coming in the middle. You're only a junior. You could retake them this summer."

Is he throwing me a bone? My watery eyes hide under my pink Ray Bans, the heat hitting me hard. I feel like raging. I have to escape.

Chapter 2

GLENLIVET & GIGGLES

Feel my body twist through the quad to find two Palm trees on the outskirts to wedge myself in between. I search for the ocean air to breath it in, but all I smell is Kapuncha Kung Pao chicken from the food truck behind me, which makes me wonder why I gave up carbs.

I ponder the scene. I know I am bad at school. When I got my SAT scores in the mail last week, it was below basic. My parents and teachers are worried and wanted to meet with my guidance counselor and the school psychologist, who still has not called me in.

Pulling out my mirror, my baby blues appear. Eyes, the window to anyone's soul; Mine: cobalt blue, veiny red and glossy most days.

"Hey." Tim's hand is like a magnet on my back.

"Hey." I close my mirror as my stomach growls and lower the volume on my Pandora that's playing Ani DiFranco's "Untouchable Face." It's one of Grams's favorite songs.

"Was that your stomach?"

"It always growls when I smell their Kung Pao chicken." I pat it.

"You could afford to eat it," he replies. "Or eat in general."

We watch Allison and Nicolette walk off to the fresh fruit stand.

Whew! I need five minutes without her. Behind them, I see Jay Felix eating Dippin' Dots ice cream while walking towards the Spanish style Building C. Dippin Dots, another question as to why I gave up food.

"Here," He fiddles in his blue Patagonia backpack as he watches Betsy Grimes walk by in her short pleated cheerleading uniform with her cantaloupes almost hanging out on display.

"Hi Timmy." She waves at Tim. "Sades."

She disappears off into the same fruit stand line as Allison and Nicolette.

The sun is hot on my back as my eyes land on his. "Wow!

Really?"

"What, she looks good in that." He hands me his water bottle full of freedom. "This will help your hunger."

My eyes squint in response. It isn't my job to correct his player behavior, especially if it's a minion. They are almost at the Pop Crowd status. My lips wrap around the water bottle as I take it in and the alcohol warms my chest. "Awe!"

He watches with desire, then brings himself back down to earth and says, "I didn't know you didn't complete your SATs." He takes the water bottle back, brushing my shoulder with his hand. I inhale his expensive coconut and pear lotion. I am tantalized by it and everything that encompasses Tim Miller.

My eyes widen. "I know. I was a little embarrassed I got so sick." I was full of it. "I was hungover . . . whoa, is that Glenlivet? I feel it in my veins." Can veins even pump any liquid other than blood? God, I am beyond stupid. Why am I trying to hide it?

"Only the best." He smiles doing a 360 panoramic view of the quad. No Allison in sight, so he mutters, "What's up with you and Big Fat Mexican?"

"BFM!" I exclaim, remembering he just fully checked out Betsy Grimes. "...Why does it bother you?"

Why can't I say what I really mean?

"It bothers me because I see you laughing at his jokes or smiling at his jokes. He needs to stay the EFF AWAY FROM YOU. He's bad news," he counts off.

"Why is he bad news?

"He just is…" he snarks.

My body jolts to his reply.

27

Seconds later, I whisper in his ear, "I'll stop laughing at his jokes if you stop looking at Betsy." My breath is minty and drenched with Glenlivet. What am I doing? What am I saying?

"Really." He slides down his sunglasses so I can see his eyes and drags his pointer finger along mine. "And, when I make out with Allison?"

This is twisted. I pull my hand away because I can feel the tension between us.

He takes a breathy sigh and puts on his best Joey Rooney face. "Well, he looks at you all the time. I can tell you think he's funny."

"He means nothing, Tim," I say confidently, adjusting my sunglasses, "like zero. He's got to lose some weight in order to get anyone's attention."

His teeth are on display. It's a smile that literally makes me warm inside, even on the coldest of Mariposa Beach days, "True dat."

"Why did you pinch my ass?"

"I pinched it because I like you," he says in his most honey voice.

"I . . . I," I say fiddling with my hands.

"Tickle your nose, pick your nail polish. Fiddle with your hands." He does the code on his cell. "I know you like me too . . . relax."

He sounds like his old man.

"You can't have your cake and eat it too, Tim."

"Gosh, what a profound statement. Did you come up with that yourself, Sadie?" He scoots away.

I look down now at my freshly painted fuchsia pink nails, trying not to chip the nail polish. I've lost him. If only he thought I was as smart as him maybe he'd give me the time of day.

He pulls my chin up. "I wanted to talk to you without interruption though."

"Okay," I say seriously. "Look at me," he commands. I do.

"Stop wearing those short shorts," he's still hoarse.

Get it together Tim. I look down at very short ripped jean shorts. "Sorry," I say in a breathy voice myself.

"No, most men from eighteen to ninety can't take the way you look in anything you wear, Sades, but I *really* cannot," he's still hoarse.

Chills run north and south of my body. He's got it bad for me. Like worse than what he has for Betsy Grimes, I mean I think.

I stand up, shimmying my butt excessively and purposefully. He backs away. "Girl."

What was up with us anyway? I think we have some major physical chemistry. I giggle uncontrollably. Glenlivet is strong whisky. His cell honks. It's his mom. I sober.

My eyes land on his cell with concern. "Your mom again?" I want him to crawl up in a ball in my lap and cry.

"What now? Is she threatening to leave your dad for the millionth time?" I say matter of factly. I know.

"His secretary is pregnant with his baby . . ." He rolls his eyes and gulps the bottle, "I'm going to be a brother. His secretary is twenty-three . . ." His fists clinch.

Tim's dad is an oncologist. He has saved cancer patients from all over the world. The man has won several awards. He is highly respected within the community, but has completely humiliated his wife and kids by "sticking it into anything sticky," as Tim says.

I maneuver my hand to his bare knee exposed from the ripped jeans. "I'm sorry, Tim."

He places his hand on top. It is warm and the warmth pumps through my veins, even though it's hot today. For a second, I try to make him feel safe.

"So that's why your mom moved out?"

"She's at Malibu Rehab Center . . ." He pretends to say it naturally.

My thumb strokes the front of his hand.

"Tim, you have the rest of this year and then senior year and then you're gone . . . just like your brother," I start to say.

"I know . . . There's Al . . . Please don't say anything . . . she thinks my mom is visiting my brother at school," He releases his hand from mine like it's a hot piece of coal and my heart fills up with blackness.

My body convulses with the mention as I see her and Nicolette within eyeshot. I grab my pink cell phone using it as a prop, "No, never, your business stays with me," I move my body away looking as covert as possible as I see Allison walking up, "but, just to be clear, the one being bullied?" I say sarcastically.

He throws his head back in laughter and finally says, "She's cray cray. Maybe you and me one day."

I feel my face light up like his dad's Man Cave sign. I imagine my eyes look like the small twinkle lights as my heart gives into his vulnerable side. It's a small piece, like the tiny amount of Oreo cookies you get in some ice creams and crave for more. God, I am famished.

"Thanks for babysitting, Sades." Allison appears, applying her Kylie Posie K berry gloss. "By the way, the SATs are offered again. You should look into it, you know, so you can get the Playa de Rico apartment with us."

Playa de Rico lies in the middle of San Diego County. It's a small, private beach city for a melting pot of the young, super trendy, independently wealthy, college and grad students. Allison's parents own a small condo on the beach. The beauty of it is there are seven colleges within earshot of it, and it's known to be a party town. That's where the Pop Crowd plans to extend the legacy.

"I will," I reply half genuinely as I don't know who is winning in the fake nice voice, but the only thing that can recharge me at this moment in time is a swig of my flask.

DRINK, DRINK, DRINK NO PAIN NO GAIN

My chest keeps pounding as I walk into my general education English class. I'm always early. Maybe because lunch is enough time to spend with the Pop Crowd. Orange is the only other one in the class at that time. She doesn't look up from her math book to acknowledge me. She continues to eat caramel and chocolate covered popcorn. Damn food! Maybe Orange hates me for what Allison did. She paid Collette, the girl with Down Syndrome, to pants Orange for whatever reason I was never clear on. I can never forget her ass, nor the devastated look on her face. Orange has always been too quiet, so maybe I don't care. She is trying in math now, because she is reviewing for a chapter test. This sparks my interest because sometimes in class she knows less than I do when called upon. Maybe, I'm panicking from what happened on the quad.

I set my tote down, breathing in a long breath from my navel and out just like my beach yoga instructor says. Orange is still looking down at her math book. I'm not sure why I let Tim tell me I can't wear the shorty shorts or say stuff like 'maybe you and me one day.' I feel bad for them sometimes with their family stuff. At least I have good parents. And, Allison, did she really want me to go to Playa de Rico with them after she sabotaged me with the SAT comment?

I pull out my three-ring notebook and flip to math and write May 3rd at the top in my best pregnant letters. The date seems significant. Is it Katie or Sarah's birthday? What would they think of me if they saw me now? They would think I was the T, ND in a Best Friends ceramic piece, I say to myself sarcastically. I pull out my cell phone to check my text messages. Nothing from Grams. She must be resting. I pull out my calendar on my phone to see about the birthday. It might be nice to call. I never visited like I said I would. I stopped calling three years ago. People go separate ways.

A picture of my old friends from Wisconsin pops up from three years ago on my Facebook. I chuckle aloud. Orange's head is still down. It was a friggin' farm girl advertisement if I'd ever seen one. I forgot I'd taken it right before I moved to Mariposa Beach. We are sitting on a hay bale all wearing jean overalls with flannel shirts underneath. I remember it was spring of eighth grade because we were at the country music festival. We were three different shades of extremely white with freckles and long blond, strawberry blond and brunette braids in our hair. I had braces and I hated braces, but I was smiling huge, because number one, I loved going to the country music festival with my friends. We would get berry shakes. And, number two, Grams had texted me to "smile big while you still have teeth" once when I texted her "I want these braces off." My eyes squint at the tiny gold choker cross around my neck and the giant knot in my stomach sloshes around.

I scroll to the picture of Allison Pratt, Nicolette Tate and I at the beach a year later. We are standing on the beach wearing our scrunch bikini bottoms. My dad thought he got rid of mine but he didn't. Our blond, ombred, and brunette hair was long on our sun-kissed backs as we turned our heads so you could see a quick side view of our faces. I was not smiling big, had my braces off. The gold cross choker was forming cobwebs in my jewelry box.

My fingers expand the calendar on my iPhone with my pointer finger still counting thirteen days left of my junior year and then 180 for senior year. The sophomores and freshmen file into our math class. I realize Orange and I are the only juniors in here. Oh, and Tommy Baker, but he got expelled. Principal Dow walks in with Jay following behind him. Jay takes a seat next to me wearing jeans and a black shirt that says, 'SUP.' I pull my canary colored rose gold ring off my middle finger and slide it back on.

"Hi," Principal Dow says, holding a walkie-talkie in his hand. "Mrs. Flame went home sick, so I will be sitting in to proctor the English test."

NO!

"I want Jay Felix to share something really quick about the ROTC class. Take it away." He sits behind the teacher desk, turning the volume down on the people talking over the walkie-talkie.

Jay uses his nonexistent inner stomach muscles and a hand to push off the desk. This guy is going to tell us about ROTC? You've got to walk the walk, BFM. He is tall and round like the six-foot plum tree we had in our backyard in Wisconsin. I guess he has lost a little bit of weight from the beginning of school. Do I really care? His face is cute: oval shaped head, shaved brown hair, big, white smile, BIG rosy colored cheeks with dimples, a ski slope nose and nice, puffy strawberry-colored lips.

"So, junior year, I couldn't believe I let myself get this big so I decided to do something irregular from my normal routine of SUP boarding, studying, and hanging with my family," he starts.

My hand fists and I bring it up to my mouth, which makes a low grunting nasal noise. Orange looks at me.

"MacPhearson," Principal Dow mumbles.

Jay cocks his head and his eyes widen at me. "I decided to start ROTC, which stands for Reserve Officer Training Corps. We do workouts like run, swim, lift weights and senior year, we will be doing an obstacle course . . . to help prepare us for the Navy, Army, Marines or whatever military branch . . ."

Next thing I know my body is shaking with laughter but no noise escapes. Is the Glenlivet finally hitting me?"

Jay watches me as he continues, "I've lost thirty pounds doing the ROTC regiment, so I encourage you to GET HARD!"

He said that on purpose.

My laughter is out in the public like a new press release.

Principal Dow stands up and points to the door. "Go outside now."

His breath smells like coffee and Bailey's.

I grab my cell and blast out of the door letting out a roar of laughter.

My body sways to the music playing in my head as I pace back and forth through the hallway in front of my class. Jay busts out of the classroom door and walks off in the opposite direction.

"GET HARD!" I yell after him.

He raises his middle finger.

I giggle.

"Civilized now?" Principal Dow motions for me to come back inside.

My cheeks feel hot as I enter the class. "Yes, sorry."

Principal Dow hands out the English tests and collapses in the teacher chair typing profusely on his laptop.

Maybe he will be more distracted than I thought. I pull out my pen and pretend like I'm reading the first question and furrow my brows in order to portray that I'm actually thinking. I casually look at my pinky nail for the answer to number one. It's B. Last night I painted the answers to the test using a tiny fine point pen in the petals of the flowers on my nails. Something I learned from YouTube.

Principal Dow's eyes shift to me as I watch him in the corner of my eye. My heart drops. He looks back down at his computer. I look at the next few flower petals. C, B and B. I jot the answers down. My hands are sweaty as I precede to the next few questions. Some people have already turned their tests in. I crack my knuckles. He watches me again. The classroom phone rings as he stands up facing the other way to answer it. Thank God. I fill in the rest of the answers and hand him the test. The bell sounds and I'm out the door.

Chapter 3

SHOTS AND SHOTS

I see BFM's body galumph down the main hallway where the highway of students scurries to get out of school. He goes against the grain of the average Mariposa High School student where most are skinny, chiseled, stylin' and brand named out.

"Yo Sades," Nicolette nudges me into me holding her cell phone in front of her face. "I'm taking a survey for Nic's Chic Blog: Pilates, Yoga, Soul Cycling or Parkour."

"Yoga," I respond.

"Soul Cycling, for shizzle," Betsy pops her head in. "But so expensive."

"Sooooo old school, Sades, and Bets, I never asked you." Her eyes roll under her black-rimmed prescription glasses, which she hardly wore, but looked good today.

Betsy steps back and talks to some minions on the side where she belongs.

"Pressed juice at Juice Farm: Cherry Treat, Dragon fruit A Go Go, Pineapple Sunrise or Acai You Silly," Nic asks.

"Cherry Treat?" I question.

"Sadie?" Her pickle-colored eyes glare at me. "I'm bored with your answers."

"What! I don't buy their juice," I watch Orange walk by with her Beatz headphones on and wonder what she's listening to.

"Or eat," she suggests.

"We all never eat," I encourage.

"Tell my mom that." She turns her body away from me. "She thinks I eat all the time."

"Nic," I take her shoulder and she turns away. She doesn't want to talk about it. I get it. Her mom writes a famous Macro diet blog. A lot of people in Mariposa Beach follow it.

In the corner of my eye, I see Tim gaping at me. I'm surrounded with my friends from the Pop Crowd so my nose gets higher and my voice escalates.

"Why were you outside your English class?" Allison asks, arms folded.

I tell them the story of BFM and ROTC.

"How funny!" Al claps, "If that guy ever joins the Navy, I'd be scared for our country . . . Let me tell you what happened in my English class today . . ." She puffs her chest.

"Okay and then my survey . . ." Nic slips her cell in her back pocket and gives her eyes to Al.

Nerds pretend to do math as she stands there, animatedly talking about how her math teacher wants to live in Mariposa Beach. Underclassmen jocks salivate at her. All the girls standing there wanted to be her. Tim Miller can't take his eyes off of her. I didn't blame anyone for it. She is absolutely stunning with her perfectly tall, slender, big-breasted body and long ombre'd hair with high cheek bones, caramel colored eyes, button nose and beautiful pink lips. And, it's not only that, she has an X-factor.

"Then I say to Ms. Ames, you're cute, you should find someone here," she pulls out her husky laugh, "because there are plenty of plump eligible bachelors, right? I mean Dr. Ford."

Nicolette cowers a little changing the subject. "Ten words to describe your Mariposa Beach High School experience?"

"Plump?" I question. "Did you say that to Ms. Ames?" "No!" she responds in one of her many bitchy voices. "Well, Ms. Ames has potential. It was like when you arrived from Wisconsin, Sadie. Ten words to describe Sadie: pale, freckles, glasses, light brown hair, naïve, Christian, homebody, no fashion sense, braces and let's see totally cool, oh, you know I love you Sadie."

My high school experience is like the Dolce & Gabbana of high school experiences and clearly it's because of Allison.

"If I had to describe it in ten words or less . . ." I read some of the shirts the minions are wearing and add some thoughts of my own. "Glitter, hickeys, flasks, cigs, tan, fashion, makeup, acrylics, beach and boys . . ." I pretend to drop the mic, "And, I'm out."

Chase pretends to pick up a pretend mic and says, "Late!" as he brushes one hand through his long, slicked back, charcoal black hair.

The minions fan themselves because anything Chase Bynes does is hot.

Chase wraps his arm around my waist, "Come over. I have some good stuff. Just follow me."

"My parents and Grams are at UCLA late today so they won't miss me," I say. Next thing I know I'm blasting Ed Sheeran's "Shape of You" in my two-door white Jeep following Chase in his red Audi Sport down the spiral street to the main Pacific Coast Highway. The palm trees, the outliers of the highway whistle as the winds trickle through. I take in the slightly fishy smell as I drive past the port and look at the construction workers as they put up the sign to the new Poke No Jokey take out joint. My laughter continues.

"I need a coffee from Java," I say aloud, "but I will get lost if I don't follow Chase." I crank up the next tune, Kendrick Lamar's "Humble," and enter the onramp of Shell Highway.

We live in a very quaint but classic beach city called Mariposa Beach. It is between Malibu and Santa Barbara and the sunsets are amazing. There is one elementary school, one junior high and one high school—all public and top notch due to taxpayer money and donations. Main street encompasses a few select designer stores in Old Spanish style settings beautifully decorated with blue and white floral Spanish tiles, antique water fountains, bronze statues of butterflies, dolphins and pelicans. Mariposa Beach has colored twinkle lights and ever-changing flower beds for every season.

Main Street held small stores like Alo, Spiritual Gangster, and St. Laurent. Once a month, a pop-up clothing store would filter in so the people of Mariposa Beach could get anything at arms reach. There were a few mom and pop restaurants like Java Coffee, Lunch Box Sandwiches and Juice Farm. Then some trendy ones like Sprinkles, Dunkin Donuts and Paul Martin's Steakhouse. None of which are in Madison, Wisconsin.

On the other hand, Mariposa Beach can feel nauseating at times with the MB Hotel, Club and Resort that was an over decorated, peach colored, posh hotel with floral Spanish tiles and big Palm trees caddy corner to the marina. The perfectly manicured parents meander in and out playing golf, tennis, water sports and schmoozing. At this point, I'm unsure what is more suffocating, the smallness of the Mariposa Beach, California or Madison, Wisconsin.

Thirty minutes later, I find myself in Chase's friend's posh three-bedroom apartment in the city of Malibu. This is where Chase keeps his art gallery, parties second identity. When Chase is here, he is himself. He is

Chasey. He pulls off this gray V-neck T-shirt and messes up his perfect hair, letting a cigarette hang off his lips.

I open the door and slip off my Havaianas sandals acclimating to his apartment full of extra large beanbags, love seats, IKEA furniture and breathtaking pictures.

Every single birthday, holiday, or special day in life in Mariposa Beach has been turned into a party and captured in a photograph by Chasey.

Picture 1 entitled: 'Back to School Bash: Circular Style' is Allison, Nicolette and me in baby pink, white and baby blue bikinis giggling and floating in a million beach balls and bubbles on the beach.

Picture 2: 'Don't Wear White After Labor Day Party' is a picture of a white backdrop and just me in a short, white, low-cut dress, sitting Indian style and biting into a red, juicy strawberry.

"Stunning . . ." he says, holding two glasses of wine. I take the wine glass and sip it.

"Awe, that's good."

"I know." He flails his arms. "I stole it from my parents' wine fridge. Pinot Grigio."

I giggle at him flailing my arms.

I look at every picture. I'm in all of them. He wraps his arms around me kissing my shoulder. I sink into his warm embrace. It's familiar.

"Where's Johnny?" I cradle his arm with my hand.

"He's at work," he rests his head on my shoulder.

"Okay, well, what stuff did you have in mind?" I break the embrace.

"Strip." He points to the copy of the next Math tests, English test, and History test. "The person sneaking into Principal Dow's office is getting expensive."

I pick up the tests and read the answer sheets of all three. "Chase, I don't want you to get in trouble."

"Hey, I need them, too." He pulls his long Vendetta Mask-pendant necklace off. "Besides, I wouldn't be able to find a girl as beautiful as you for free."

I shove them in pink tote. "What am I wearing today?"

My thoughts race . . . I knew Chase was getting the answer keys somewhere but I didn't know he was paying someone.

He throws me a black bikini triangle top with a cheeky black bottom.

"Dude, these are bold," I say, pulling off my shorts, tank top, and lingerie in front of him and slipping on the bikini.

He stares at me and smiles. "How bad do you want the test answers?"

"Chasey?" I protest.

He adjusts his camera lens. "As always, I promise no nude shots. It'll be side shots only, not your full cheeks." He points behind him to a snow scene backdrop and says, "slip on your Uggs."

I sip my wine, letting it settle in my veins as it helps with the angst and fear.

"To the left . . . like to the right . . . puckered lips . . . good job, baby," he screams with excitement hands flailing, "GOD, YOU'RE BEAUTIFUL!"

I'm giggly from the wine. If only Chase could see himself in action maybe he wouldn't be so scared to tell his dad. This goes on for a solid hour.

"Shit, Johnny is home." He motions for me, "You gotta go."

I grab my clothes and I'm out the back door like Wednesday's trash bag. "Bye."

"Bye, Sades." He kisses my cheek. "Thanks."

I run barefoot to my Jeep down the way, so I can be out of eyeshot of Johnny. I'm always accommodating people. I'm wearing the bikini only. My dad can't see me in this. Some young college guys drive by in a BMW and whistle at me.

"Ew," I squeal as I slap the air.

My eyes feel heavy like I want to sleep. Maybe if I lay my head down on the headrest. I catch a glimpse of myself in the rearview mirror.

I mumble, "I look like a poster child of what not to do." My long, blond hair is in a messy bun, my mascara is smeared and my lips are red. "Chase should capture this."

I see the guys turn around in their BMW. A proverbial red flag is lifted in my mind so I throw my jean shorts on as quickly as possible and start my Jeep, grabbing my white tank top.

"Hey," a tall, fit, good looking brown-haired guy with full tatted sleeve of a tiger opens the door. "Do you know where I could buy some…"

'Drugs,' I finish the thought in my head.

There are three other guys in the BMW as well as a girl who looks really young.

"No." I pull the gear in drive. I shouldn't drive. This goes against everything I was taught from my father and school.

"Awe, come on, you're smokin' and we all want to have a little fun." He takes two steps closer.

My eyes focus on the road and I slam my foot on the gas. "Dear Jesus, please take the wheel."

Chapter 4

BELOW AVERAGE

The next day, I dig in my purple Coach tote bag for my cell phone, chipping my freshly manicured black nails. "Crappy, my nails," I say in the privacy of my own waiting room outside the main offices the Mariposa Beach High School. I sit on a wooden bench with pretty white and purple Orchids hanging in small baskets. My cell read 12:30 p.m. Update: No text messages in thirty minutes. I had to return to fifth period in thirty minutes. I know my meeting with the administrators has something to do with my SAT scores. My legs shake so badly I knock my water bottle on the ground.

"Sadie," A long-bearded gentleman pops his head out, narrowing his eyes. He has been at Mariposa Beach High School for fourteen years. Students think he started growing his beard when he started. He guides me in his small office next to Principal Dow's. It's a small box, colorless and smells like cigar smoke. The wood shelves are full of stacks of books and about a hundred coffee mugs. All this guy does is work, read, drink coffee and smoke. Gross!

"Hi Dr. Plumb," I slip the water bottle back in my tote. Did you do it in the library with the wrench? I laugh at my own internal joke. I need to ease my anxiety a little.

"Hi," he replies shortly. "I'm the school psychologist on campus. The school counselor is unable to join us. Come in, take a seat." He points to the ugly polyester chair across from him. "Principal Dow will be taking notes. Your parents will be here, too, in a minute."

"Hi Sadie," Principal Dow opens a window as he yawns. "Excuse me . . . late night with the family."

"That's okay." My legs are still shaking.

My parents walk in. My dad tugs on his red and white flannel long sleeve while my mom flattens down her new, red Tory Burch slacks. She is long ways from the flannel shirts and jean overalls she wore in Wisconsin.

"Hi." My voice is small.

"Hi, sweetie." My dad kisses my forehead. I wipe it off.

"Oh, are you rubbing that in?" My dad smiles. It's his eternal joke.

I'm annoyed.

Dr. Plumb smiles at the exchange and folds his hands promptly on his lap. "We wanted to talk to you about your SAT scores. I'm just really concerned because they are below average for your grade level and GPA," He passes me the test scores.

"I was nervous." My thumbs rub together. "Plus, I wasn't feeling good."

My parents' eyes are on me and finally my mom says, "She was getting over something. However, she did complete them." "You need to get higher than a 1300 to get into any California University," Dr. Plumb says flatly, "A 900 won't cut it."

Principal Dow clears his voice, "San Diego University is the college of choice?" "That's still the plan . . . with Allison and Nicolette?" My mom looks at me while adjusting her gold chain with a fireman badge charm.

"Yeah." I sound matter-of-fact, although, slightly hesitant in my head.

My eyes zero in on the test results looking at the two bars, one of which showed the average for my age level the other was my actual test score: BELOW AVERAGE. My burritoless bowl makes its way up my throat.

"We might be thinking of other colleges, too," my dad says firmly, "like Malibu JC."

I try to spit out words in a rebuttal, but then my mom interjects. "Can we see fliers for some up here and some down in San Diego?" My mom puts her hand on my dad's arm.

"Okay, what junior colleges are down in the San Diego area?" he caves.

Dr. Plumb swivels his chair around to the fliers of the junior colleges and colleges behind him.

"There are quite a few . . ." Principal Dow interjects.

"Thank you," my dad takes the fliers, narrowing me in the eyes.

"Sadie, the chances of you getting into SDU are slim. Maybe you can try really hard one year at a junior college and then apply," Dr. Plumb suggests.

The words felt like a butcher chopping my heart in half.

Could he be any more frank? My hands are slimy.

"What about my GPA, it's a 3.1. Doesn't that count for something?" I ask.

Mrs. Flame, my bitchy English teacher walks in. "Sorry I'm late. I had to get my students started on a test. Hi, Mr. and Mrs. MacPhearson, Sadie."

Is Freddie the maintenance guy going to join us as well?

Thoughts shuffle in my head.

My parents exchange handshakes with Mrs. Flame.

Principal Dow catches her up by reading the typed notes thus far.

"Well, it looks to me like the last three papers you have written show below average skills for your grade level. Here's an example of an up to par essay, and here is yours. The topic was a time where you decided the path you were taking wasn't a good one." Mrs. Flame hands me the paper.

My eyes zero in on the last name Felix.

Water almost spews out of my eyes. My mom recognizes it and puts her hand on my knee.

"Sadie . . ." Mrs. Flame sits at the edge of her chair like she's ready to attack me.

"Yes," I belt out.

She turns her body towards me. "We, meaning all your teachers and I are concerned about your work and confidence level here. Have you ever been evaluated for a Learning Disability?"

I shake my head, no. A Learning Disability?

"Okay, Nancy, I'll ask her those questions?" Dr. Plumb says gruffly, tugging on his beard.

Mrs. Flame sits back in her chair, nostrils flared, mouth shut. Every teacher at Mariposa Beach High School is super passionate.

"Do you feel like words or maybe new concepts are hard?" Dr. Plumb asks.

I sniffle. "Like every math concept."

"Do you have a hard time taking tests? Notes in class? Verbal lectures?" He asks more questions.

My head bobs.

"I see," he glances at the paper with a large 'transcripts' sign. "Your grades are Bs and one C in Math and, as we discussed, your SAT scores are low. What were you planning to do career-wise?"

My mouth feels like it is sewn shut.

My mom jumps in. "Well, she loves fashion and makeup." "That's great!" They say in unison like I pooped on the potty for the first time.

"She's going to college first," my dad says flatly.

Mrs. Flame has to add her own ideas. "Well, I wanted to tell you that I'm concerned about your writing and test-taking abilities," she says. "You seem to get all B's on the multiple choice tests, but some of the essays aren't up to par." She shows a lopsided grin.

It's because I have to come up with the material on my own.

Maybe Principal Dow feels the tension rising and feels the ping pong ball discussion going back and forth, so he says, "We could open a case-study to assess for a learning disability."

"What the . . ." I say.

Dr. Plumb looks at me, "If you are found to have a learning disability, you could receive help with your writing, and some classroom accommodations for tests," he says.

I look down at the three papers I had written for Mrs. Flame's class.

"I know this is a public high school but it's one of the best in California and our special education team is top notch," Mrs. Flame adds, as my parents nod.

My body is numb. I am speechless. They cannot find out my secret.

My mom puts her hand on mine, "Do you really think she has a learning disability?"

"I agree," my dad interjects. "I mean she's seventeen. How did she get by with the past twelve years being in the school system?"

"There isn't any rhyme or reason," Dr. Plumb says frankly to my dad. "I mean she was in a private school in Wisconsin with extra help for so long and then once high school hits, it's hard for teachers to zero in on that."

"We may have higher education standards . . ." Mrs. Flame starts and then stops as she sees my dad's reaction.

He looks flushed as he loosens the top button of his button-down shirt. I know my dad wants Mrs. Flame to exit stage right. "Mr. and Mrs. MacPhearson, I have been a school psychologist for thirty years, and I have found that many times, students make it through portions of their educational career without showing any signs of disability. There's no rhyme or reason to us evaluating kids. When the material becomes more difficult, it becomes apparent that they qualify for Special Education. Some get evaluated when they're young and some when they're older."

My dad unbuttons two more buttons.

"Plus," Dr. Plumb says, "she went to a private school with no special education resources."

I sit still as the tears run down my cheeks. Everyone stops talking for a second.

"What will it look like if she's evaluated and does qualify for special education?" my mom finally asks.

"She would have an IEP, which is an Individualized Education Plan, that will probably put her in Standard classes with a more remedial type learning, smaller class sizes and plenty of classroom accommodations, for instance, allowing her more time for tests, another student to take notes or a copy of teacher's notes, among other things. We will have to pinpoint the severity of the disability." Dr. Plumb pauses as he looks at me.

"My life will be turned upside down," I talk softly through my tears. "I would be in special education classes."

"Not all standard classes have special education students. But, yes, all your classes next year will be changed aside from cheer," Principal Dow says sweetly.

"I know a social life means a lot in high school, Sadie, but, you need help academically," Mrs. Flame says outright. "You will drown in college or any basic trade school for fashion, if that's your choice."

"This assessing? How long? Where?" my mom asks point blank. I think my dad is done with the convo.

"We will pull her from lunch or nutrition or possibly Ceramics," Dr. Plumb suggests.

"Well, I think I'm fine." I stand up and dust off the proverbial dirt. "And, by the way . . . you guys think you're the shit out here and standards are higher, well, screw you! And, peace out!" I raise two bunny ears, grab my purse and bust out the door.

"Sadie Lynn!" My dad takes my arm. "That is no way to speak to adults."

I pull my arm away.

"It's okay, Sadie, go back to fifth period," I hear Principal Dow say. "We'll talk to your parents and get back to you."

Tears streak down my face as my black, low-heeled sandals click on the pavement across campus and head to the bathroom. I need a shot. I open my tote and grab the water bottle full of vanilla flavored vodka. I open it and pour it into the little Diet Coke I had left from my drink at lunch. Sitting in the bathroom stall sniffling, sipping, thinking and praying, the little red anger devil image I have in my head has slightly subsided.

Before I moved to Mariposa Beach, my parents sent me to a private, Christian school in Wisconsin. This was another thing Grams paid for. My parents believed I needed the Christian foundation, which was absolutely correct. However, this is my rebellion stage where all morals go out the window and I mean literally chunks of rebellion have gone out the window.

Back in my private, Christian school, I was always put in the low group at school. My teachers would always do a winky wink to the parent volunteer. The parent volunteer would smile, nod and they would exchange some words like 'I always thought she was a little slow.'

That was not even the beginning of my humiliation. I was always in the low group from kindergarten to sixth grade. ALWAYS! I would always do the worst on tests and getting new concepts. In fact, by the time the teacher started a new concept I would finally get the previous one. I had trouble with reading comprehension and understanding math word problems. In fact, my old Wisconsin friends Katie and Sarah would say on the yard, 'why'd you get a D on the Math Packet. It was so easy.' 'Why'd you get the wrong answer if you used the calculator and I didn't even use one?' When I had the chance to move somewhere new, I was happy no one really knew my intelligence level and I could continue to fake it.

Chapter 5

MATH JOKES, AND,
MISS POTENTIAL

I smell cigarette smoke, so I wipe my tears and unlock the bathroom door. I see Orange. She's dressed in ripped jeans and a long sleeveless shirt that says Alabama Shakes. I want to tell her I like that band, too. She's actually kind of pretty with the dark chocolate colored skin and eyes. She gives me sad looking eyes.

"Can I bum one of those?" I point to her Marlboro Lights on the counter.

She takes a long hit and blows it out in my face handing me one without speaking. I put it in my mouth and she lights the end.

"Have a nice day, Orange," my voice cracks. She giggles and walks into a bathroom stall.

I take the long way to my fifth period class to make sure my eyes are dry, the vodka drink is in my system and the bottle is in the trash before I step foot into the class. My sunglasses slip into my purse and my body slides next to Tim in Ceramics. I take a deep breath. Thank God Mr. Cooper was in the middle of a how to mold a Ceramics piece. I can't believe what those jack-asses had to say anyways. They had absolutely no sense of tact. They were underpaid, overeducated, dressed in Kohl's professional clothing line, still paying student loans, cheated by the system and education, going down the drain, negative people. They are not going to ruin my life by assessing me for a learning disability. I. AM. FINE. Then again, the classroom accommodations of someone else taking notes sounds like a sailboat ride.

"Why does Orange not speak?" I ask Tim. I change the subject in my head because I need to maintain stature.

"I don't know," Tim says as he rests his chin on my shoulder. He's only doing this because Allison is currently missing from fifth period.

I push him off. "Does she?"

"I don't know but her mom's new workout line for Stretch is absolutely breathtaking," Nic shows me images on her cell phone of the beautiful colors—orange, green and pink on the crop top tank tops and Yoga pants with three hearts on each leg. "Chantel Robbins is her name . . . you have to have the bod to wear the new line."

"You have the body, Nic," I scroll down the images of the models on her phone.

Al snorts, appearing out of nowhere. I smack her shoulder.

"Chantel Robbins, an uber Christian, has the heart for special needs children," Allison glares at me, "Maybe Orange is mute."

"Or maybe she doesn't speak to us because you paid Collette, the girl with Down's Syndrome, to pull her pants down," I say.

I instantly regret saying it. My heart rattles in my chest. Her face is the color of the red Skittles again or the little red devil image in my mind. I'm not sure which one is darker. I try to breathe in the clear ocean breeze before I start to hyperventilate.

"True, Sadie," Allison breathes in mechanically like she does. Maybe she learned it from therapy. She breathes out and says, "but Orange has kicked so many innocent girls' asses, she deserved it."

'Who?' I ask myself. I drop the topic. I have bigger fish to fry mentally. I pull my hair back in a ponytail, reposition myself in my swivel chair, scraping the sides of my new sculpture, a wine glass, and wonder where my comic relief is today. Isn't he a big fan of being at school because he is such the exemplary scholar . . . with all the effin' perfect essays???

"Hi Sadie," Betsy comes up to me and whispers.

I nod, giving her permission to speak, but I don't look up from creating.

"I just wanted to tell you, my younger sister graded your Geometry quiz and you got a 3/10." She had been the one grading mine in Period 4 Geometry.

I close my eyes praying they didn't hear that.

I need to have a serious talk with Chase for a bogus answer sheet before the day was over.

"3/10! Isn't this the second time you've taken Geometry?" Allison walks in, "I think I completed that Freshman . . . or wait . . . in eighth grade."

Tim raises a brow at her. What kind of brow is it? Is it a shut up Allison brow you're hurting Sadie's feelings, or is it a shut up Allison brow?

Nicolette giggles as she sculpts her newest ceramic piece, a pink sprinkled donut. She says if she can't eat them, at least she can look at them.

I blink a few times to dismiss the tears. I am sure I am all out of tears anyway. Maybe my intelligence level is more apparent to the Pop Crowd?

My gold Aviator sunglasses hang out the side of my purse.

Jay pulls them out and hands them to me.

"Thanks," I whisper making eye contact with him through the lenses.

He nods and sits. I should have helped him with his broken chameleon the other day.

Tim clears his throat. Why does he hate BFM so much? Allison and Nicolette continue to crack jokes about my math skills.

"Al, what's four plus three?" Nicolette asks Allison. "Um. Nine," Al puts her arms up acting like she's slow.

Betsy's loud laughter bounces off of the four walls. Soon a third of the class is laughing at my extent. It takes everything inside me not to break. I wish someone would knock me over by accident so I could break into a million pieces.

From the table next door, Jay yells, "STOP."

Mr. Cooper is over instantly and everyone is back at their seats.

At the bell sound, my Havaianas hit the cobblestone floor as I try not to focus on Allison plunging her tongue down Tim's throat like it was a stopped up toilet. Yuck! Is she the bad kisser? I really think the jokes have gotten to me as well as the vodka.

Was it the math jokes? I can't I say I'm not a math person and more of an English person. Why is that unacceptable and worthy of joking? My dad is a firefighter and not a surgeon, lawyer or politician like theirs.

"He'll never leave her for you." Nicolette taps my shoulder, holding a half-eaten protein bar.

"Nic." I nudge her. "Don't be cray."

She grabs my arm and we link arms to the gym. "I saw you staring at Tim, Sades."

I look behind her to see if Al is in my periphery tomfoolering, as I put it with Tim. Tomfoolering, Al's playful way of playing with Tim that makes me want to vomit. We walk in silence in the girls' gym as there are a lot of people around.

Nicolette revels as I pull off my shirt in the locker room. "God I wish I had your body," she stares an extra long amount, "Perfect boobs and rock hard stomach. Maybe these protein bars will suffice the constant hunger I have. Summer beach body is on the horizon."

"You look great," I say to her. She really does. She is a solid 5'4 and curvy but with a flat stomach, nice legs, perfectly rounded boobs and has a pretty face with green eyes and darker mocha colored hair. When she eats, which seems minimal, she eats vegetables, fruit, protein shakes and protein bars. She tries so hard to fit in. It reminds me of Colbie Caillat's song "Try."

"Back to our convo, he is off limits." She ignores the compliments I seem to dish at her 24/7. I need to shake her and say, 'you're amazing, Nic.'

"Tim?" I say, pressing my lips together. I try to play dumb. "Yes." She says impatiently. "Tim said he wanted you, but he can't because of Al."

"Okay." I shake my head. This is not news.

"Anyways, he told Chase that he would never date you because you're dumb," she shrugs. "Sorry . . ."

"Um, I'm getting a 3.1," I defend myself.

"Well, I'm getting a 4.2 in AP classes." She presses two fingers on the bench to balance herself while she pulls off her brown Coach converse. "That's why he'll never leave her. Sades, you need to get over him. Al has already asked me three times if I think there's something going on with you and Tim. I never said anything to her about it, but I don't want to lie to her."

"He flirts with me." I clench my jaw. I am so dunzo with today.

"Stop gritting your teeth," she says. Her hands shake like a fat girl's bum on a treadmill. "Don't forget who brought you in. She's your friend. Get it together. Al is coming." She pulls her cheerleading outfit on.

"I'm getting it together," I say, as I adjust my C cups into the Lululemon sports bra Grams bought me. It's just the wrong day to mess with me.

"Your skirt is so wrinkly," Allison swoops in doing the combination on her locker. "Get it together."

"I am," my octane is a little higher, as I flatten the C.A. embroidery on my shirt.

"What's with the screaming, Sades?" Allison removes her skintight zebra-printed tank top and short white tulle skirt, showing her perfect boobs in her magenta Victoria Secret lace bra and underwear, "Who flirts with you? What were you saying to Nic?"

My mouth is dry, hands are still shaky and my eyes are tired from this two-minute conversation.

"Sometimes Tim and Chase flirt with me," I mumble as I sit down, pulling my left cheer tennis shoe on and then right. I'm getting ballsier and ballsier by the minute.

"Tim and Chase?" Al sits next to me doing the same mechanical breathing from earlier. "Maybe Chase? But isn't he flirty with anything that walks?"

If she only knew . . .

"Dude, Tim is trying to please me by checking in with you. I can't always handle Sadie and all it encompasses." Her hand does a circle in the air.

That one landed hard. I plop down like it hit me in the heart. After this conversation and today's events, I feel worthless. I feel grimy and dirty, like I've been slimed, rolled around in the dirt and poop, left to my own demise. I've shut down and I'm out of the conversation.

"ANYWAYS," Al annunciates every syllable. "I heard something today . . ."

Nic looks at her and squeals.

"Chase," they say in unison, laughing. Dude, they were meant to be friends this long. They are always on the same wavelength.

"What?" I ask, wanting to be in on the secret, wanting to have more letters in the Best Friends Ceramic Piece.

"I like him back. You know how he said I look cute in the picture he took," she says. "Well, he came over last night later. We kissed. He said he wanted to wait until school was out but he couldn't."

Allison pulls the cheerleading outfit over her head and flattens the letter C over her right boob. "He's really a catch and I'm not saying that because he's like a brother to me. He's had his eyes on you for quite some time . . . I was kidding when I said he flirts with everything that walks earlier . . ."

I see my skin turn ghostly pale in the mirror. What happened to Chase last night that's making him need an instant girlfriend?

"Say something." She nudges me. " . . . I know Chase likes to stay single but he's cool . . . Oh you look pale, Sades," she pulls out her flask and hands it to me.

"You should give it a try, Nic." I take a sip of her flask, tasting straight-up Tito's vodka.

"Let me have some of that." Al grabs it. "I have to pull an all-nighter for that oral presentation on Osama Bin Laden for AP World History . . . after I study for other finals."

Nicolette grabs it back from her and lets out a roar.

"That's the spirit. This game can't cheer itself." Al slaps our asses. Friggin' OUCH!

"Hey Al." Betsy walks up in her uniform with a smile plastered on her face. "Since I've had two years on the cheerleading squad, do you think next year I could try out for Captain Assistant?"

Allison is the Captain of the cheerleading squad and Nicolette and I are the Captain Assistants, although, Nicolette probably shouldn't have been a part of it, considering, she was the least coordinated on the team.

Al's eyelids droop. "NOPE!"

Betsy blinks a few times and scurries off.

I feel bad for her.

Seconds later, I gallop out onto the baseball field as the supporters in the stands yell and clap for Mariposa Beach's Varsity baseball team. We are playing our biggest rival, Malibu High School, and the crowd is full of charisma, foam hands and bubbles. I watch Allison as she directs us to our first cheer song to rouse the other team. I pump my body at every beat of the song, "We Will Rock You." I feel awkward cheering and dancing next to Allison. I feel she is the prize and everyone is always looking at her, although, I see a particularly arctic blue set of eyes on me tonight.

My mind wonders back to the first time I met them. I was thirteen years old and visiting from Wisconsin for the Fourth of July. Of course, I was all Wisconsin'd out with my freckles, glasses, paleness and Midwestern attire jean overalls. I remember sitting on a blanket by Grams at the Mariposa Beach watching the men barbecue shrimp on a grill while women drank white wine. My parents partook in the activities. I stared at a group of boys around my age playing soccer and a group of girls doing each other's nails. Grams nudged me to go play soccer but I shook my head no. The ball went swiftly towards the ocean. Grams told me to get the ball. I grabbed it, and Tim walked over.

"Hi," I said, dribbling the ball to him, "I was trying to get your ball for you."

I internally kicked myself in the head, 'I was trying to get your ball for you? Dumb Sadie, Dumb! I may have been as stupid as Baby from *Dirty Dancing* saying I carried a watermelon.'

He kicked the ball back.

I kicked it back to him.

"Wisconsin can play. Why don't you join us?"

I spent the next hour playing soccer with Tim Miller, Chase Bynes and a few others. Surprisingly, I could keep up with their soccer skills. I didn't say much during the game. I just played. The girls gave me a few dirty looks during the game but Allison and Nicolette shushed them. At the end, my dad got the call that he was accepted to LAFD Academy and we were staying here.

One summer day, Allison and Nicolette were walking to the beach and saw Grams and I outside clipping roses from the garden below our swing around front porch. I was home with her all summer while my parents packed up everything to move. We watched old movies, listened to Classic Rock, looked at fashion magazines, went on bike rides, ate out, shopped, drank coffee, did Yoga on the beach, read books to each other, sat on the beach, swam, played tennis and cooked high-cuisine meals all summer long.

Allison started to ask Grams about her career and all the celebrities she's met. Who wouldn't? I remember thinking Allison was so pretty and sophisticated. Nicolette was more reserved but asked questions intermittently. Grams suggested we go get ice cream while she stayed back to take a nap. We rode our bikes to Main Street. I followed them like a lost puppy. They had these cute floral rompers on that I didn't even know existed. Luckily, I had a cute, white cotton dress on that was a prize favorite for the hot, muggy summers in Wisconsin.

At the old-fashioned ice cream parlor shop, called Cherry On Top, we ordered Cookies and Cream ice cream. We licked our ice cream cones and sat at the wood picnic bench outside. They talked about high school starting in a month, the extremely hot guys who went there, who they'd kissed already, the elaborate vacations they went on that summer, Back to School shopping in Beverly Hills and the Back to School Bash at Allison's house.

I didn't speak. I was so happy they invited me to the Back to School Bash.

I remember Allison saying. "You have a lot of potential, Sadie."

What she meant was she needed to transform me. First things first, they took me to the salon at the Mariposa Hotel Day Spa under Allison's family account and gave me a complete makeover. The stylist cut my long, dirty blond haired mane and dyed it platinum blond, plucked my eyebrows, softened my freckles, and gave me self-tanner. Al said I could borrow her black triangle bikini for the Bash, but she would convince Grams to take me shopping to a few choice places in town.

The Pratt House was behind the gates of the most expensive neighborhood in Mariposa Beach. It was close to 8,000 square feet with high vaulted ceilings, marble flooring and crystal chandeliers. In the backyard was her humongous square-shaped pool where she had lounge chairs and cabanas set up for the Back to School Bash. There were rafts in all shapes and sizes for all the Pop

Crowds of each grade level. The Pop Crowd encompasses the most beautiful, smartest and trendiest students at Mariposa Beach High School. This was our audition to be the freshman Pop Crowd.

I remember the smell of the sushi: fresh water eel with Ahi tuna, a candy bar with fine candies from Lolli and Pop, and one-hundred-dollar wine bottles. My first glass of wine was probably $30 in a restaurant. I smoked my first cigarette and then barfed. But, the best part of the Back to School bash was a hot, popular senior boy wanted to kiss me. We were playing Truth or Dare with an empty champagne bottle and someone told him kiss the hottest girl there and he pulled me out of a raft and kissed me. I didn't even care I wanted to belong so badly. Was my life in Wisconsin really that boring?

Chapter 6

GRAMS AND JACUZZI JABBING

We won 4 to 1. The game was done by 7 p.m. The Pop Crowd went for pizza afterwards. I let the warm water droplets from my shower wipe away the day. I have to talk to Chase. I have to talk to Tim. I have to see where I am with the both of them.

By 7:30, I am curled up in my warm bed like an al dente piece of macaroni. Luckily, my parents are at a birthday dinner and the 'a talking to' with my dad, Wyatt MacPhearson, will be had later. I crack open my door to the patio outside my room to smell the ocean air. Since I am on my own wit, I try to read a book for English. Maybe I can actually get a C on a pop quiz tomorrow. As far as I know, Chase is not returning any of my calls or texts, and the school is on to my intelligence level, so I have to try in school. My eyes are heavy from the day and the vodka. I am wrecked. I feel like a Mack truck hit me.

"Hey." Grams pops her head in.

"Hey." I sit up against my pillow. "Go back to bed."

"I'm good." She sits on the edge of my bed. "Good chemo day. I took a nap this afternoon. Mom made you a sandwich."

She points the turkey and cheese wrapped in a paper towel on my pink nightstand. Ugh, carbs.

I turn to look at her so she can see my face and take her hand. "Good, Grams."

She takes a deep breath and fixes her black beanie with *The Big Apple Cookoff* etched in red stitching, hiding her missing hair. "What's wrong, Sades?"

"Long day. I'm tired," I draw a few hearts on the paper with my watermelon scented pen. "And, no matter what, I can't seem to ever understand what this William Shakespeare guy has to say."

"It's okay. Everyone hates him." She half smiles.

I try to form my mouth into a smile. Grams can be really funny sometimes, but tonight I am really held back by today's events.

"What it is?" She strokes my arm and grabs my hand pumping it. "You can tell me anything. Pregnant? On drugs? Jail? Prefer women?"

I put my hand up. "Okay, stop. Tim said I was dumb."

"Well, I don't think you're dumb." She leans against my one hundred pink pillows as she makes a goofy face. "Your bed is very comfortable."

I stare down and eyes water.

"Sadie Lynn MacPhearson . . ." she pulls my chin up, "Tim, he's not even worth your tears . . . besides isn't his dad like a nympho . . ."

"Probably . . ." I agree.

"Look, all the little crushes you have on boys, men are just crushes, but when you meet your husband, it'll seem so different . . ." she says.

I nod. "It's just everything that happened today with Dr.

Plumb, Principal Dow and Mrs. Flame, too."

She hugs me for a few seconds. "Your mom said that they may assess you for a learning disability? I think it would be good to know if there's something . . . and to get help . . . I can't speak for the other two, but Principal Dow is a nice man. His father was one of my best friends before he was murdered."

"Really? That's terrible."

Her sparkly, cobalt blue eyes peer at me.

"That, and my secret will be out . . . and Al . . ." I start rationalizing out loud.

"What secret? What is her obsession with you, your grades, classes and SAT scores?"

"I dunno." I blink back tears. "I'm tired, Grams." I have no more words, not even for Grams.

The corners of her mouth curve into a smile as she pulls herself up. "All right. I'll drop it, because I hate to see you cry and besides *The Big Apple Cookoff* is on."

"Okay, we can watch it tomorrow. I have to read a little more."

She jokingly rolls her eyes. "Okay, and, Sades, no more alcohol."

"I'm . . ." I start.

"No, the parking on your Jeep last night . . . really? You could hurt someone or yourself," she says, walking toward the door, "and, eat your sandwich. You're not an Ethiopian child."

The other half of my smile from the other day appears.

Grams is a one of a kind lady. She was the youngest of seven children and her parents were poor. She grew up in Brooklyn, where she started cooking anything in her refrigerator and made it good. Later in life, she became a world-renowned chef. She worked at a famous restaurant called Nova in New York City where she made delicatessens for everyone from John Travolta to Sarah Jessica Parker. She was also very beautiful, social and extremely independent. From time to time, she would travel to different parts of the world and cook for different famous people. When she was in New York City, my grandpa (Gramps) was stationed in Fort Hamilton Brooklyn, but his parents were independently wealthy living in Mariposa Beach. She was catering a military ball and Gramps ditched his date to hang out with her in the kitchen. He won her over with his good looks, wit and charm.

Less than three months later, she told him she was pregnant and they bought the apartment she still owns in Battery Park to raise my mom, Cindy. Grams continued on being a fabulous chef like no baby ever got in the way. Gramps basically raised my mom with an upper class New York City lifestyle.

Years later, once my mom met my dad when he was in New York City for March Madness, she moved to Wisconsin to be with him. My grandparents still lived in New York City. Once my parents had me, Gramps came to help my mom raise me since my dad was occupied as the fire chief of Madison, Wisconsin. Grams stayed in New York City as she was a judge on a reality TV cooking show called *The Big Apple Cookoff* that filmed twice a year. We did this triangular traveling: Wisconsin, NYC and Mariposa Beach for thirteen years. New York City was my favorite. I remember the rainy weather, sophisticated dressers, fast-pace, excellent cheesecake and the gorgeous or gargantuan floats at the Macy's Thanksgiving Parade. On my thirteenth birthday, Gramps passed away from a heart attack.

The beach house in Mariposa Beach was owned outright by my grandparents handed down from my great grandparents. Although we would go back and forth for vacations a few times a year, we could never get enough of it. After my Gramp's death, my mom was depressed in Wisconsin because everything reminded her of my grandfather. My dad's parents died within the same year about a year before Gramps. We needed a change so we moved to Mariposa Beach the summer before freshman year. My dad went from Madison Fire Department to the Los Angeles Fire Department. Grams decided to retire from the reality television show with Gramps' death.

I was so excited to live with her in Mariposa Beach. I loved hearing the stories she'd tell about her adventures with all the boyfriends she had, the parties she went to, the people she met and the places she traveled. She'd run her fingers through my hair or we'd hold hands as we'd talk. She slowly became my role model, my confidant and my best friend. Last year, she was diagnosed with breast cancer. When my dad found out, he inappropriately laughed at the situation. Timing is everything. Her chemotherapy is helping and she is doing a lot better, so there is hope. I savor moments.

I listen for her soft snore through the wall. I have to turn it off, too.

My body melts into the cold sheets on my bed. I close my eyes, letting the day fall over me.

My dad grounded me for two days for the way I spoke to Dr. Plumb, Principal Dow and Mrs. Flame, and made me apologize in an email to them. I spent a long day at UCLA Medical Center for Gram's chemotherapy on Saturday. I am happy that Sunday has rolled around. I'm not grounded anymore and am ready for a party. My head feels clearer about the events at school the prior week.

Tim lives in a beautifully restored tri-level Victorian-style beach house on the north side of Mariposa Beach. It's tall and the most beautiful shade of nautical blue, holding all the infamous nooks and crannies of a classic beach house. It has a nautical theme throughout, light wood flooring and Brighton white, classy beach furniture. It also has a touch of modern-life: stainless steel, plasma televisions and recessed lighting. It's gorgeous and pretty much the house to be at any night. Tonight is the Memorial Monday party. This party happens on the Sunday night before Memorial Day. It consists of people wearing red, white and blue bikinis and board shorts, and blue and red drinks with dry ice coming out of the top. In honor of the military, we drink and play a war game, where we battle each other on the beach with war paint and games, red verses blue.

I drive over in my Jeep. My mom and Grams released me after a long dinner with garlic and rose-mary-marinated chicken over Jasmin rice, and cucumbers and squash. I told them I planned to spend the night at Allison's and my mom nodded her head. My grandmother winked at me, whispering in my ear to be careful. My dad was at work. And, my mom was a little up in arms about Grams fighting cancer. So, I could say the house was burning down and my mom would nod and say, "okay, don't forget your sweater."

Meanwhile, my dad texted me a lovely message, "Be good now."

If my parents only knew . . .

I walk into the beach house a few minutes early taking two shots as I pull off my new Michael Kors American flag cotton dress with my skimpy American flag bikini, ready to rock and roll. Grams says it is too scantily clad, but I don't care. I walk toward the spa on the lower deck overlooking the ocean, where I know the girls are all sitting in the spa. I guess Allison and Nicolette have already started with some of our other close friends. I'm about to turn the corner to join them in the spa but stop when I hear the words, "extra credit."

"Extra credit?" asks one of the minions.

I pause in my tracks, crouching down behind an oversized blow-up Uncle Sam pointing his finger at me. I know he's got one of those annoying features where he speaks a recording, "I'm Uncle Sam and I want you for the Army," so I try my best not to set him off.

"Yes, I guess so," Al replies, sipping her dry ice drink.

"Well, I heard she stepped into the office and they told her she can't graduate unless she continues to earn extra credit," the minion continues.

"What, no, how sad?" Nicolette replies.

"How much extra credit?" another one of the minions asks.

"I don't know. There's not enough in the world for her to pass." Al's rings clink against the glass.

The minions giggled.

"She's lucky she's hot," another minion giggles. Glasses clink. "To be honest, she's always been a little dumb in my book," Al says.

"Yeah, Al, but you're an Honors student," a minion says back. The blow up Uncle Sam sways back and forth as a gust of wind comes in through the door opening on the other side of the floor. I panic.

"True," Al scoots her back on the jet like nothing that has been said in the conversation phases her. Nicolette licks off the sugar in her dry ice drink.

"She's probably coming soon, so let's change the subject," Nicolette states.

My heart stops as my hand naturally covers my mouth. I feel like a million needles hitting me, perhaps similar to a joining the Army with Uncle Sam. I slip back around the corner, planning my escape without talking to anyone.

"Sades," Tim's sultry voice sounds as I'm nearing the hall. He does his usual head to toe checkout. "We missed you the last two days." He is shirtless, wearing a pair of red O'Neill shorts.

Dang.

"Yeah, I was grounded," I say, hearing nothing. The girls are silent. I am too far to see them. I continue to walk, grabbing my dress and purse.

"I have to go, Tim," I see Chase by the entry holding a beer. "I'm not feeling very well. I think my grandma undercooked tonight's chicken."

They watch me as I pull my dress back on scurrying to the front door.

"Let me drive you." Chase's arm naturally goes around me.

"Funny, you're still alive," I pull his ear to my mouth. "We need to have a convo soon."

"Let's do it tonight," he whispers back, trying to hand me his beer.

I shove it away.

"Sades, what's the matter?" Allison appears in her beautiful, gold, shiny bikini.

"I feel like crap. I just want to go home." I make it to the front door, opening it.

"Let me call you a cab," Tim takes a step in front of the door, but I rush past him.

I run to my Jeep, start it up, and wait for clearance on Pacific Coast Highway. The good thing is I've only had a few shots, so I think I'm okay to drive. Grams once told me, "Have a good cry, wash out your heart. If you keep it inside, it'll tear you apart." I jerk my Jeep to a safe spot on Pacific Coast Highway and light a cigarette, trying to inhale deeply. I try to calm my tear ducts, but they continue to water.

Chapter 7

SUP BOARDING

As I open the Jeep door and swing my legs over so I can have a full view of the ocean blue and the dark cloud on the horizon. Something in the corner of my eye catches my attention and distracts my mind from evil girl bashing. I watch a tall, beautiful, blond woman dressed in a half wetsuit and a pink bikini top talking into her cell as she leans against a black Chevy Suburban. She laughs and tugs on her bracelet, anxiously. I need to laugh more I conclude. A tall, darker man with shaved hair, wearing a half wetsuit starts unloading Stand Up Paddle boards from the bed of the truck.

"Heeeeeee-eeeeeeeey," I whisper. "Move those paddle boards." He stops to look at her and smiles. She smiles back, squeezing his hand. One tall, blond girl, about eight years old, with her mom's face, opens the door and turns back around to help younger siblings. One looks like her twin, there's a second blonde, a third dirty blonde a few years younger and a fourth brunette a few years younger than that. They all have their half-wet-suits on with matching pink bikini tops and are jumping up and down screaming with excitement as the sun hits perfectly on their gorgeous blue and green eyes and blond to brunette hair. Their dad takes out their mini pink, turquoise, purple and yellow SUP boards.

"They're so cute!" I take a drag. This is the epitome of what most people want, a perfect-looking family dressed in designer wear.

I see another figure make his way out of the Suburban and I hear, "Come on, Uncle Jay."

He's out and jumps up and down with the girls. The tall bungee cord holding the SUP boards tightens and it unsnaps, bonking Jay in the head. The woman narrows her brows at him, covering her laughing mouth. Jay frowns at her and rubs his head in the rearview mirror. To my surprise, he sees me.

"Is that Sadie?" he mouths. The white Jeep is a few cars back. He throws on a white T-shirt over his folded down wet suit like he's not trying to show off the muffin top, and walks towards the Jeep.

I light another cigarette and lean against my Jeep. I wipe the black mascara marks dripping down my cheeks. I really need to purchase the expensive waterproof mascara from the Too Faced line.

"Hi." He waves.

I turn away from him. "What's wrong?" he asks.

I grumble, and hopes he gets the message, a solid go away.

The woman, who is off the phone now, walks up, looks at me and then Jay. "Jay, we're heading out. Joey really wants you to go with her."

"Okay, be right there." He smiles. "Gorgeous," I say as she walks away.

"Disgustingly so." He places his hands on his waist. "That's Mel. She's my sister in law. That's her husband, my brother Josh, and their four girls."

"Oh yeah." I'm now looking off in the distance, "Her body is rocking and she has four daughters."

"Yeah, she was a Victoria's Secret model but quit after kids," he watches me smoosh my cigarette with my red Coach heels.

"I need to look into that," I say.

"What, having four kids? Or being a model?" he says, trying to formulate some resemblance of a real smile.

I throw my cigarette in the trash, not replying. Ignoring people sometimes trains them not to say stupid stuff. It's what Al taught me. Although I'm not sure what Jay said was stupid.

"Awe," he says sarcastically like I responded.

"Probably too short to be a model," I say.

"Nah, you're perfect," he says, mouth open a little. He gasps for air, like he's trying to pull the words back in his mouth.

OFF. MY. JOCK. PRONTO. BRO. I. WILL. NEVER. WANT. YOU.

I've been told to stop laughing with this guy. I stare at him for a second and pull my 110 pounds back into my Jeep.

"Well that sounded weird, my honesty precedes me. I'm going to head out." He points towards the ocean as if I am unclear where it is. "If you want to join us, I have an extra SUP board. It's a good way to blow off steam . . . That's one of my favorite songs by the way." He throws it out there rambling on.

"I'm not supposed to be . . ." I turn Led Zeppelin's "Stairway to Heaven off."

"You're not supposed to be what?" he persists. Now that I think of it, he does look like his brother.

"Fine, I'll go. My plans got cancelled anyway." I step out of the car, pulling off my American dress leaving it in the car.

He clears his throat and quickly looks at me in my skimpy bikini, which has twenty stars on the bottoms covering my butt and 25 stripes on the bikini top covering my boobs. It's time to show up this perfect little family.

He takes a deep breath, "Let's go Betsy Ross."

I want to smile.

The break is rough, but I get myself out there. Jay has the twins Joey and Tyler paddling on his smaller Sun Life Seabreeze paddleboard. Once I'm out there, Jay introduces me to the family.

"Nice to meet you, Sadie," Mel's Australian accent shines through. She is in the front of a fifteen-foot turquoise Sun Dolphin Seaquest board with the six-year-old Noah and the four year-old Billie strapped in and her husband bringing up the rear.

"You too," I say softly. I haven't forgotten my manners.

I paddle to keep up with them.

"I love this view," Josh points to the orange, yellow and red horizon.

Mel shakes her butt. "This too."

"That's what I was referring to," he yelps.

Jay paddles next to me. "Don't mind them, they're lucky in love."

I say softly to Jay, "it's all good." What I would do to be lucky in love?

"Uncle Jay, since you gave our board to Sadie, can I at least ride with her?" Joey asks.

I panic. Thank God I had only a few shots. Mel's head bows, showing the okay.

"If it's okay with Sadie," Jay says loud enough for me to hear.

Joey does a swan dive into the water and swims her best breaststroke to me.

She pops out of the water, and I scoot back on the board. "Nice swan dive."

She pulls the second paddle off the board like she's eight going on sixteen. "Thanks, let's go."

I beam at her cuteness.

The winds help with our paddling.

Good thing I know how to SUP board from spending a lot of summers at Lake Kiki in Wisconsin. Every once in a while we see a jumping fish and Joey and I squeal. The deep ocean blue waters remain semi-calm, three hundred feet out. Joey tells me all about her second grade class at Mariposa Elementary, her swim team, how she doesn't like to share with her twin sister, what she likes to draw, her gymnastics and her new cocker spaniel, Kale. Oh, and how her aunt works at the school. I listen to her giggling, saying oh and yes at appropriate spots. Jay follows a safe distance behind me; Josh and Mel lead the way.

Josh takes us around to rocks, a huge one that stands about two hundred feet and one that's one hundred and fifty feet above sea level with a connecting arch and a cave. Its umber colored rock is covered in lime green moss all around. Some white, pretty flowers give off a scent wafting through the air, reminding me of the smell of lavender. The water is bluer and clearer over here, allowing us to paddle board through and see a smorgasbord of tiny red, purple, yellow and blue fish. The coral is light purple, dark purple and brown. It looks like it would be a photograph on the wall of a beach hotel room.

I wonder why I've never done this or seen this in the three years I've lived here. My dad and I talked about it but we could never find the time.

"Beautiful right?" Joey says. "We paddleboard as a family once a week."

"Josh, it's so clear today, " Mel lies on her board and looks down at the water.

"Yeah, it's not always open to the public," Josh says to me. Now that I'm in closer proximity. Jay has the same facial features as Josh. The only difference is Josh is thin and fit.

"Stunning," I find a good word.

"Yeah, the Arch of Love is one out of my two favorite spots, breathtaking," Jay starts. "In fact the old Hopi Indians used to use this cave for ceremonies: baptisms, celebrations, holidays and weddings," he rambles. I sit Indian-style, listening and kind of want more information.

"Your eyes match the blue water," Tyler looks at me. "She really is pretty, Uncle Jay."

Mel, Josh and Joey laugh. I feel sweaty, even though I'm the only one without a wetsuit and it's getting really brisk.

Jay sits with legs floating in the water, looking at me. I just remember that I may have offended him the other day in class. His waterproof iPod plays Foreigner's "I Wanna Know What Love Is."

I love that song!

He points to the arch, "the bride and groom would stand there with the guests dispersed onto the mini chairs . . ." he continues.

"Do people get married there now?" I eye him nervously and pull more hair over my shoulders.

"I don't think so . . ." his voice is low and nervous.

"It's probably a liability now," Mel suggests. "Everything is money, money, money these days."

"Well, it's stunning," I reply.

"Despite the money, right!" Josh says, sitting behind Mel. I smile.

I felt a little of the Wisconsin girl coming back.

We sit, lay and kneel on our paddleboards while Jay and Josh dive to the bottom. Sets of big waves roll through. Mel starts a game of I Spy to keep the girls calm.

"That's a good idea," I feel an anxiety bug throughout my body as the set ends. The youngest girl, Billie, grabs onto Mel.

"After being a mom of four for years, I still don't know what to do," she looks at the next set of waves.

"It seems like you guys have the perfect family," I suggest. "Thank you. You only live once," she admits.

"Tyler, luv, can you jump on the board with Miss Sadie and Joey? I'm going to buzz Josh, so we can get going," Mel's face whitens, as we simultaneously look overhead at a cumulous cloud rolling in hot. The sun has disappeared, even though the sunset for today is supposed to be one hour from now, at 8:05 p.m.

"Holy, okay," I pull Tyler's board towards me helping Tyler jump on mine. I wrap one arm around Tyler and one around Joey.

"Your breath stinks," Tyler says to me.

"Uh thanks," I say.

A wave jerks me and the girls off my board and into the cold, rocky water. I've lost the twins. I feel my body turning in the washing machine of the waves as I reach for Joey and Tyler. I try to swim to them but the current pulls me down. I feel arms wrap around me. It's Jay. He pulls me up and up to the top of the surface as I cough out some water screaming, "THE TWINS."

"They're fine. They have life vests on." He pulls me onto the board. "Are you okay?"

"Yeah, I tried to grab them," I say through my shivers.

My body feels goose pimples as he cradles me in his lap. I see Mel with the twins on their board and Josh with the two younger ones paddling ferociously through the all of a sudden constant winds and waves.

"Sadie, listen, the girls are fine." He yells over the noise of the storm. "You're shivering. You've gotta stay here while I paddle." He points to his lap.

A second later I adjust myself in between his upper legs holding onto the grip handles while he paddles hard through the small but constant waves. He is strong and his large paddle strokes cruise us along. The shivering stops and starts like my dad's old Mustang. This goes on for about ten minutes. My chin rests on his leg, I try to focus on the board. I see in small black decals on his board In Loving Memory of Candice Rashi 1999-2012.

He shifts his weight and I look up and see land. "Thank God."

"What?" he yells as the heavy rain hits us like a paint ball pellets.

"NOTHING," I yell back.

He waits for the break to soften, as soft as it can be in this instant monsoon.

He cradles my ear, "HOLD ON AND I PROMISE YOU WON'T FALL."

I grip the handles tight as he squeezes my body with his upper legs. His big arms pound his paddle through the water like a boxer taking that first swing. I peek through his armpit and see an eight-foot wave behind him. He ditches the paddle. "READY." He is still crouched down and my legs are wrapped around his. "DON'T LET GO!"

The wave barrels and he uses his arms to push us along. I catch a glimpse of his green eyes. He cracks a smile. Perhaps to let me know it's all good or that he's enjoying the thrill. Water suspends around us in the barrel. It is an incredible out-of-body experience to be in a barrel this large. The barrels spits us out into shallow water. I'm still holding onto him as he's now standing in a foot of water.

All I can say is, "WOW! I won't ever laugh at you again."

He doesn't say anything, and I'm still letting him hold me like a baby.

"We're safe. Let's get you warm." He helps me stand up. "Sorry," I say. "Maybe I should wear a life vest next time?"

"Or, maybe be sober . . ." He lets my feet hit the ground.

Oh.

"Like I don't already feel guilty . . ." I yell back in the rain. He shakes his head, carrying the SUP board to the Suburban.

Mel runs out with a large, warm, pink towel with a big Minnie Mouse on it.

"Mel, I'm so sorry," I wrap myself looking at the four girls covered in towels in the suburban.

"What do you mean? That was awesome!" Joey yells.

"It's all good," Mel tucks Joey in the Suburban, slamming the car door. She covers her forehead from the water droplets pummeling her. "That rain came out of nowhere. Jay needs to take it down a notch."

Larger raindrops hit my face. "I should probably get home." "Okay, take the towel. Do you want us to follow you?" she asks.

I step out. "No, that's okay. I'll give the towel to Jay at school." The rain and wind prevent me from making it fast to my Jeep, but I finally make it. I pull on my seatbelt as I blast the heater looking at the rearview mirror to wait for clearage on Pacific Coast Highway. I click on my Pandora: Classic Rock. I felt bad not saying goodbye but I would hate me too if I put any of my family members in danger. Maybe next time he does a presentation on ROTC, I won't laugh.

I arrive home around 7:30 p.m. from the SUP sesh. I feel guilty about the girls but Mel made me feel a lot better. BFM was right. It was a good way to blow off steam. It felt like a natural high, something I need more of: twinkling water, beautiful green-colored moss on the rocks. After a warm, defrosting shower, I lie in bed for more warmth and try to find the lyrics of the song "I Wanna Know What Love" is and a few other classic rock love songs. I couldn't help but wonder if they'd written these songs for me—songs of wanting to feel something raw and real. I need these lyrics to help me wrap my head around what I overheard at Tim's. I am dumb (period).

Therapeutic waves of music trickle through my now sober veins and then come to a screeching halt as I hear some yelling.

"What the hell, Cindy," my dad's voice penetrates the hallway.

I wonder if Grams is sleeping and want to shush him.

"Wyatt, no, she said . . ." her voice cracks. My heart hurts for her. My dad is so strong sometimes.

"No, we move all the way from our happy, normal, farm, small town life where Sadie was happy at her private school with her normal friends. Now we have to keep up with the Jones' in Beverly Hills Ville by having her privately assessed for $6,000 because your friends are telling you what to do? Isn't it the high school's job?" he sighs.

"I am not trying to keep up with the Jones. I'm trying to figure out what's wrong with my daughter," my mom says in rebuttal.

Who are the Jones anyways? Do they live in Mariposa Beach?

Is there something wrong with me?

"Yeah, you are." I peer through the crack of the door. I watch my dad do a head to toe stare down. "You, your mom, Sadie . . . I don't like your friends and I don't like Sadie's friends or their parents." He's buttoning his uniform shirt for work. "It's all fake."

With her head in her hands, she is crying.

"We don't even go to church anymore, Cin," I watch him cup her face through the cracked door.

She wraps her arms around him and cries. She walks him down the hall. My eyes squeeze shut as my world comes crashing down. The flask under my pillow meets my mouth and the alcohol trickles into my mouth and then my veins.

"There's always tomorrow," I mumble, as my eyes close to the world.

Chapter 8

RUMMY CUBE AND PB & J SANDWICHES

The next morning, lightning flashes against my bedroom window and thunder rattles my window awakening me earlier than I wanted to wake up on a Saturday morning. My hand makes its way up to my favorite rectangular plush pink pillow that says BFF. Allison gave one to me and Nicolette for Christmas last year. I find a loose string on the B and start pulling it off. That's for talking about me.

I throw on some flannel pajama pants, my pink Victoria Secret robe and slippers, and shuffle my way down the hall. All the pictures on the wall are of me and my parents and grandparents in Wisconsin or New York. I enter the great open room where two rooms are separated by a pony wall. Both rooms encompass a coastal style design of light blue walls, white loungy blue L-shaped couches and nautical blue and white striped pillows with accents of starfish, pelicans and surfboards. I pull out my favorite blue fleece blanket and throw it on the couch for later, coaxing my one hundred percent Rhodesian Ridgeback dog Lucy off the couch with a toy.

In the kitchen, I pull out my favorite Disney mug with all the characters on it and press start on the Keurig coffee machine. The kitchen has white wash cabinets and sand granite countertops. The coffee is ready in a minute. I click on the TV finding *The Big Apple Cookoff* on my DVR as I pull the fleece blanket over me.

Usually, living vicariously through other people's lives makes me take the focus off my own, but this morning, my heart feels like a million people have stepped on it and any screaming or fighting over ingredients isn't going to make me switch my train of thought.

I'm not upset that my friends are talking about me. I know some of the things they have said in the past, and my mom/ grandma would chalk it up to jealousy. It was the subject of their conversation that makes me feel numb. Would they understand that I have a learning disability, if I have one? Would I understand it? And, when would my favor exchange be found out? Will this endless pit of guilt in my stomach ever subside? And, will my parents ever forgive me?

My grandma maneuvers her way with a cane.

"Crazy storm," I say, thinking thank God she was the one who interrupted my thoughts.

"Hi, scrumptious," she says, kissing my head "My gosh, I thought the roof was going to come off."

I stand up, helping her to the couch. "Want me to get you a cup of coffee?"

She shoos me away. "Not yet sweetie, how was the party?"

"I came home early," I sigh looking away. "The chicken did me wrong . . . I think."

I feel her peering at me with her tantalizing blue eyes, "Oh. I didn't hear you throwing up last night but then again I had a glass of wine, so I slept like a baby."

I giggle, focusing my thoughts back on who is making the best salmon dish.

I can tell Grams is onto something but she has to work for it.

She looks at the screen, "Who is she married to now?"

"Cameron? I think she just divorced . . ."

"Bryan Green," she answers. "That's right I remember meeting him."

"Grams," my eyes widen as I lower the volume to the TV. "Dish.'

She turns towards me, like an old grandfather telling a war story to his grandsons. I was ready for the war story, a.k.a. the scoop.

"I catered Cameron's birthday party one time. She was really sweet. She lived in a humungous house in Hollywood Hills. Everyone was there. Julia Roberts. Brad Pitt and Angie, Jamie Foxx."

"Wow." My hands grip the coffee mug as Grams shares her blanket with me. This warms my heart.

"I know, Jamie Foxx!" she says. "Secret crush."

"Brad Pitt was the one I was referring to," I say. "He's old but still has it going on."

"So I was in the kitchen with my crew and we were preparing bacon-wrapped mushrooms with Bourbon, just the works and I believe it was a birthday party for her agent's one-year-old daughter."

My brows furrow.

"I think I wanted to melt the butter, but the microwave wasn't working and all the burners were taken up. Cameron popped her head in and led me to the guest house kitchen."

"Whaaaa? The guest house kitchen? Fancy!"

"Yeah, so she was so sweet asking me about me and saying the food so far was great. We walk into the guest house and low and behold there is Bryan Green kissing some chick."

"What?" My shoulders slump.

"Cameron put her hand over her mouth and said let's go before they could turn around and see who it was. I stayed and melted the butter."

I giggle, "You had a job to do," I suggested.

"That's right. The girl looked at me and buttoned up her shirt. He scrammed. The party went on. I didn't see Cameron all night but the girl Bryan was kissing was the wife of Cameron's agent so . . ."

"The mother of the one-year-old Cameron was hosting the party for?"

She points to me, "Yeah, they are together now. I guess the agent didn't make as much money as Bryan Green did."

"Money makes people doing such crazy things . . ." I admit. "Power, and fame, too," she points to me.

"Are you pointing to me because you want me to learn a lesson from your story?" I ask.

"Sweetie." She takes me hand. "I'm old but still hip you know." She winks. "Now tell me the real reason why you left the party? Because girlfriend, I've catered for the president and never once got a complaint about any undercooked chicken."

I reveal everything about the suspected learning disability and my friends' conversation. Probably way too much but she is the only person I trust right now. Grandma has a way with pumping info out of me. She has a way with pumping info out of anyone. It is like there is no judgment on her part, just concern. She has lived a full life and always tells me to not judge people.

"Sadie, it doesn't matter how you get there, you'll get there academically, but I think you should get tested to see and maybe you can get help. There's no shame in that," she smiles.

"Yes, but I don't want anyone to know." I hug the pillow. It is the first time I say it aloud. I literally spent years hiding my grades from people or making excuses for them. I spent the last three years cheating to show that I had good grades in order to maintain Pop Crowd status. I spent more years making fun of myself when people would say, 'oh you just got that joke or you just got that.' I would say things like, I'm the dumb blonde.

"I get it," she squeezes my arm, "Just say you're doing some extra credit to build up your grades when they ask you where you are at recess."

I smile. "Recess? Its called nutrition."

"See, you're correcting people already." Holding both hands, she looks at me. "Sadie, those girls are not your friends. Nicolette, I never liked her. Her mom's blog sucks anyways."

My body shakes with laughter.

"Who wants to learn to be paleo or macro anyways? White bread is good," she continues.

"Yes," I stab my fist in the couch. She laughs at me. "Calm down."

I laugh even harder. If Grams were my age, we'd be best friends in school.

"And that Allison Al is jealous of what you have with Tim," she says.

My body freezes. "Which is a friendship only."

"No, it's not, Sadie Lynn and you know it." She points her finger at me. "But if he calls you dumb, then maybe you shouldn't like him?"

I swat her finger away jokingly. "You're acting like mom."

She narrows me with her eyes. "Sadie Lynn, you have to start standing up for yourself." She reveals a smile at the end of the sentence.

I nod.

"In five years from now all of this won't matter. And, the nameless man who wants favors in exchange for tests? That needs to stop," Grams narrows her eyes. "I don't want to know what these favors are, but it needs to stop."

"Okay," I whisper.

I lean my head back on the couch as I hear the shuffle of my mom's big bear slippers. The convo was over as soon as the shuffle hit my ears. She just can't know. She already has a lot going on. The rain outside continues to come down as the wind rattles the house. My body shakes with chills this time as I pull the blankets over my anguish and Grams.

We exchange a few words. I watch my mom start a fire. As she stacks the firewood into the fireplace, my mind is stuck on what Grams said, 'In five years from now all of this won't matter.' Was she right? Would my friends shine through if I did have a learning disability? Have I truly lost the ability to decipher between mean people and nice?

Later that afternoon, after several hours of *The Big Apple Cookoff* and a few games of Rummy Cube, the lights dim.

"Whoa," I say.

"It's okay." Grams looks at the television. "We will find out if Heather from Dallas is good at making creme brulee . . ."

"Tito is from South Hampton, right?" my mom says.

"Yes, he lives in the Borchard track," Grams recalls.

"Your dad and I have always said we want to move there one day," my mom states.

"Beautiful place," Grams says.

"OH, we lost it." My lips pucker as we lose the power.

"Okay, my two television-watching teenagers, dad called, he's been recalled because of the storm." My mom lights the nearest coconut pear candle.

"Okay, Mom," Grams smiles.

I put my head next to hers and we both look at my mom.

"I see your cuteness," She fiddles with her iPad, cueing up her favorite Pandora's Carole King.

"You make me feel like a natural woman," Grams sings.

"A glass of wine, Grams?" I feel my cheeks thicken with a smile.

"No, this is all natural woman, Sades," she giggles, "I don't need no wine to help this singing along."

I shift my gaze to my mom, now pulling out bread from the fridge.

My mom smirks, "I'll get you a glass, Mom."

Grams and I focus back on the game. I make my last move and win.

"Oh man," Grams says.

"This might cheer you up." My mom hands her a plate of peanut butter and jelly sandwich slices, tortilla chips, and cut-up apples.

"Send it back. I want white bread," she smiles. I giggle.

"Haha, your wine is on the coffee table," she replies, handing me my plate.

I smile and take the plate, "Thank you".

My mom sighs. "So we playing another game of Rummy Cube?"

With coconut candles lit, the warmth of the fire permeates the small room. We continue to play intense games of Rummy Cube until the sun goes down and into the night. Between the footsies Grams plays with both of us and the Carole King music sounding through the room, I feel happiness. True happiness and I don't have a drink in my hand or an expensive piece of clothing on.

"I want to be assessed for the learning disability . . . or whatever," I say, "at Mariposa." My eyes meet my mom's.

Grams looks at me, bread crumbs surrounding her lips. "Good girl, Sades."

My mom nods.

"Sadie you can do whatever you want. Don't ever settle," my Grams says with the most seriousness in her eyes despite the breadcrumbs on her face. "You're too smart to settle for anything."

"I agree," my mom says.

It was a moment of seriousness, so I look at Grams and wipe her face. "Bread crumbs."

"Awe shit," Grams belts out.

"And, that's where my daughter gets her personality," my mom adds in.

I giggle and then courteously smile at my mom.

"You know what I always say, study or you will have to be a stripper," Grams smiles.

Laughter attacks my body and I let it take over in all its vulnerability. My mom and grandma look at me as I'm trying to catch my breath. They lose their breath, too. My mom falls on the floor with laughter and Grams doubles over. That evening, I tuck Grams into bed. She shouldn't have had that wine because of her chemotherapy but she asked if we could let her live a little.

"Night Grams," I pull the warm blanket over her fragile body.

"Night sugar," she puckers for a kiss.

I lay one on her, "Grams."

"Hhhhhmmmm." Her eyes close.

"I don't want to you to ever think less of me because I was cheating."

"Never Sades, because I will never know what storm God has asked you to go through. I just hope you choose the right path from now on." She is as clear as day and then adds, "I once made out with JFK Junior."

I take her hand, "What?"

She's already asleep. I will have to wait for that story in the morning. I click off her light and walk out the door.

My mom leans against the hallway door. "She is lucky to have such a doting granddaughter."

"I'm lucky to have her," I whisper, walking across the hall and plopping myself on my bed.

"Hey Sades . . ." she leans her head in my room. My mom looks tired. "Dad said Mel Felix called to check on you after paddle boarding last night?"

"Oh yeah, I skipped the party and ran into the Felixes at the beach, so we paddle boarded a little until the storm hit." My voice is flat, informational only.

"Oh wow! That's great." Her voice had a little excitement filtering through. "I realized you were home during my conversation with your dad. Sorry you had to hear that."

"It's fine," I reply frankly. My eyes feel tired. I'm not in the mood. What was I so mad at her about?

"Well, okay, I will sign the assessment plan, and we will be on our way to having you assessed." She uncrosses her arms and moves towards the darkness of the hallway.

I pull the string for my pink lampshade and all is black except for the fake stars on my ceiling that my dad put up to help me remember the stars in Wisconsin. I remember my other lampshade in my room in Wisconsin. It was in the shape of a pig with a really adorable snout. My room in Wisconsin was double the size of this one.

It even had a loft with a ladder where at one point I set up a Barbie town and had massive amounts of sleepovers with Katie and Sarah. It even had a skylight so I could see real stars. I wonder what it would look like now if I hadn't moved. Would I have stayed with the farm animal theme like a lot of kids had? Or would I have a sports theme and lots of trophies from soccer or softball? Would Katie and Sarah be talking about me at a party behind my back? Would I have to be assessed for a learning disability? Would my parents be fighting about me?

Chapter 9

EXTRA CREDIT

The next day the sun illuminates my room. The storm has passed. A lightning bolt laid across my heart and a thundercloud had roared in my head. I wash and dry my face with the nearest towel. I take in the lavender smell of Arbonne's face wash, plus a hint of Dreft laundry detergent in the pink Minnie Mouse towel. I think about how to return the towel to him and a split second about how brave Jay was about approaching that gargantuan wave. And, maybe I should apologize again for not having control of Tyler and Joey.

I walk on campus. Palm tree leaves are everywhere from the storm. Chase sits on the stone wall in the quad.

"That needs to be put away," he mumbles, as he slips his cell into the pocket of his blue skinny Moscow jeans and stands up to say hi. Chase is fly. He is average height, with a nice upper body, brown hair, brown eyes, square jaw, and a nice smile.

He puts his hands under my loose off the shoulder T-shirt. "Whad up?"

"Not much. Your hands are cold." I remove his hands. They smell like Dolce & Gabbana cologne and cigarettes, which reminds me of a sleazy Italian who worked on the set of *The Big Apple Cookoff*.

"Your body is rockin . . . I couldn't help myself," he removes his hands.

I elbow him away. I'm not in the mood for his displays. I sit down next to his backpack.

"What's wrong?" He steps in front of me and forces me to look at him. "Why'd you leave the party and you're like leaving abruptly all the time these days?" At this moment in time, out of the group, he is the closest to my friend maybe because he's actually taking time to ask.

"What's up with you and Nicolette?" I pause for a reaction.

"She's not my type, Sades," he responds with a blank stare.

"I know," I giggle. No female is . . .

"Why are you laughing now?" he asks, angrily.

"It's okay to be who you are, Chase . . . Chasey," I put my hand on his bare knee.

"Nic was all over me at the party. I guess she wants to make it public knowledge." He holds my hand.

"So this secret friendship where we do things that no one from the Pop Crowd knows about . . ." I point between us. "Has to pretty much be over?"

"No," he replies.

"So we live a double life?"

"Sades." He rubs the palm of my hand. "Nic is a friend. She knows we had a little something going when we first met but will freak out if she finds out what we've been doing."

"What? Taking provocative pictures for the answer keys . . ." I remove his hand. "At your lover's house."

"STOP!" He throws his hands on his head, clearly agitated. "Okay," I reply. We are silent for a little while. The thought of Chase, or rather Chasey, trying to be attracted to females seems ludicrous to me. I change my clothes in front of him all the time and he doesn't even look twice. I feel bad that he's struggling with his sexuality and can't express it.

I take his hand. "Calm down. How was the party?"

"Good." He brings himself down and lowers his black Ray Bans. "But I missed you. Tim got pissed at Al and was hanging with Betsy Grimes. Al disappeared for a while. Were you sick or is there something I should know?"

I pat my stomach. "Undercooked chicken."

It's a stupid lie. Grams is an amazing chef. She's catered a hundred parties for his dad.

He runs his fingers against my stomach, making me have chills to the touch—like chills you would get from riding on Haunted Mansion at Disneyland when you're four years old. "Glad you're feeling better and still alive. I texted you a hundred times."

"Thanks, my phone died, so Tim and Al? And, Betsy?"

"Yeah, big fight something about talking crap about people.

They bore me now. It's boring." He squints his eyes as the morning sun peeks over Building D. "And Betsy was on Tim's jock."

"Really?"

"I gotta go be at a debate class but feel better," he says.

If Tim only knew that we had never slept together and that Chase preferred males, maybe he'd want to be with me. But then again, he thinks I'm dumb.

"Wait, so we can't . . ." I suggest.

"Nothing's changed between us, Sades. I had to cool it because I almost got caught with the answer keys and then Nicolette wanted to hang a lot. She's a good girl to be photographed with." Chase wraps his arms around me. "Come over tonight." He releases his grip. "I have a copy of something you'll want. My parents are busy with campaign stuff, anyways, so we can sneak over to Johnny's."

I stare at him blankly, unsure of what to say and eager to leave.

At nutrition, I sit at my zen tree away from the Pop Crowd. I used to pray to God when I was struggling with something. It was a very simple. Dear Lord, please help me with blah blah, but now I don't deserve Him. Now, I get zen from trees, which is silly.

Nicolette, Allison and the minions are close within earshot and on their best behavior. Nicolette is telling me how food poisoning is an awesome diet. Tim sits on the quad staring at me under his baseball hat and sending me text messages. I pull my cell out of my pocket.

Tim: Feeling better?

Tim: Are you mad at me?

I don't respond. I know Al and him were off for a minute and would be back on. Plus he called me stupid.

For the next week or so, I don't go to the quad at nutrition. I don't go off campus with the crew at lunch. Instead I am pulled in for intensive testing in Plumb's office. He tests me in timed multiplication, timed math, timed written sentences, timed reading sentences, paragraph writing and so much more. It hurts my brain a little. I've forgotten I had one because I hadn't used it in so long.

Tim: where are you? Why haven't you texted me back?

Sadie: I'm doing extra prep for SATs.

Chase: u ok? I need my photogenic model. Nicolette is on my jock . . .

Al: Are you coming to cheerleading?

Sadie: Yes.

Nic: We're going off campus for lunch today.

Sadie: I have to stay for SAT prep.

Every day after testing, I call Grams to let her know how it's going. Because the truth of the matter is that it isn't good. I'm freaking out. What if I have this learning disability and can't go to San Diego with my friends? Or my entire life changes because of it?

On the last day of testing, I finish early. I see a few minions in the office, so I slip in the bathroom to call Grams but she doesn't answer. I opt for some Malibu Rum to ease my anxiety of the Pop Crowd finding out. I know if I qualify for special education, my classes will change from College Prep to Standard. That's a whole new set of answer keys. Chase won't even be able to help with all his new ideas and photos.

On my way out of Math, I trip over someone. My Havaiana flip flop goes flying. I recall the wild look in his eyes when we were in the barrel together.

"I'm sorry," Jay says, standing up and trying to pull me up with him.

"Well, you should be careful where you're walking," I say curtly, pressing my pink cotton skirt down and searching for my sandal and a smidge of dignity I am hoping to find in the grass.

He smiles. "I was sitting."

I glare at him. "Why are you talking back?" I need to mellow out on the Malibu rum. I still have his niece's towel at home.

He hands me his Java coffee, "I haven't even sipped this, but I think you need it more than me. It's a caramel macchiato."

"Whatever, stop trying to rescue me all the time," I say, locating my sandal on the grass.

He gets close to me. "You smell like a mini bar."

"Well you smell like . . ." I stop when I see his eyes. They're intriguing. I never did thank him for the SUP boarding.

His brows furrow. "What? Drink half and put this piece of gum in your mouth. It'll take away the alcohol smell."

I grab the coffee and gum before entering Mr. Cooper's class. After all, he is a keen teacher and Principal Dow frequents the classroom as well.

"You're welcome," Jay yells after me.

I curve my hand like I am holding balls and shake it.

"Well there you have it, classy," Jay follows me into Ceramics. He probably hates me.

I sit next to Tim, smacking BFM's gum and sipping BFM's coffee. My gum now. My caramel macchiato from Java. I throw my folder down, plop my folder on the desk and watch the show that is always the Pop Crowd.

"How's the SAT prep going, Sades? You've missed Ceramics and Nutrition and Lunch all week?" Allison turns her head towards me as she loudly scrapes her ceramic piece that's fitted to be a mirror. It's like nails on a chalkboard.

I cringe, turning my head towards the crew.

"Good."

"Funny you're taking the SAT prep course, I'm on that committee and I don't recall hearing there's one on campus this week." She looks at Nicolette, smiling like she should say Eureka.

"You know what . . ." Jay mumbles. "Why does she need to tell you? I'm on the committee, too, and Sadie is in one of our small prep courses." His eyes meet mine just like the day we went SUP paddle boarding. It almost feels like if you waved your hand in front of our eyes looking at each other, we wouldn't budge.

"Did you actually say something?" Allison stands up, walking over to his table.

"I did, Allison." He stands up at least a foot taller than Allison inches away. "You don't intimidate me."

Everyone remains silent.

"Allison," Tim orders, "Sit down. He could crush you."

Allison and Jay glare at each other like they're having a staring contest.

I put my hand on his chest, backing him up a little. "Al, I need to improve my grades," I say.

My hand is still on his chest. He looks at it, smiling with his eyes. . . . slow your roll, BFM, Felix, Jay. I remove it faster than I can count to 1.

Allison's shoulders relax as she struts back to her seat. Jay smiles like he's won. We all sit.

"Pussy," he mumbles while looking at Al.

Nicolette chimes in, "you'll get there. I had to kick it up a notch in AP Bio this year."

"Yeah, AP," Allison threw in her two cents, "She is in CP Bio."

I try to smile. At least it was an effort. Nicolette smacks her arm.

"Hey, stop with the abuse," Allison says, smiling. "I'm sure you'll be just fine, Sades."

Mr. Cooper starts talking. My hands are a little shaky. I began sculpting my newest ceramic piece, even though I'm not sure I know what it is yet. I work in silence. I don't know which is worse: Nicolette's fakeness, Allison's brutal truth or my inability to stand up to her.

Chapter 10

SWIMMING IN CHARDONNAY
AND LIES

That night, there's another charity function at Chase's house for breast cancer awareness. Chase's family is well-liked because his father is ex-military and is Mariposa Beach's mayor. Chase's mom is an independently wealthy, very proper, church-going lady. The Bynes family basically does a lot of philanthropic work for the community. Chase is generally the nicest person in the Pop Crowd and is nice to anyone by default: jocks, mad scientists, mathletes, lesbian softball, fighters, metros, headbangers, Pop Crowd and people with hot bodies that need answer keys to tests. But he has a secret that only we share.

He lives in a three-story house close to the beach. His older triplet sisters are at UCLA, and USC. The décor in his home is beautiful: marble flooring, upscale Joss and Main white and grey furniture. The backyard is larger for Mariposa Beach. White tents cover catered food from Maggiano's. Long strands of twinkly pink bulbs connect from palm tree to palm tree.

Chase's parents, dressed in elegant formal wear, sift their way through the crowd of Mariposa Beach's finest. Chase and I sit at a table with a plate of bacon-wrapped mushrooms, crab cakes and eggrolls. I switch from feeling like a lightning bolt cracked in my heart and a thunder in my head to feeling better. The testing for the learning disability is completed, Grams is on the mend with her chemo and the Pop Crowd, including Allison, are being exceptionally nice to me this week. Grams bought me a short, bubblegum pink tulle skirt, a pearl-colored, shimmery tank top with a big, black belt and black heels for the occasion. I feel Chase's hand slip in mine. He has gray slacks on with a light pink shirt, like the color of a ballet slipper. Sleeves rolled. Sometimes, I wish he didn't bat for the other team, that his spectacular wide dark amber-colored eyes would be glued on me.

"You look amazing. Maybe we can slip off and take some pictures later," he says in a quiet voice, slipping a bacon-wrapped mushroom in his mouth.

"I may need to be done with that," I say. The pit in my stomach has now turned to the size of a peach.

"C'mon Sades, I have to get a photo of you in this skirt," Chase pulls the tulle.

"Maybe, Chasey," I take the glass of wine he is slipping me under the table, "Why do you let your parents call you son . . . it's so proper and you are . . ."

"So not . . ." He smiles at me.

"Stop kidding yourself, Chase." I do a once over. "Just tell them."

"Sadie, I can't . . . so . . . STOP PUSHING." His tone is testy.

He can be nasty sometimes.

I pull my hand away from his.

"Sorry, babe." He takes it back. "Sorry."

I nod, "Someday, people will know, Chasey."

"Please my parents are suspicious enough. They saw a text from Johnny and I had to lie and say it was a girl from San Diego."

That's why the all of a sudden interest in dating Nicolette.

I nod as we both watch Allison's parents walk in. It's like a scene from a *Great Gatsby* movie with her pink fur shawl and his pink top hat. This conversation is long gone. I felt sweat in my heels as I know Tim is coming.

"Drink Sades. It'll relax the Tim nerves," Chase says. "I don't . . ." I say in rebuttal.

"Yeah. " He smiles and sighs. "You will always have Tim nerves."

"Are they back on?" I nestle into his shoulder, looking at the sky. It is a really warm and inviting shoulder. The sun setting is a beautiful pink.

He shrugs his shoulders. My heart falls to my knees.

"Sades." Allison grabs my shoulder. She is wearing an extremely short magenta leather dress and black heels from Valentino. Her hair is in a high bun.

"Dude," I say.

Why does she always have to physically abuse me? Chase stands up to welcome his dad's colleague.

She sits in his place. "You have to let it go with Chase."

"I don't have anything with Chase," I lean against the back of the chair and whisper in her ear. If she only knew . . .

"And I don't look hot tonight," she giggles uncontrollably and wacks my leg with her matching wristlet. "You guys are always caressing each other and . . . I know . . ." She's slightly nicer when she is buzzed and she is buzzed. "C'mon Chase told Tim, and Tim told me."

"Told you?" I'm flush. I'm sure I'm flush. It could be the wine or the fact that my secret could get out.

"Told me that you had a weird little thing going on. Now we all know you hooked up freshman year but Nic thinks it stopped then. I'm trying to look out for my bestie," she wraps her arms around me, "And, you're my bestie, too . . ."

Huh, why is she touching my arm? "No, we're friends only . . . like that's a fact." I pull my shoulders back, trying to show confidence.

"Okay." Her brows furrow. "Whatever the friends thing only is, Nic is into Chase and feels like there's something more between you guys, so back off."

I nod. "Yeah." Wow, this is kind coming from Allison. "Great, I love you." She stands up. "Bitch." And she must be sober now.

She prances over to Nicolette who looks really pretty in her long, pink, silk dress with a slit going up her leg.

I walk over and pull Chase's ear to my mouth and divulge. "Okay, so, Nic is on your jock. Your secret is always safe with me."

"Yours too, Sades," he wraps his arm around my neck.

"Chase," I say coyly, "We're friends no matter what."

He looks at Nicolette who is trying to own the slit on her silk dress. "She wants me, huh?"

I go back to his ear. "Bigtime."

"I don't know how to . . ." He pulls my ear to his lips and kisses it.

I inch away. "Do what you have to do Chasey."

I watch him machismo his way to Tim and the other guys. He high fives and says 'bro' and 'dude.' He wraps his arms around Nicolette's waist, and her face beams like a baby tasting candy for the first time. I watch Elliot Bynes and his wife watch in excitement. A sense of delight takes over Chase's face. And, the fake plastic world moves on.

A tall, good-looking, fit African American man in his early thirties wearing black slacks and a long sleeved white button down with a pink tie slips in the seat next to me. "That is the finest piece of ass I've seen this side of the Mississippi. Is he an underwear model?" He points to Tim who stands next to Allison. He's wearing a silk, very light blush pink, long sleeve shirt, with pecs and arms exposed and a pair of grey slacks. His blond hair is slicked back. Allison pulls Tim's pocket, moving him towards her.

I shake my head watching her mouth move as she animatedly talks to her parents and the others.

"Want to pretend we are in a serious convo so you can take your mind off of him for a minute? I want to make someone jealous too." He points to my gawdy silver necklace. "Beautiful."

"Thanks." I turn my body towards him holding my stomach with a pretend laugh.

He does the same. "Oh my God, that's so funny."

I bust up. "Yes, it is. I saw a bear poop in the woods one time." "Oh yeah?" He puts his hand on his hip.

"I was riding my bike to work and I stopped at a stoplight . . . Do you love him?"

I throw my head back in laughter for real this time and answer in an honest voice. "I have no idea."

Tim turns to look at me, lips pressed together.

I have no idea if I love him. By watching my parents, I know love is unconditional like a dog's love for its owner no matter how much it gets ignored. Love is putting your needs before someone else's, even if it's difficult.

"Just so you know GQ has been looking at you all night. And, she," he points to Allison on his side, "has nothing on you."

"Really?" I ask looking at her cackle and throw in her animated looks.

"Yeah, but let me tell you it is not only about the attraction.

Love is from here," his hand fists over his heart.

I pretend to smile. "So how do you know Elliot?"

"Well, everyone knows Elliot in one way or another, but I am his campaign manager, John Marthonian." He extends his hand, "My people call me Johnny."

I shake it. "Sadie. I go to school with Chase."

"Oh," he says distinctly.

"Oh?" I repeat.

"Oh, that didn't mean anything." He hides behind his wine glass, "Chase is a good kid."

I squint as if I could investigate the situation. I want to say I think I've been in your apartment a few times, but I opt for, "so campaign manager? Elliot is taking it to the next level?"

'Ew!' I'm a little disgusted if this 30 something year old is taking advantage of Chase. I want to say Chase can handle it. I try to escape but he keeps talking.

"Yeah, so he plans to run for state senate . . ." he proceeds to babble about Elliot's plan to be president one day. I'm swimming in my wine at this point and I need a donut raft to let me rest my head and count the ways of Tim Miller.

It takes Tim a good half an hour to walk over to talk to me. He spends a lot of time with Allison and her parents. Johnny excuses himself from his conversation with me about politics. He mutters something about Elliot and a phone call from someone fabulous for moving Elliot's campaign further along. I praise Jesus because I was a little lost in the convo about the public schools in America, a little tipsy keeping up and picturing him and Chase together made me want to hurl.

"Hi," Tim says, sitting next to me.

"Hi," I turn to face him. His eyes, my God, the way he stares at me makes me want to dive in and swim for hours. The "Sadie is dumb" comment can be shoved to the bottom of the pool and sucked down the pool drain. I'm swimming tonight.

He half smiles still. "Drink?"

"A glass of Chard sounds splendid," I try to say without slurring my words.

"Splendid then." He pours me another glass under the table.

The crowd disperses as waitresses pour more wine and the band continues playing Adele's "Rolling in the Deep."

He takes my hand to get my attention and talks into my ear. "You look insanely hot, like I would have thought you were 21." "Like you want to pinch my ass again."

I take in his minty wine breath.

He rolls up his sleeves, showing his nicely toned forearms. "I had no idea that was your ass."

"Whatever," my voice squeaks as my lips rub together nervously.

"So . . . it's like crazy loud. Wanna go for a walk? I want to talk to you." He holds his hand out ready to take mine. Allison is nowhere to be found, so I take his hand. His hand is so soft and lotiony my hand almost slips out.

He walks me through a long hallway outside to a bench on the veranda out front.

"What's up?" I sit down.

He winks. "So you and Chase all this time?"

My shoulders curve in, and I want to crawl into a hole and die. Oh my God, what did Chase say to him? Was he desperate because his parents saw a text from Johnny?

"What did he say?" I ask.

"Well I had an inkling . . . about it." His voice is strong.

"About what?" I say slowly.

"Nothing, but he confirmed it when he said you hook up once a week." He suspends his information, waiting for me to say something.

This moment in time was crucial. Should I sell out my tightest friend from the Pop Crowd and say we haven't been sleeping together because he is hhhhhhm-mmm, or, I've been cheating for three years because I have zero intelligence?

I do my usual shake of my head and say, "Yeah, but I think it is over now that him and Nic might be something. It was a weird physical attraction thing." I couldn't believe it.

"So friends with benefits?" he adds.

"Why do you care?" I say. "You have a girlfriend."

"I don't care," he jokes. "I would never date you anyways."

"So I heard . . ." I can't help but get emotional. It was a mean sentence.

Lightening splits my body apart and the thunder-cloud in my head releases mass amounts of rain out of my eyes.

He pulls me close to him, whispering in my ear. "Don't cry . . . Sadie. I didn't mean to say that . . . it's just you're Al's friend. That's why."

I break away. He is such an asshole.

"Timmy." Chase pops his head around the corner. "Al needs you."

And so it goes . . .

He presses his lips together nervously.

"I didn't mean to say you were dumb . . . It just came out," Tim says.

"Go," I cry. "And, whatever happened with Chase and I, it never stopped my feelings for you."

There it is out like a picnic lunch on a blanket: full sandwiches, apple slices, wine. I have feelings for you, Tim.

"Whoa," his hands act as a human stop sign, "feelings?" I want to scream profanity at him.

I can see his cheeks flare. He's smiling. He thinks this is funny. This whatever this is was the ultimate question. My life is crumbling before my eyes.

"Feelings? I don't know what that is." He turns around. As he's walking backwards, he sticks his tongue in between bunny ears. "But we could explore those feelings further."

"Stop acting like your father . . ." I mumble as I watch him walk.

My body rattles in my arms as I'm running to nearest bathroom. Truth is I need to cry in peace And, maybe the other real truth is I want to check the look on my face to see if I am buying it. It meaning this life I am living. This life of giving giving giving and people taking taking taking.

I sit in Chase's bathtub fully clothed, sipping a wine bottle and eating Sees chocolate molasses from the candy dish. There's nothing like a good Italian imported wine and some Sees candy chocolate to bring a girl to her happy place—this girl—Sadie MacPhearson. I look at my face from every angle in the mirror surrounding the bathtub: right side profile, left side profile, frontal. I'm not buying it. I am buying it. I am not buying it. I am.

Truth is I love Tim. He's hot, sexy and really smart. He is the guy that I never thought I wanted to date because he is such a player. But I literally cannot ever stop thinking about him. It's like the small speck of light coming out of a thundercloud painting that Chase's parents have in their guest bathroom. Maybe I think I could create a bigger light in him. Every now and then I see the light in Tim and then it gets crushed by a dark cloud moving in.

About a minute later I hear pounding on the door. I wipe my eyes.

"Yo," Chase's voice sounds on the other end.

I wipe the mascara off my face wondering if I can rip my entire face off and get a new one, and somberly open the door.

"Hey," Nicolette giggles as she's draped around Chase, "OH, it's Sades."

"We need this bathroom," He pulls Nicolette in. I put my hands up. "It's yours."

I am beyond hammered. I need a ride home. Or better yet, I need a boat to sail through this storm I have created. Better yet, I need an Army vessel.

"Thanks," Nicolette squeezes me.

Chase rolls his eyes at me. I want to roll my eyes back at him and say, good luck with that. It's not that Nicolette isn't pretty with her voluptuous body. It's just Chase prefers a different type, a man with a ding-a-ling.

"You better believe it," I look at her and then Chase. I grab the wine bottle they brought in and book it. I sip the wine as my bare feet hit the stone path leading to the opposite side of where the party is. I position myself in Chase's tree house lighting up a cigarette, I press the Uber app on my cell but it doesn't work. Tears roll down my cheeks as I sniffle and smoke and watch Tim and Allison dancing. Maybe there's something I don't know about them, like they have a special bond. Maybe if I'd grown up in Mariposa Beach or was smarter . . .

Chapter 11

TREEHOUSE CHATTER AND BIG FAT CUSHIONS

I sit criss cross apple sauce on the wooden floor with my white sweater over my bare legs. Why don't I dress for the cold beach nights? I sing along to 4 Non Blondes "What's Up."

"Hi," a male voice whispers.

"What?" I pop up, my heart jack-rabbitting out of my chest as I bang my head on the roof of the tree house.

I recognize him at once. I've only known him for three years and spent two hours with him last Friday night paddle boarding. He has black jeans on and a long sleeve black shirt.

"Oh my God, what the hell are you doing? You just scared the crap out of me," I belt out.

"Sorry," Jay says.

I rub the bump on my head.

"Sorry I was going to be quiet but then we were hiding in the same place and I thought it would be weird not to say something, especially because you're crying," he rambles on.

I hold my head. "That's gonna hurt tomorrow."

"You okay?" He shines the flashlight on my head. "No blood.

That's a good sign."

"I wasn't crying."

He turns his flashlight off and looks at me from the streetlight. "Just a bump. And, there must be a condensation leak from the tree above us," he splashes water on his face from a water bottle, "I got it too."

My mouth forms a half smile.

A few seconds pass. I wipe my tears and take a deep breath. "Why do you have a flashlight?"

"I'm helping with security for this party." He looks at me and then points to Elliot Bynes in the crowd below. "His detail is my ROTC coach and needed some extra big guys to sit on people in case things get testy."

"Oh," I say nonchalantly, "at least you still get to come?' "Really," he points to himself, "You think I care to come to a party like this, or, do you think I'd rather be at home playing a game with my nieces?"

"That's a tough one," I reply. "Your nieces are pretty cute. Also, I'm sorry they fell in the water."

"It's over." He shrugs.

Crickets chirp and the echo. The music vibrates the tree house.

My lips make a slurp sound as I sip the Chardonnay bottle. He puckers his lips.

"What?" My words are getting a little sloppy. "Why are you smirking?"

He puts his hands up. "No reason."

We are silent for a second. We sit in the treehouse with the streetlight shining down on us. We watch the scene below. It still smells like lasagna and cheesy garlic bread. Elliot has his hands around his wife's waist laughing, is smoking cigars, and sipping fine wine. Chase's older sisters stand there properly with their boyfriends and college friends. Tim, Allison, Nicolette and Chase are in a circle laughing and drinking what's supposed to be Pellegrino soda water but I know is spiked Pellegrino. They all fit into a puzzle if you had to put the pieces together. I'm the piece with barely any color that matches with the entire picture. Something happens in the crowd, which makes Tim, Nicolette, Allison, Chase and their parents chuckle.

"Ugh," I look at my cell with my screen saver of Grams and I. "Fake . . ."

"What? Miller, Pratt, Bynes . . . the parents?" he asks.

"Yes." I lean my head on the back of the wooden treehouse.

He smiles. "What about them? They all bother me . . . they have since I've lived here."

"Why?" I ask.

"Ever heard of the Radiohead song, "Fake Plastic Trees . . ."

"Yeah," I sway forward to put out my cigarette, "I love Radiohead . . ."

He takes it and officially puts it out, "Well it's them." He points.

"No one is real. Allison's and Tim's parents are here because they have put out a lot of money for Elliot's campaign, but I don't think Mr. Bynes can stand Mr. Miller. And, Mrs. Miller doesn't know what day it is. She's Lucy in the Sky with Diamonds. She should be in rehab."

I shake my head.

He breaks my intense staring. "And, the Bynes . . . Elliot he's an intense guy. I mean respectfully a decorated Marine, deacon at church, has a good family . . . She's sophisticated, independently wealthy . . . three beautiful triplets all going to college and a perfect son . . . It's too perfect. Something's gotta to give."

I can feel the wheels spinning in my head. "Like? . . ." I say.

"I don't know . . . it's his only boy."

He flips the flashlight on and off.

"There's something that wouldn't make this so perfect. I can't put my finger on it. I may have half a finger on it. Chase doesn't seem happy."

I shut my eyes.

"His dad is hard on him . . ." I motion for more as I sip out of the wine bottle.

He points to Nicolette's parents. "They are some-what normal, although, Dr. Tate is a tad overweight according to Mrs. Tate and she puts pressure on her husband, daughter and son, hence the diet blog she runs."

I mumble, "If you only knew."

"Huh?"

"Nothing," I say. "Go on."

"And, Mr. and Mrs. Pratt, the attorneys at law," he changes his voice to deep and dramatic. "Douche bag number one and douche bag number two." He strings the not-so-lovely names together. "They're both intelligent and good looking but extremely narcissistic. I can't imagine growing up in their home."

I agree.

"Where are your parents?" he asks.

"My dad's at work, and mom and Grams are at home." "How come you're taking a break? Same reason you were bawling the other day at County Line?" He lays it out. "None of your business," I say automatically.

"Oh," he says sarcastically, shining his light in my general direction.

I turn my head. I am silent. What is my problem? I should walk away. Obviously, the Pop Crowd hates him and I should, too. Instead I hand him the wine bottle.

He pushes it away looking down at my cell as it illuminates. "I can't drink tonight."

I put my lips on the wine bottle and gulp the remainder of the wine. My face feels numb.

"Is that Annie Styles?" He looks at the screen saver.

"Yep, my Grams . . ." I try to hold the cell up to his face and put another cigarette in my mouth.

"I met your Grams the other day. She was helping Mel plan the menu for teacher's appreciation week at Mariposa Beach Elementary School."

I sigh with frustration, lighting the Marlboro Light cigarette. "Yep, she got into some trouble for that one."

"Really? Why?"

"She has stage 4 lung cancer," I blow smoke out, and I can't help but smile at his shock.

"Right," the word falls out of his mouth. I shrug.

"So maybe smoking isn't the best idea . . ." he motions towards the cigarette.

"Yeah, but she's not seventeen." I tilt my head.

"Awe, so, that's makes it okay." He grins. "Anyways, she was pleasant."

I hand him my cigarette, as I pull the gawdy necklace off. He pretends to cough.

"Ten pounds lighter?" he asks. "I can borrow a forklift to help you next time."

I giggle. He's just as funny as he is in class. My head falls to the side. I am sleepy.

"Oh," he responds, as I feel him positioning my head against the wall. I am shivering, but I can't speak. I feel his bomber jacket on my shoulders and my eyes shut in his warm embrace. For the first moment in a long time, I feel safe with a teenage boy.

Chapter 12

THE TRUTH REVEALED

The next morning I open my eyes. They feel like Triple E boobs are stuck on the bottom lids. I feel for my phone, discovering my same outfit from last night still intact, blanket over me, lying on Chase's couch. I do not recall how I got there. I look at my phone. It reads 9:05 a.m. I try to remember how I got to the couch or what time I passed out. Blank. My phone buzzes with a new text and I it reads:

Mom: Sades, we have to talk about how tomorrow at school is going to look. I ran into Principal Dow at the store and he said you are going to qualify.

My mind flashes back to the meeting at school. If I qualify, that means I would be in Standard English, Standard Math, Standard History, Standard Science and Cheer.

Nicolette jumps right on me, "WAKE UP. We're going to Vegas, baby," Nicolette says.

"What time is it?" I yawn, slipping my phone casually under my legs, "Vegas?"

She nudges me. "The diner, bakery? You know the one we've been going to for centuries."

I pop up. "Crème Brule pancakes and coffee sound like my best friends."

"Easy pumpkin." Nicolette pushes me back down. "Dish."

"What?"

"BFM," she sits next to me, "Chase said you were passed out in his car."

"Really?" Tim stands in the doorway.

I look at her, "I'm changing the subject . . . Chase."

"A lady never talks . . ." She jokes, trying to snap out of it.

"Ladies, Uber ten minutes . . ." Allison yells.

"Ugh, I can't be ready in ten minutes. I have mascara under my eyes still. Why do I always only get ten minutes?"

Tim flashes a look at me. "You look beautiful like always. Okay, brush your teeth and hair and meet me at the front door."

I remember what he called me last night. Is he trying to make up for it? Ugh, I feel sick.

I walk to the bathroom.

"Sades, I love you." Nicolette grabs her purse and follows me. "Really," I brush my teeth.

"Yeah, last night was amazing with Chase," she says, pulling her pants down to pee.

I text Chase: what the hell did you tell Tim? Then I get a text from Tim.

Tim: U ok? BFM?

Tim: Where were you like all night? I start typing back.

Me: None of your business. Screw him!

I slip my cell in my oversized tote, pulling out a pair of Von Dutch jeans and an oversized off the shoulder, black, long shirt, heels from last night quickly changing and am out the door.

Chase meets me in the doorway before every one has arrived there.

"Tim asked me about you. I told him it was plainly physical."

"Okay." I dip my head.

He whispers, "yeah, well, then I fake made out with Nic."

"Oh Chase, you have to tell everyone," I say.

"Tell everyone what?" Allison puts her arm around Chase, "We all know anyway."

"Know what?" Chase asks.

"That your dad's campaign manager Johnny is hot and gay." She puckers her lips with her Kylie Jenner gloss.

Chase's cheeks flush.

He's saved by my cell ringing. "And now this is my mom."

"Hi," I say.

"You okay?" she asks.

"Yeah, going to breakfast with the crew," I talk quietly in the corner of the room.

"Okay, enjoy and then come home when you can." Her tone is different. "I spoke with the school psychologist, too. You will definitely need an IEP but I guess we have to meet as a team to figure it out."

I feel myself turning green, light green, yellow and now white.

"Love you," she says.

I hit end and place my cell back in my purse.

"What?" Allison asks with a high-pitched voice. "You look like death warmed over."

"She just wanted to check in . . ." I instantly hid behind my sunglasses.

Allison rolls her eyes. "Doesn't she trust you?" she laughs. "Why weren't your parents there last night?"

"I don't know," I mumble, trying to remember last night. "I think my dad had to work."

"Table for five," Al says to the hostess, plopping down in between Nicolette and I while the boys stand outside smoking. "I'm so bored of our lives. Tim and I are back on."

"Yay," Nic claps. "Double date."

Al looks at Nic and says, "So?"

Nic laughs. "Chase said he's always wanted me. He had something going on with some mysterious girl but that's over and done with now."

I look down. Yes, it is, but he certainly has something going on with a guy.

Al wraps her arms around Nic. "Oh Nic," she yelps, "it would be faster if they had us drive to the Vegas Restaurant in San Diego and sat us . . . I mean I have to leave for my intern interview in Playa De Rico soon," she says, annoyingly loud. I want to put my hand over her mouth.

"Allison, party of five," the waitress yells. Thank God.

We settle into a booth at the trendy restaurant, Vegas, painted red with blue and white dice and a ton of slot machines. People in their Sunday morning best are diving into their gourmet coffee. I sip my coffee, cringing at my upset stomach. "More creamer please." Maybe I can add enough creamer to dive in and disappear, I think to myself, trying to get rid of what my mom said about having a little something and needing an IEP.

Tim is across from me, peering at me. He looks pissed. Chase passes me a piece of bread. "Eat." It's a gesture. The table is silent.

"So, great party," I say.

"What's up with BFM?" Tim asks. So he wants everyone to hear.

"We found you in his car with his bomber jacket over you. He said he would drive you home but instead my dad said you could sleep on our couch," Chase said, "That guy is . . .," Chase jumps in.

"Fubared," I suggest.

"Yea," he says.

Tim, Allison and Nicolette look confused.

"It's from the movie *Saving Private Ryan*," I say. "My dad says it all the time."

"Mine too," Chase suggests, looking at me. "It's a military term."

A simple connection but worlds apart. Tim and Allison proceed to sip their coffee like they could care less that people died for their freedom. I want to share my dad's experience in the Marines during the Gulf War but I opt to stir my coffee.

"Are you in Army?" Nicolette hangs on his arm.

"Do you want me to be?" He barely kisses her on the lips. I can feel his repulsion.

"Barf," I say aloud. "Oh that was supposed to be in my head."

Nicolette picks at her egg whites with veggies omelet. "Awe,

just because you don't have someone, don't be jealous." It won't last, I say to myself.

"So why is Jay fubared?" I ask. "Long story," Tim suggests. "Another time?" Chase says.

"Basically, this girl Candace died because of BFM and his twin brother Jack," Nicolette replies. "It was before you moved here."

Jay has a twin.

"That was really sad," Allison says.

We all look at her. I look at her to make sure that came out of her mouth.

"You don't think anything is sad," Tim looks at her.

"I know. It was, okay, I sort of crushed on Jack, like hot, in elementary school," Allison reveals.

"So Jack has a special place in your heart?" Tim wraps his arm around her.

"You do," she looks at Tim.

Barf city. I shift my eyes over to the next table. I finally smile. "I like that girl's shirt."

They all turn to look and Allison reveals, "Free People." I nod.

"Okay, so we crossed that bridge safely. No BFM for Sadie," Allison says.

"I don't know . . . I haven't had a chance to give my opinion," I joke as I wave my hands against my face. Tim and Chase glare at me.

"You don't have an opinion," Al says plainly. "Just joking, stop looking so pale."

And there it is . . .

"Al," Chase says in rebuttal. "BFM."

"I'm not interested, that's my opinion," I finally say. No matter who I am trying to make jealous or get back, I cannot justify liking BFM to this crowd.

"No, retard." Allison turns my head towards the front of the restaurant. "He is here."

Gotta love being called a retard?!

There he is with black slacks and a long white button down with black boots and hair shaved. Is there a hot Jack under the fat suit?

"Crap, he's coming over . . ." I say.

"Well, Tim is waving him over . . ." Al kicks his leg under the table.

"Knock it off, bro," I punch him in the arm and then compose myself.

He stops to sit down at a table with Mel and the four girls who are dressed in cute pink Sunday school dresses.

"Oh hello," Tim says, casually sipping his coffee as Mel bends over in her short pink skirt and white lace oversized shirt.

Allison glares. "Who's that?" Al's brow points towards beautiful Mel. Jay says something to Mel and she turns to look at us. They both laugh. Mel waves.

I wave back, "That's his sister-in-law Mel, who happens to be an ex Victoria Secret's Angel," I close my eyes, wishing I could spontaneously combust before the next interrogation starts.

"How do you know them?" Nicolette asks.

"Mel's husband works with my dad," I lie, "So I've seen them at the fire station."

Al sits on the information, "BFM as a firefighter?" She throws her head back in laughter. "Just like the ROTC thing . . . ABSURDITY."

"No, his brother is the firefighter . . ." my voice is low.

"Well, he is an oversized fake SAT tutor by morning," Al pretends to peruse the menu, "or Big Fat Cushion for Sadie to pass out on."

"Allison, that is rude," I say. "Give up on the fake SAT tutor thing . . . half of the school did better than you."

"WOW." Her hand slips from the coffee and next thing I know my lap is on fire.

"Awe, HOT." I grab napkins to put over my jeans. "HOT!"

"ALLISON!" Tim yells handing me more napkins.

"No, wait, first of all, you are gone all last night probably screwing Jay in his old car like you did with Chase for the last three years, " Allison starts.

"WHAT?" Nicolette yells.

"Say something Chase," I look at him.

He runs his finger around the rim of the coffee mug, not looking up.

"And, you're really not retaking the SATs, are you?" Nicolette asks.

"You're being evaluating for a learning disability?" Allison brings out her sweetest baby voice for that one.

How did they find out?

I grab my tote. "Please move." I nudge Chase to move, "MOVE!!!" I scream. The restaurant stops at the commotion and everyone stares.

"Sades!" Chase stands.

"We were wondering if you have to repeat junior year . . ." Nicolette says.

I run passed Jay's table and through the emergency exit, letting off the alarm and start speed walking on the street. I wipe my jeans as I walk. It still burns my legs. I hate her. Like with a fiery passion I hate her.

RUN, RUN, RUN! My heels pitter patter on the cement sidewalk. I taste the tears. My soul is in a million pieces. I want to go back to the last time I felt alive. I run to the park and hide in the concrete tunnel, pulling my flask out of my purse and sipping until I feel alive again.

"Sadie," Jay peeks his head in the tunnel, which is ten-feet in diameter and painted gold.

"We're not friends. You can't keep talking to me like this.

They think we slept together . . ." I sip my flask. "Why?" he plops next to me.

I run my hands on my jeans trying to dry them. "I don't know because I was passed out in your car all night."

His voice is defensive. "You slept there until 6 a.m. this morning. I carried you in before the reporters came to Chase's house. Elliot wanted me to move you."

"What?" I sip my flask again.

"Sadie," he looks at his cell. "It's 10:30 in the morning. Why are you drinking?"

"JAY, GO AWAY," I scream.

"Okay, I will, but do you realize that no one in their respects you? Maybe, Chase, a little, but I bet he'd be willing to sell you out, too."

I shrug, letting the tears roll. "You're wrong. It's just . . ." I pull my knees to my chest, bury my head and sob.

His big ass body is bent in the tunnel. He pulls out a corner of a tissue from his tight pocket and hands it to me. "Hang on, it's in there." He tries pulling out the rest but it's stuck in his pocket.

The other half of my smile from last night appears.

"Okay." He's pulling it out micro-piece by micro-piece, handing it to me. "This should do it."

I hold my stomach, doubling over in laughter. "Thanks. This is really helpful," I manage to say.

He catches the contagious laughter and says. "Anything I can do to help a friend out."

And, it's silent for a while. Birds chirp. Clouds move over away from us as the sun peeks out. The beautiful daisies blow in the wind. It reminds me of spring in Wisconsin. We lived on a small farm that had a small pond that froze in the winter and in the spring colorful daisies popped up all around it. My dad said it was because the previous owners had a Rhodesian Ridgeback named Daisy.

"Whatever it is, it will be okay, Sadie." He leans his head against the tunnel wall.

"No." I gaze out at the clouds moving quickly over the park and the earth gets dark again. "It'll ruin me."

"What?" I feel his stare.

"They know I have a learning disability and it's just leverage for Allison." I fidget with the tissue he gave me.

"She's a bitch," he sings out and then slams his hands against his head. "Who the hell cares. And, you know how many brilliant and famous people have learning disabilities? Bill Gates? Albert Einstein?"

He is so nice. My cell plays Led Zeppelin's "Stairway to Heaven" as I dig in my purse to find it.

"Hi Mom, I'm coming, meet me at the park," I say clicking the end button. "I gotta go."

"Okay," he says. "Whatever happens on Monday, just know you're worth gold."

"Gold, huh?" I mumble.

Chapter 13

CHRYSALIS AND THE KISS FROM DEATH

"Who's that?" my mom asks as she rolls down her window.

"No one," I reply putting on my seatbelt.

"That's Jay Felix," my dad says, "And, hi, to you, too." "What are you doing home?" I ask.

"I called Plumb. He wants to meet on Monday to talk about next year. I'll explain what he said when we get home," my dad says.

"Okay," I comply.

"You did qualify," he adds.

"I know, Dad," I say with an attitude. "I figured all these years of struggling chalked up to something."

I zone out for the rest of the conversation as my mom talks to me about what the school will probably say about my testing and what it could possibly look like. Same deal. Standard classes with mostly special education kids. Once we get to Chase's to pick up my Jeep, my mom adds, "One more thing, Sades."

"What now?"

She turns to me. "Grams is in the hospital. We have to go see her."

"What happened?" I plead.

"The last round of chemo didn't do her good, and she's still fighting off that bronchitis."

"That she got from the last event she did." My memory flashes to my conversation with Jay about the white party.

The sky turns grey. Thunder rumbles. I try to blink back the tears. I need her. I need to tell Grams I'm afraid of what everyone is going to say on Monday about my learning disability. I need to tell her Tim called me a slut and Chase called it off. I need to tell her I am scared.

The afternoon is a complete blur. The hospital feels like icky stuff crawling on me. Walking in and passing each room with a sick patient feels like a bad dream. I hold my mom's hand as we enter Grams' room. Grams lays there fragile and frail, white and wrinkly, like a chrysalis ready to fly. Like another one of Kennedy's women dying. All she can do is look at me. Her blue eyes, my exact color, a window to her soul. I hold her hand for hours.

"Baby," my dad takes my hand out of Grams.' "You've been here for ten hours. You need to rest before school tomorrow. Shower and change. The doctor said she will make it through the night. Just come back in the morning before school."

I squeeze my dad's hand as tears well in my eyes. "Okay." I back up from the bed.

"Hey, it's gonna be okay," he kisses my cheek.

"Yeah." I back away.

"And, I'm so very proud of you with the school thing," he says.

If he only knew how scared of myself I am. I kiss Grams and say bye to my parents.

"Hey," I sniffle, starting up my Jeep and a cigarette.

I'm not sure why I call him. Maybe because Tim wasn't trying to bring me down at breakfast.

"Hey," he replies. There is something in his voice. "You okay?"

"Can I come over?" I ask with a crackly voice.

"Yeah," he replies.

The hospital is down the block from Tim's. I change out of my coffee-stained jeans and into my jean shorts. I know Allison is away with her dad at an internship interview in San Diego. I go into the kitchen where he is pouring himself a glass of Glenlivet. I want a double. Through the kitchen sliding glass door, I see Chase on the sand leading Nicolette in a Yoga routine.

Tim looks at me head to toe, handing me a double. If looks could undress . . .

I sit at the marble kitchen table balled up in the blue upholstered chair with a floral pattern going through. I look at the table set up with fancy hand-painted plates, three different sized forks, spoons, wine glasses and knives. I wonder if it is ever used.

"How's your mom?" I ask.

"Going back to rehab in a few days. Let's not talk about her though." He sits next to me, holding my hand. He sways a little from the drinks. And frankly, I am almost there after that strong drink and zero food in my stomach.

"Alcohol makes you sweet," I say. He squeezes my hand.

"Another one," I say holding up my empty glass with tears in my eyes.

I look up at him and he uses the pads of his thumbs to wipe away my tears. His hands are soft, unlike my dad's. This guy is a white-collar worker in the making. He made my heart beat heavily at the young age of 14 years old and it has continued every day since. My body aches for more of his touch when his thumbs touch my face and every moment before that.

I sigh as the tears fall. I am vulnerable in front of him and uncomfortable. It is the first time I've cried in front of him. I remove myself, standing up and walking away. I can feel his eyes on me like they always are. He always undresses me with his eyes. People would tell me in private that they'd watch him do it all the time. I'm not stupid in some ways.

He stands up, walking unsteadily to me. "Sadie, your grandma is in the hospital. It's okay to cry." He takes my hand, kissing it with his perfect sun-kissed lips. "We don't have to talk."

"She's my best friend." Tears well in my eyes. I don't feel like talking either.

He pulls me close, our stomachs touch, and he sighs. His eyes are red from drinking all day. This is the moment I have been dreaming about.

He pulls my chin up.

We have stood like this once before. Eyes locked. Heavy breathing. Hormones raging. Ready to do something high school kids do all the time. This time is different. I'm not sure why. I don't want to say stop. He puts his hand on the back of my neck and pulls me to his lips. Bare Chicka Bare Rare!

"No Tim," the school uniform pig-tailed girl in me says quickly. I hadn't seen her in while.

"It's okay," he whispers, biting my lower lip as he grips my face with his soft hands.

I am like out-of-body pulsating. Grams, my learning disability and my secret with Chase are on my mind, but his BITE alleviates any thoughts.

His kiss: wet, sensual, slightly aggressive. He uses his tongue to feather, dig and lick like he is looking for something, lips to soften and teeth to bite. I melt inside like candle wax all throughout my body. It reminds me of the wax that drips from a long candle on the dining room table on special holidays.

I sway back, looking in his hungry eyes. If I could wrap that kiss in a bow and show it to my grandkids, it would be a big set of pink lips on a bed of red petals with very small spikes. I'd really have to explain the spikes in a gentle way.

Despite the bottle of Glenlivet I am swimming in, the continuous pulse takes over my body, the pig-tailed girl comes back to remind me of Allison. "What about Allison," I ask?

"I don't care about her. I hate her sometimes." He moves closer, kissing my neck and running his fingers along the top of my jean shorts.

"I want you," he breathes alcohol into my ear. "Like more than I've ever wanted someone. It's always been you, Sadie. You're so beautiful."

I wanted to hear smart but the alcohol, oh man, the alcohol, the way he kisses me and touches me, it makes me forget.

Allison, him calling me dumb and breakfast can go out the window.

I let him kiss me hard again, wrapping my legs around him as he grabs them. He kisses me like he is turning himself in for murder tomorrow. He pushes me against the Goddard painting in his kitchen, hands on my butt, waist, face and then lets my legs down.

"Ever. Since. We. Met." He manages to speak through kisses he's placing on my stomach fiddling with the button on my jean shorts. "God, Sadie. "

"I know," I close my eyes, my body saturated with candle wax. I start to take my left boot off with my right boot.

"Boots stay on." He smirks. "Please."

I rub my lips together, pushing back into my boots, "Fine, but we need to go somewhere besides the kitchen. If Chase and Nic come in here and see us . . ."

"Okay." He removes his shirt and backs me up to the guest bedroom by the kitchen, lips locked with mine. He lands on the bed. I look at him. He could have done an ad for Under Armor underwear like then and there without working out for the audition.

I walk back, twisting and twirling with my tshirt pushed up, jean shorts hanging on the waist and black boots, G-string lacy underwear and black boots. I know he's turned on, just by looking at me. I can feel his eyes on me as they have been for years. I feel hot and sexy. I pause as I feel Allison, Grams and my learning disability diagnosis stacked up like a Neapolitan ice cream.

"Girl." He buries his head in my pillow. "Get over here."

I smirk, trying to not take my eyes off him, but the door creaks open slowly. At first I see a dark shadow.

It's a familiar dark shadow.

"Al?" my voice curves around her name like I need to be pinched.

"What the hell, Sadie," Allison's voice transcends throughout the hallway as she looks at me and then at Tim.

'What the hell, Sadie, or what the hell, Sadie, and Tim?' I say in my head.

Tim jumps up. "Get out." He orders me like I am his sex slave.

I nod profusely like I am his sex slave.

"Allison," we both say in sync.

"What?" She turns, tears enveloping her almond eyes. "It just happened, right?"

I nod profusely throwing my shirt and shorts on.

"Sadie, I am not surprised . . ." Her bitchiness returns. "Chase, Jay and now Tim."

"I . . . I . . . never slept with Jay or Chase, for that matter."

I say. "You guys are so misguided."

"Misguided?" Al asks in an octave voice I'd prefer not to explore. "You were hooking it up with my boyfriend."

"We were broken up Al," Tim mumbles.

"For like the day . . ." Al says.

Chase appears in the hallway sweaty, shirtless; Nicolette follows quickly behind.

Allison screams, "Both of you never talk to me again." I'm silent. She's heard enough from me.

"Al, stop," Tim's voice is desperate as she makes her way down the hall.

I look at him. He doesn't even make eye contact with me. "I think you'd better go," Nicolette squares me.

"No, Nic, I'll leave," Allison yells as she makes her way to the front door.

I grab my car keys and my purse to follow her. "Sadie, don't drive right now," Chase grabs my arm.

"I have to," I walk through the house as quickly as possible and scream at the top of my lungs. "Party is over."

Is it really over?

"Sadie," Chase grabs my arm.

"Ouch, what?" I say pulling my arm away. "Tell them and I'll stay."

He pauses with a torn look on his face. "Tell them what?"

"Thought so . . ." I stumble down the stairs. He tries to help me up.

"STOP!!!" I scream.

Chase backs away, "I care about you."

I point to him. "No, you don't, and you know it."

He looks at me like I just stabbed him in the back and says, "Go then, slut."

"Sadie leave?" Nicolette looks at him.

I'm behind the wheel. I start my Jeep in the driveway and put it in drive, hands shaking. I pull forward toward Tim's garage and realize reverse is what I wanted.

My nose sniffles. My eyes blur from tears. My life is a smashed bug on the windshield.

"If Tim could just see my abilities maybe he'd stay," I mumble as I manage to get my Jeep on the street following Allison in the brand new, red two-door Mercedes her parents bought her for her sixteenth birthday. Spoiled brat! Why am I'm even bothering?

"Pull over, there's always cops on this street," I yell. She pulls her car over and I follow suit.

"Allison," I jump out.

"You want to talk," she jumps out of her car lighting a cigarette,

"I pulled over because I want to know what happened."

"He was comforting me because of Grams." I sit next to her. Her voice is grumbling and low. "I could care less about your Grams."

"We just kissed." My hand is on my forehead.

"You were about to sleep together though?" She turns to me, looking at me. Her eyes are watery. "I need him, Sades."

I am quiet. Allison has never needed anything in her life. She has everything. She's like Barbie but with freshly brown ombre'd hair. She will probably have 734 careers, be good at every one of them and live in a Barbie Dreamhouse with a real-life Ken.

"It's been going on for a while now, huh, Sadie?" She looks me in the eyes. "You're just a piece of meat to him, just like you are with Chase. He will never want anything more than sex from you. He thinks you're stupid. They think you're stupid. I'm the only one who tries to get the truth out of you so we can at least have that."

The candle wax slips out of my toes.

"I . . ." I manage to say.

"I . . . I," she mimics, putting her hand up. "Save your brain waves."

Tim and Nicolette come running down the street. "NOW GET OUT OF MY SIGHT!!!!" she screams.

I exit stage left.

"Sadie, let me talk to her." Tim looks at me out of breath. "All this time sleeping with Chase." Nicolette turns to me with hands on her hips. "For the answers to the tests? Yeah, Chase just told me."

Tim looks at me like I am a piece of trash with extra poop on it.

My head spins and I'm spiraling downward. "That's not true, Nic."

Nicolette turns around, giving me the evil eye and pointing her finger. "Screw you! We created you," she says, like I'm a Frankenstein project.

"And, she stops hooking up with Chase and goes for my boyfriend." Al shakes her head and points to my Jeep. "You have lost your mind . . . GO."

"I have lost my mind." My body sways. "Tim, what about texting me like every day all day," I say. "And, Allison, remember the twins from San Diego? Not to mention the guy the other week from UCLA."

Tim gives me his infamous icy look he usually gives Al and roars, "GO," as his mouth cracks with ice. He walks over to Allison hugging her even though she tries hard to resist. My heart cracks. He always chooses her over me.

Chapter 14

BLACK

I start the engine to my Jeep and skid past them. I crank up the volume to the Rolling Stones favorites, knocking over a half-drank Java in the meantime, bobbing in and out of the cars on Pacific Coast Highway under the dark night sky. It's exceptionally dark tonight. I search for the stars. The stoplight forces me to stop and then I turn left into the Mariposa Beach Elementary School parking lot so I can light my cigarette without crashing. I glance at the picture I have of Grams and I in the center console. We are dressed in designer Michael Kors white dresses at a fancy wine-pairing event she catered for the insanely rich city of Montecito. We are laughing in the picture because we just saw Oprah and are slightly star struck. But the even funnier thing was, the DJ must have had a lapse in judgment as he flipped on DJ Snake and Lil Jon's "Turn Down for What." I remember Grams singing the words to me and laughing that she knew the song. The music quickly switched to classical.

I look behind me to see if any of my friends are chasing me, following me. Nothing.

"Screw them!" I scream. "They are not my friends." Tears gush down my cheeks. "We are over!!!!"

I feel a wave of nausea, which for some reason, forces my foot on the gas pedal. Radiohead, "Fake Plastic Trees" pops on Pandora as I cruise the parking lot of the school. I sing to the song.

I want to call Grams. I pick up my cell phone; seven missed calls I read my mom's text message 7:58 p.m. Mom: She's gone.

"NO!!!!!!!" I scream, throwing my cell down.

The next thing I know my eyes are fogged with buckets of tears coming out. I need to stop this Jeep. I feel for the brake with my right foot but something is stuck and I can't press it down. I'm heading for the front office of an elementary school building with my Jeep at 25 miles per hour.

"Why isn't this effin' Jeep stopping?" My foot slams down and next thing I know my Jeep smacks into the window of the front office. My body jerks back and then forth as my head smacks against the dashboard. My world is black.

Chapter 15

FLOATING

"Hello Sadie." A nurse dressed in purple scrubs pops in my peripheral. "I'm putting this IV in your arm."

"Hi," I am still floating in a bottle of Glenlivet singing, Radiohead's "Fake Plastic Trees."

I'm not going to lie. It's a good song.

"She looks pale and green at the same time," a familiar male voice sounds. "Let's get this mascara off her face."

Someone is wiping my face and someone is pulling my hair back. I smell throw-up. And, someone is holding my hand.

"Jay," the nurse says, "we gave her some anti-nausea, anti-anxiety and anti-itch so we can let her sleep it off."

"Jay with green eyes," I belt out opening my eyes.

"I'll stay until at least one of her parents gets here," Jay says. A minute later my mom walks in.

"Oh baby."

Jay lets go of my hand. "Mom," I mumble.

I sober slowly just from the sound of her voice. I look at my mom. She looks beautiful wearing a white velour outfit. Her blond hair reminds me of an angel's.

"You look like an angle," I say softly as I take her hand, "AN GEL . . ."I whisper in her ear.

My mom doesn't speak. She just puts her hand over her mouth and cries.

"It's okay." I reach for her, but the stuff they gave me makes me relax.

"Nurse," her mom's voice urgent, "Who called?"

"Jay," the nurse yells. I hear footsteps but I am too tired to open my eyes again so I listen. "Can you tell Mrs. MacPhearson what happened?"

"Go ahead, Jay," another voice sounds. "Hi Mrs. MacPhearson, I'm Officer Sob. I was first cop on the scene. I'll be handling her case."

"Her case? Is she in some sort of trouble?" my mom asks. "Please sit down, Ma'am," he says.

Jay speaks. His voice is velvety, like expensive drapes I want to wrap around my body. "My sister-in-law Mel was at a meeting at the church at 8 p.m., across the street from Mariposa Beach Elementary School when she heard the crash. She is in the waiting room right now if you want to talk to her. When they all ran out of the meeting, she recognized Sadie's white Jeep, although, it was pancaked to the building, so she immediately called 911 and then me, because we know each other," Jay says in a low voice, "from school."

"Is she going to be okay?" My mom voice shakes. I want to reach for her but I can't move.

"She was unconscious but breathing and pretty intoxicated," Jay says.

"Well, thank you, Jay. We have it from here," my mom says. "I'm sorry it took me so long to come. My mom passed tonight and I was with the doctors at this hospital on the seventh floor. I just had my phone in my purse in another room because I didn't want to disturb anyone. My husband is coming . . . there he is . . . Wyatt."

Oh great . . .

"It's okay," Officer Sob says.

"Okay, I'm going to leave," Jay says, "And, by the way, Mrs. MacPhearson, I'm sorry for your loss."

"I have yours and Mel's information," Officer Sob says. I hear my dad's voice and Jay's voice in the background.

A new male voice sounds. "Her blood alcohol level was 0.18." Maybe it's the doctor.

"God, kids these days. She's so small for that level," Officer Sob says. "Okay, I'll get all the paperwork done. Thanks doc."

"She needs to stay overnight and sleep it off. We can check that concussion in the morning," the doctor says.

My eyes close.

The purple blob is checking the aching spot on my head and the merry go round is spinning faster and faster. I ralph again. The nurses inject me with anti-nausea meds and I feel better instantly.

The night passes in a blur with nothing left in my stomach, not even green acid. Glimpses of the Glenlivet girl trickle through, and I giggle. Then there's the silence of the car ride in the morning, the old me frowning as I sober.

"How much trouble am I in?" I manage as my mom holds my hand in the backseat. Mispronouncing words is something I've always had to concentrate at not doing but today it's something I let slide.

"A lot," my mom replies, putting a washcloth on my head. It makes me feel so cooled down.

"My brake wouldn't work." Silence.

"Your cell phone was wedged in there and you crashed into the side of an elementary school building," My mom's voice gets an octave level higher. "So, you're basically screwed."

I want my flask.

Chapter 16

DEAR GRAMS

In the northern hemisphere, summer is especially warm because during this time that part of the earth is directly under the sun and its rays are focused on the area. Summer brings lots of outdoor social activities: picnics, beach days, summer camps, water park days. This season the days are longer and nights shorter. In Mariposa Beach, summer solstice is my favorite. I usually end up at the Mariposa Beach Club for days full of beach activities swimming in the pool, boy watching with my friends, nightly bonfires and party after party. But after what happened with the car accident, I am basically on house arrest from my parents and under my parole officer's care. Stuck at home all summer, I write Grams letters she'll never see.

Dear Grams,

This summer, I barely left my room. Mom and dad took me off of all social media. Took my phone. Took my television. Took my iPod and iPad. Took my heart out of my chest and stomped on it. I will be a prisoner in my own home and have no contact with the outside world FOREVER. At least I have the Birds of Paradise flowers we planted that first summer. You're right, the color of it reminds me of the inside of a mango. But mostly words cannot express my desire for your touch, to hear your laugh, to talk to you. Did I mention I have a parole officer, 360 hours of community service and eight weeks of AA meetings, basically a judge who wants to make an example out of me.

Love,
Your favorite grandchild, Sadie Lynn

Dear Grams,

Every day I wake up to feel the sun in my room teasing me. Mom and dad leave a breakfast item and hot coffee on the floor outside. At least I still get food. My dad hasn't spoken to me since the night you died. I'm a bad daughter.

I'm sorry you had to leave. I am a slut. I am a bad friend. I am dumb. I am nothing.

Love, Your Favorite (only) Grandchild, SLM

Dear Grams,

There are 234 stars on my ceiling, although, I may not be counting them right since I don't know how to count, since I am dumb and have a learning disability.

Miss you, SLM

Dear Grams,

I love you here and there and everywhere upside down and right side up to the sky and around the whole world (Just like you had stitched on the pillow case).

Sadie, Sades, SLM

Dear Grams,

My mom went through my closet and pulled all the crop tops, short skirts and shorts, knee high boots, and basically anything that screamed slut and burned it all. She took out all the alcohol in the house. We are dry. We have several conversations about moving back to Wisconsin. I wanted to call Katie and Sarah this summer and tell them I want to go the country music festival and drink berry shakes. I heard mom on the phone with Sarah's mom. She was crying. I often wonder how I would have ended up in Wisconsin. I need to go to church.

SLM

Dear Grams,

Another part of my punishment from the judge was to take my driver's license away for a year. Not driving all summer was really embarrassing considering my parents sold my Jeep, too. Not going to the beach, boat trips, parties were extremely embarrassing. But the most embarrassing was attending

AA meetings at seventeen years old. I was the youngest one there. Not to mention I decided . . . I mean we decided that I should take an online Health class so I can lessen my load my senior year and concentrate better on fewer classes (per IEP). Plus, I had to fit in my volunteer hours. And, my parole officer, special education staff at Mariposa Beach HS and my parents said it would be good for me to learn about health and nutrition for my sobriety. Well, mom said that.

Loser MacPhearson

Dear Grams,

My dad drove me to every single AA meeting, which was close to his work. Talk about Toto, we are not in Kansas anymore. He'd sit in his car while I went in. I listened to people who were HIV positive, homeless, raped, abused; things far worse than my measly learning disability, some bad partying/friend choices and you dying. I felt like I was a fish out of water so I just listened. I never stayed for coffee and donuts at the end. I left as soon as it was over. I didn't feel like I belonged there anyway. I didn't have a problem. I hated the way alcohol tasted but loved the way it made me feel. Did that make me an alcoholic? Or was it just experimentation and a judge's orders?

Love always and forever, SLM

Dear Grams,

Truth was my life was pretty good. I lived in a lovely private beach community with anything a teenager could ask for. I had two loving parents. Dad won't talk to me, still. Mom barely does but she cries a lot. We all miss you.

S

Dear Grams,

Once I met the Pop Crowd, I became selfish, insecure, envious and desperate to be part of it and close to Tim Miller. I get it now! And after having zero friends visit me in the hospital and no one checking on me all summer, I'd allow them back in my life just to feel the high. To picnic on the beach with margaritas and catered Mexican food with my friends on a random Tuesday afternoon. To charter a boat to the island because we could. To throw a Back to School Party at the second biggest pool in California because the owner was my friend's parents. Being with the Pop Crowd meant getting me things I couldn't get before. And, continuing to be with them meant I could get anything I wanted in the future as well. I have let material things take over.

SLM

It has been two months since Grams passed. I begged my parole officer to attend an AA meeting in town so I can ride my bike to and not make my dad drive me to one in Los Angeles, where I really learned that my life was not so bad. And, maybe, the continued awkward silence wouldn't be so awkward if it didn't have to happen.

I ride my bike to the church across from Mariposa Beach Elementary. My eyes glance over to the construction workers rebuilding the frame for the side of the office they are trying to get done before school starts. ALL MY MISTAKE!

I walk in the church room and find a seat in the furthest square chair out from the circle. It feels weird to be back at church. Step 6 of the program is to believe in a higher being. I never stopped believing in God.

An older man I recognize from working at the grocery store explains how summertime is hard for him because he runs out of non-alcoholic drink ideas. A teacher from Malibu talks about how her week is always tough at work and she wants to unwind with a glass or wine or twelve at night but she settles for a warm bath and Twinkies. I want to laugh but I maintain. I see a tall, slender female dressed in a long black dress and a pink baseball cap. I recognize her instantly.

"Hi, my name is Mel, and I'm an alcoholic." She pulls her Good Vibes only baseball hat off and looks around.

What the hell? I make eye contact with her.

"I know I haven't said much... I like to listen. I've been in AA for ten years. I was attending Malibu's AA group but I decided to attend this one because I guess I'm not embarrassed anymore to go to AA in my city . . . after ten years . . . only took ten years." She smiles.

My eyes meet hers, and I feel my lips parting my teeth.

"I'm proud to be a part of it. So here's my story just so you all know. I was born in Sydney, Australia. My parents were extremely poor and made very bad decisions, so I bailed when I turned 14. I haven't talked to them since. I blame them for my brother's suicide. That's a whole 'nother conversation. Anyhow, I made my way to New York City by living on the streets and selling my body, if you will."

I feel my head shake.

"When I turned 16, I was hounded by a customer to do some modeling and eventually got to the Victoria's Secret Angels level. At least my parents gave me a pretty face."

More smiles appear.

"When I was 25 years old, I had traveled all over the world modeling, drinking, partying, VIP here, limos, champagne and men. I never ate. I drank vodka for every meal and smoked like a smokestack. Well, one night, I was drunk in the Sky bar in the Wilshire Hotel. I saw this gorgeous, extremely famous man who shall remain nameless. At the time, he was charming and rich. We got drunk and went to his hotel room. He drugged me and did some pretty horrible things to me. I will spare you the details."

My hands sweat. I think of the wild look on the brown-haired hottie with the tiger tattoo outside of Johnny's house that one day. What if I had gotten in his car?

"The next day, my friends saw me and we called the police. They sent the fire department and paramedics because of the events that happened. I met this young paramedic/firefighter early on the job who held me in the back of the paramedic van all the way to the hospital and the entire hospital visit. That was my first day of sobriety. I quit the modeling business and decided to start AA. That was ten years ago."

"What happened to the guy?" An older gentleman asks. "We were friends for a long time. But, he became my husband and we have four daughters," she points to her wedding ring and necklace with all their birthstones.

I grimace nervously. I like her.

The meeting is over. I stay back to talk to Mel. "Hi," I say.

"Hi Sadie." She reaches for a hug.

I give her a quick one. "Thanks for sharing your story. I had no clue . . ."

"Sometimes you have to go through it to get to it." She smiles.

"I'm happy you're here," she says. "I've been worried about you." I nod.

"Mel, I never said thank you for calling the police.

I know my parents and I sent you and Jay a thank you card, but I wanted to say it in person."

"Oh Sadie, I'm happy you're getting help. You're lucky to have such loving parents. Hey, let's sit and have some coffee together."

She gingerly takes my wrist.

I sit next to her. She seems so put together.

"Sadie, do you have a sponsor?" she asks, passing me the creamer for the coffee.

"I did at the other AA meeting but never used her. My parents are pretty on top of it."

"Well, I can be yours," Mel suggests. I agree.

Chapter 17

FIRST DAY OF SENIOR YEAR

It has been eight weeks or so after everything went down. The Gerbera Daisies Grams, mom and I planted died. My friends haven't talked to me since the night I crashed into the building. I didn't go to the last three days of school as I was in the hospital and dealing with Mariposa Beach Police Department. I pat down the bags under my eyes that show the sleepless nights and anxiety and wipe leftover makeup on my white legs hoping to make them look tanner.

I smear it all over my legs.

"Dumb ass," I say to myself as I rub.

This morning on the first day of school, I should have been across the street at Starbucks with the Pop Crowd swimming in the sea of popularity. It's a tradition the morning of the first day. We'd meet at Starbucks, get a skinny whatever and smoke cigarettes, kissing ourselves because we were too pretty.

#tooprettyforthisbeachcity, we'd say.

Instead, here I am hiding behind a purple fountain grass tree, thinking Kuwait in the summer would be better than here. The ten-minute warning bell sounds and the fog layer forms chills all over my body. I double check my bike lock on my strawberry-colored cruiser. I feel like a nerd. After all, I have until June to ride it. My Jeep, or what's left of it, belongs to someone else now.

My parents can't drive me. My dad has to be at work at 6 a.m. and my mom doesn't want to. No, she seriously said, "I would drive you Sadie, but I don't want to."

I sort of laughed inside when she said that. I think she wanted to laugh, too, but she hid behind her oversized Disney coffee cup. I was trying to give her the benefit of the doubt since we had lost Grams and oh, yeah, I became known around town as the DUI teenager.

Nonetheless, it's my senior year and up until eight weeks ago, I had been enmeshed with the Pop Crowd. Do you know how it feels to have everyone want to be you? Look like you? Dress like you? Hang with you? Act like you? Want to sleep with you? Want to destroy you?

And this was our senior year and it is supposed to be the year of years: cheerleading, prom, football games, bubble parties, senior trip to Disneyland, senior trip to Mexico, snowboarding trips to Mammoth, boat parties and pool parties. Or just being sexy and beautiful, the thing I was known for ever since freshman year when I walked into school the first day of school with a short skirt on that I didn't want to wear but Allison forced me to. Was I still that girl that could get away with JUST being sexy and pretty, or did I have more inside?

I pull myself up in an incognito fashion. Standing up, I pull out a ripped paper from the pocket of my ripped jean shorts reviewing my new schedule as I walk swiftly on Mariposa's campus, like there are snipers in the trees about to shoot at any moment.

Period 0: Standard English

Period 1: Standard Math Period

2: Standard U.S. History

Nutrition Break

Period 3: Standard Integrated Science
Period 4: Standard Psychology

My life, STANDARD at this point. Fifty-six days of sobriety, zero friends, fourth year of high school. I take a seat on the cement outside my Period 0 English class. The cement is cold. A text message slips through my old cell phone, one I literally received back this morning. My mom reminds me after leaving my breakfast on the floor outside of my room like I'm the family dog. "The only reason you have it Sadie is because you're riding your bike to school. I will be checking it nightly. It's for text messages and phone calls." The words appear in my head one at a time like it's an advertisement at a baseball game. My thoughts, at least they're still feeding me.

Dad: Officer Sob will meet you at Mariposa Beach Elementary School at 1.

> 11223 Peacock Drive every day until graduation.

Dad
Me: Thank you

I shake my head and a smile appears. He hasn't spoken more than six words to me. Those six words divulged from his mouth this morning after eight weeks: "Have a good day at school." My jaw dropped. I think my dog was even surprised to feel vibrations of him talking to me. My dad and I were always close in Wisconsin. Ever since we moved to Mariposa Beach, he started to work more and our relationship became robotic.

People whisper as they walk by. The cement is still cold, but I sit, so I can keep my head low and I put my backpack under my legs, keeping them from touching the cold cement. Another text message chimes through on my cell phone. It has to be my dad again. What now? Can I offer you a messed-up daughter with a side of sorry I ruined your life and career, again?

I look down. It reads 818 555-2233, a number I grew to memorize, which belonged to Tim Miller.

Tim: Have a good first day of school, Sades.

I freeze and become one with the cement, "Holy heart failure Batman . . ." I whisper to myself. At least I have my sense of humor.

First of all, he's thinking of me, but, more importantly, he hasn't talked to me since the crash, eight weeks ago. I can't process it right now; my heart is heavy. I have to wait until I am out of the sniper zone. I shake my head, trying to pull myself up from the cold cement at the sound of the bell.

A tall, slightly overweight African American girl with horribly dyed orange hair stands next to me and interrupts my thoughts—Orange.

"I can always count on you Sadie to be in the dumb classes." She smirks. She is dressed comfortably in a pair of tight yoga pants and a long loose tank top. She looks pretty cute.

She speaks. I've never heard her speak. I've heard her grunt and make noise.

I half smile at her, "It's nice to see you too, Orange."

The only reason I know to call her Orange is because she is Orange Crush, the girl fighter at our school. Maybe that's why Allison paid the kid with Down Syndrome to pull her pants down?

EWW, why is the name Allison in the four front of my brain??

"I heard you slept with Allison's boyfriend and you no longer belong in the Pop Crowd." Her body towers over me. "Good for you."

"We never slept together and I'm not sure where I stand with them," I say.

I almost want to say to Orange, 'I don't owe you jack. I'm just afraid you'll crush me to death,' but I just stand there, zipping up my white Roxy sweatshirt, still cold.

Orange looks over at Allison, Nicolette and her minions walking like an army to English. Once they see me, Allison puts her hand over her mouth, whispering. They all laugh.

"I don't think you have any hope, Sadie. Once you wrong Allison, she will not stop for anything to ruin you." Orange giggles uncontrollably. "Who cares though? She's a ho. Nicolette and the others are scared of her. I could care less about you either," she says, taking her seat.

That was almost as funny as when my mom said, 'I would drive you but I don't want to'.

I nod my head in agreement. I wish I could roll my eyes, but I'm afraid to. Orange has no clue what she is talking about.

Orange laughs, "I'm being serious."

"I know, what do you want me to say?" My eyes widen as I realize I just said what I meant. The little girl inside says, 'please don't crush me, please don't crush me.' I catch a glimpse of Allison and Nicolette going out of their way to walk by my classroom.

"What a retard drunk!" I overhear Allison yell.

Orange gets up, runs to the door and yells, "BITCH!" as loud as possible.

Allison trips over Nicolette as they scurry into Mr. Hotsy's AP English class.

I hide my face with my hands and shake with laughter. It's a laughter that has been trapped in for a while and feels good to let out a little at a time.

"That will be the only time I say something for you," Orange sits back down, looking at her iPhone, "I really hate Allison. I'm serious."

My body still shakes with laughter and finally I find words in the break. "Do you have to say I'm serious after everything you say or can you just talk normally?" I feel my cheeks fire and my eyes widen. "Oh snap."

Orange stands up and walks over to my desk, standing a few inches from my face.

At this point I'm shaking from laughter as I stare back and say, "Well, I am dumb but not that dumb, I'm serious."

She backs up and laughs, "Dude, I didn't know you were so funny, Sadie."

Then she sits down and all the air in my body comes out of my mouth in relief. I am funny.

Mr. Clark walks over to Orange who surprisingly sits next to me.

"Hi Orange, how was your summer?"

"Good, my mom took me to New York City for a few weeks," she says.

Mr. Clark squeals like a little girl, "What?"

Orange laughs, "I thought of you because we went to this . . ."

I was surprised to hear a nice voice come out of her.

"Hi Sadie, I'm Mr. Clark." He bends to his knees next to my desk.

"I know, Mr. Clark." I smile.

"I know you qualified for an IEP at the end of last year so I wanted to go over those areas of weakness with you and set some goals for reading and writing. You'll probably find this curriculum to be a lot easier than College Prep. Anyhow, I'll get a packet together of worksheets you can work on at home."

"Thanks." I nod my head, writing the date down on a piece of paper.

"I think you'll like my class. Most students do, especially Orange, and she doesn't like much." He stands up.

"So I hear . . ." I mumble.

Mr. Clark purses his lips. "Oh yeah, I heard about your grandmother. I loved her on *The Big Apple Cookoff.* She used to cater the teacher appreciation luncheon and I looked forward to it every year. My condolences."

"Thanks," I say quietly, scurrying to write the writing prompt.

I miss her food, too.

At nutrition, I walk near to the grassy area behind building B, where Nicolette, Allison, Chase, Tim and some minions have been hanging for the last three years to see if he's there, where we ruled for three years. Nicolette, she sips her skinny Starbucks Latte and pretends to drive drunk using one hand on the wheel. What the hell did I do to Nicolette? Allison watches her and then laughs. She jumps into the fun pretending to be a cop pulling me over. "License and registration, please. Oh wait, you're from the special needs school," Allison laughs at her own joke mocking me. Tim and Chase shake their heads but laugh.. I can't believe it. After all the crap I went through. "Comedians," I start turning the other way, quickly pretending to look at the huge Expressive Word Wall as I hide behind a palm tree positioning my sunglasses so that I can take another look at Tim. He looks good: tan, shaved head for football, black shirt, blue O'Neill board shorts, same burly arms and six pack. He caught me because he lowers his sunglasses and looks right at me. I turn away and duck behind Building C, the old Spanish style building with an wooden arch holding beautiful, yellow lantanas.

"Hhmmm," a voice clears from the other side of the lockers. I turn my head to see BFM scrunched in a corner eating a protein bar and reading *American Sniper*. He looks older this year. His acne is gone and he is wearing an oversized brown Quiksilver hoodie with a pair of jeans and a baseball cap that reads Dodgers. Did he lose weight?

I look down at my backpack, feeling like pulling out an invisible water bottle of vodka and downing it. Maybe I need to text Mel. But, instead I pull out my math book. I guess it's time to pass high school on my own wit.

"Hi," I respond curtly.

He looks up again and looks at me. "How are you, Sadie?" I like the way he says my name. He has such a clear voice.

"Just ducky," I reply, slipping on my sunglasses at the sun peering over the auditorium. I'm surprised at myself. I'm being honest. Like sarcastically honest but honest.

His cheeks fatten with a smile. "I'm sensing some sarcasm."

"I hope you don't mind if I sit here?" I ask. I'm basically starting from the bottom of the barrel.

"I don't mind, if you don't mind," he says, resting his book on his lap.

"I don't mind," I agree.

"I don't mind either," he adds. "If you don't mind, I don't."

I can see his mouth cracking into a smile. Silliness surrounds him. I feel my mouth cracking into a smile but I stop it. Maybe I need to smile a little more. Besides I am depressed after the summer I had.

I wonder if he knows Mel and I are in the same AA meeting, although, it's confidential.

Chapter 18

MEETING GRACIE AND JUDGEY PEOPLE

Later that afternoon, I find myself at the front desk of Mariposa Elementary school. They reconstructed it over the summer after my Jeep ran straight through it at 25 miles an hour. WHAT. A. MODEL. CITIZEN. I. AM.

"Hi I'm Sadie MacPhearson,"

I look at the older lady behind the computer.

"For who and what?" She finishes typing an email, not even looking up.

Is it mandatory to have zero manners when being a secretary at a school?

I feel like doing multiple eye rolls but contain myself. "I am doing my mandatory volunteer hours." I look at her. My patience has become thin these days.

She looks up at me and yells, "Dan, Concha."

Officer Dan Sob is my parole officer who is over-seeing my case. Concha? Who's that?

"Sadie is doing her mandatory volunteer hours here." The office lady continues to type.

My cell vibrates. It is my dad. I wanted to salute him and say thank you for signing off on me for working at the school I literally crashed into. There's something about the saying "Don't bite the hand that feeds you."

"I'll wait," An older, pretty Latina woman wearing a black pantsuit rolls her eyes.

"Sorry," I square her. "It was my dad making sure I arrived here."

"Without hitting the side of the school?" she mumbles. Bitch, I say in my head.

Officer Sob nudges her.

"Right, well it's a little easier to avoid that much damage on a beach cruiser and with water in my system," I nod my head in the general vicinity of my pink cruiser, "Everyone makes mistakes."

I learned that from AA. Not everyone is perfect. I can feel her staring at me as I look down.

She makes the same sound I made earlier to Orange, "Hhhhmpph."

Funny, I know she is trying to cover up a laugh and wants to be serious.

She extends her hand, "My name is Concha Felix, I'm the Vice Principal here, but mostly I have the students with IEPs, so I'm awfully busy. Why don't you come in here?"

I shake her hand following her into the office that had on oversized cherry wood desk, white walls, tons of pictures and several shelves of books.

Concha Felix?

"Hi Sadie, good to see you," Officer Sob walks in, "This is Chantel Robbins. She is Gracie's mother. She wanted to meet you." She looks very Mariposa Beach. She's an attractive botoxed-out, blond lady in her late forties wearing Stretch exercise gear.

"Hi sweetie."

I shake her hand firmly like dad taught me. "Nice to meet you, Mrs. Robbins."

"Oh sweetie, call me Mama Chantel. It'll be easier for Gracie that way." She sips her Dragonfruit A Go Go drink from Juice Farm.

I nod, fiddling with my Chan Luu wrapped beaded bracelet, a gift from Grams.

She looks over at my court papers. "Holy moly, Officer Sob assigned you 380 hours to do. Do you care to do them over the span of this school year? It would be about an hour and 15 minutes a day plus you could work some of the fundraisers after school and weekends to make up the extra hours." She pulls the calculator app from her phone, typing in some numbers. "Monday through Friday 1:15 to 2:30."

"It's fine," I reply.

"Her classes are from 7 a.m. until 1 p.m., so . . . is that enough time to have lunch," Mama Chantel asks.

I nod.

My sad, little life . . .

I think about my afternoons last year where I was on the cheerleading team and had practice or a game every day after school.

"Okay, well I'll just walk you around today since you're not dressed accordingly," Concha glares disapprovingly at my ripped jean shorts. She may as well have poked her pointer finger through the holes of my jean shorts saying 'you're unacceptable all around girl,' "You can meet Grace and Nicole, the girl and other teacher's aide you'll be shadowing."

"Sorry, is it the ripped jean shorts? I will be coming after school every day so I need to be mindful of what to wear," I look at Officer Sob who shrugs his shoulders.

Minus that, I'm not sure how I feel about working with a girl with behavior issues all year wearing nothing but prude clothing.

She nods likes it's already a forgotten subject. "I'll show you the campus and some of the teachers you'll be working with."

"Okay, I have to get going, so Concha send me the paperwork." Officer Sob's cell sounds.

"I have a flight to catch." Mama Chantel grips her car keys. "Nice to meet you and I love that bracelet."

"Thanks." I hold the door for her. "Nice to meet you."

Concha walks me through the school campus and shows me the lay of the land. She points to the bathrooms, playgrounds, and where the principal's and nurse's offices are. I walk by room 6 and on the wall outside the classroom in red paint is Jay, Jack, Tim, Chase, Allison, Nicolette, Ariana & Candace = FRIENDS FOREVER. I guess they were tight from the get go. But, why Jay and Jack? And, who was Candace, again? Ariana, was that Orange?

"Ready to meet Grace?"

"Uh." Come back to Earth, Sades. "I guess."

"And, just so you know, Sadie," she says my name like she is literally sending me to my room for a timeout. "You will be in training for two weeks ABA Training."

"What?"

"Applied Behavior Analysis, it's for kids with Autism."

I follow her into Mrs. Keller's third grade classroom full of perfectly lined up single desks with pencil boxes set on the right side and names on the left. To the right is a large bookshelf full of books organized by color tabs. To the left, red, yellow and green colored plastic bins with labels like, multiplication tables, geometrical shapesing words, blends, digraphs. On the walls there are colorful rectangular posters of life cycles of frogs and butterflies, grade level sight words, adjectives like what to use instead of good, and what are mammals?

I feel the multiplication tables rumbling nervously in my stomach. All the stuff I hate.

A tall girl dressed like she is the female version of a clown doll meets us. She has on red jeans, a pink polka-dotted shirt and huge pink Converses. She has curly red hair, white skin, and freckles. She sits on the floor doing somersaults on the tile.

"And, this is our one and only Gracie," Concha says, as she pulls a chair out for me.

"She always wears red." She smiles at me like we're friends now.

"That's her aide, Nancy."

"Gracie, sit in the chair," Miss Nancy says. Nancy, a middle aged woman dressed in pair of Von Dutch jeans and a beautiful Free People blouse. She's very Mariposa Beach'd out with her Brazilian blowout blond hair, Botox face and a stick up her ass. She fills out a notebook that says Grace's Communication Notes on the front.

"No way, bitch." Gracie throws a squeezy ball at Miss Nancy. The students in the class laugh.

I minimize my laughter by making the noise, "Hhhhh mmmph."

I see Joey Felix walk in. She is wearing jean overalls and a pink tank top with matching pink Converses and a high ponytail.

I wave.

She waves at me, "Hi Miss Sadie . . .Hi Auntie Concha." What the eff . . . ?

"Gracie, you need to listen to Miss Nancy," the teacher chimes in.

Concha watches.

Gracie stands up and pushes Miss Nancy over in her chair.

She falls back, hitting her head on the corner of the desk with a smack. Nancy falls on the rainbow carpet. The class remains silent. Concha grips Gracie's arm with one hand on her elbow and one on her shoulder, walking Gracie out of the room. "No Gracie."

"Miss Nancy, are you okay?" I ask, holding my hand out for her to grab.

"Yeah, when is your training over, because this girl is crazy." She shows me the scratches on her arms. My eyes widen like I've found a snake in my bed.

"Good luck," she grabs her purse and scurries out. Concha motions for me.

I walk out, and Joey whispers in my ear, "Gracie's cool. She needs a younger person I think . . ."

"Thank you, Joey." I squeeze her hand, "Good to see you."

I shut the classroom door behind me. What have I gotten myself into?

"That was not okay, Gracie," Concha says as she's walking Gracie down the hall.

"I hate her Mrs. Felix. Miss Nancy is a bitch," she says, singing the words as she skips down the hall.

I put my hand over my mouth. She needs to stop saying bitch or I'm going to lose it to laughter.

"Who's this bitch?" She stops puffing her chest at me. "Nice ripped jean shorts. You don't have money to buy the entire pair?"

God, is she related to my ex-best friend, Allison?

I smile at her. "My name is Sadie. I don't like you calling me bad names though."

She gets inappropriately close to my face, "Like BITCH?" "I've been called worse," I say to her.

Her eyes finally meet mine. She takes a deep breath and backs off.

Concha shakes her head as she's corralling Grace like she is a herd of twelve flamingos with time bombs strapped to their chests walking around. I follow safely behind. We sit in her office. Gracie calms down after headphones are placed on her head.

"Well, this will be fun?" I crack a half smile. I'm not sure if Concha deserves my entire smile yet.

She nods. I nod.

"I want you to read her school psychology report."

I take the report and start reading. I just read one of these for myself in June. It said my skills are two years behind in almost everything: math, reading and writing. My social/emotional are all in the average range. My executive functioning, which includes attention and processing speed, is below average. That's why I fail with test taking and public speaking.

I read Gracie's key points:

Gracie has autism and is labeled emotionally disturbed.

She had fetal alcohol syndrome.

She was adopted by her foster parents when she turned two.

She lives with her four adopted siblings.

She might have to be sent to an alternative setting soon based on her behavior.

Aggressive. Physical.

Angry.

Verbally abusive.

Needs positive reinforcement, breaks, one-on-one attention.

Loves refrigerator manuals, Playboy models and anything Disney themed.

My learning disability isn't looking too shabby in comparison.

"What's an educational therapist?" I look up from reading the report.

"A private therapist that parents pay for who specializes in autism, behavior, academics . . . like a glorified after school tutor but they make a lot of money." She adjusts her glasses.

"Doesn't she get everything she needs at school?" I ask. Concha shrugs. "Unfortunately no."

"Will she ever live independently," I ask, "Like when she is older?"

For the first time she makes full eye contact. "No."

"That's a bummer." I slump in my seat.

"Yep." She stands up, walking to the door. "Excuse me, my nephew is dropping off lunch for me."

I press my lips together when I look at Josh. He's gorgeous! He is broad shouldered muscular, brown skinned with big lips, basically Jay in ten years but skinny.

"You're 17, Sadie?" She guides him in.

"Yeah, I'll be 18 in July," my voice cracks. "Hi Josh."

"Hi Sadie, how are you?" His voice is as clear as Jay's. He is wearing a surf shirt and board shorts.

"I'm good," I reply.

"Gosh, Sadie seems to know everyone," she comments.

Josh's eyes show annoyance as he sets the Chinese food down. "There's Kung Pao chicken in there."

"Thanks, you heading out to surf?" She doesn't look up from her report.

He kisses her cheek, "Yes, see you tonight for dinner. Mel is trying a new recipe."

"Bye." She kisses his cheek back.

He waves bye and I do the same.

"K, we will call today your first day. The ABA training starts tomorrow at 1:15 p.m. A behaviorist, someone who holds a master's degree, will come here tomorrow to train you on behavior strategies. Come dressed appropriately." She hands me a dress code flier and a volunteer packet and opens the door.

I stand up. "Thank you."

She nods, "And, Sadie, I know we have mutual friends, but, can we keep it professional?"

"Uh yeah," I say in a perplexed tone.

I walk out the door, throw my backpack over my shoulders and ride my beach cruiser the half-mile home. My hands grip the handles and when I hit a street that I think no one can hear me on I let out a long scream. I cannot believe I am stuck with a girl with major behavior issues. And, kind of a bitchy boss that is Jay's aunt? All. Year. Long. If I don't finish the mandatory volunteer hours, I will never get my license back and my record will not be wiped clean. If only I hadn't driven drunk. If only I hadn't semi-hooked up with Tim. If only Grams hadn't passed. If only I hadn't been diagnosed with a learning disability.

My legs pedal fast and with every cement slab my bike rides over, I picture the faces of the Pop Crowd and even add Gracie and Concha to the list. My bike hits my driveway and I slide it into my one-sixteenth portion of the garage. The rest is my dad's toolboxes, an old car he's restoring, bikes, surfboards, SUP boards, and things I forgot we had. Almost every weekend of my freshman year, my dad asked me to hike, garden, ride bikes or SUP board with him. He stopped asking after a while.

We did so much together in Wisconsin: rode bikes, SUP boarded on the lake, played soccer and ice hockey. I feel a sting in my heart remembering the last time he asked me to do something. He wanted to go on a bike ride with me. It was freshman year, and I had just made the freshman cheerleading team, hence the Pop Crowd tryouts, and I wanted to have pizza with the Pop Crowd at Champagne's Pizza.

I carry my oversized pink tote into the house, slamming it on my bed. I need a serious release. My parents aren't home, so I light a cigarette and sit in my Tommy Bahama adirondack chair outside with my feet propped up. I breathe out the layers of hurt from the day. The pain. The loss. The anger. I may need a second cigarette and then I think of the entire reason why Grams died and put the pack away in my underwear drawer.

I pop a mint in my mouth and spray perfume on my body. Our grandfather clock chimes four times. I should be at the first football game cheerleading. I remember the cheerleading manager calling my parents and telling them I was no longer welcome on the squad. I blinked the tears away listening to the conversation my mom had with the manager. All I remember my mom saying was, "yep, no problem. We agree." The tears rolled down my cheeks as fast as the tires on my Jeep. This wasn't fair. My life wasn't fair.

I don't know how to talk to my mom and dad about it because they're angry still. I have no one to talk to about it. So I write another letter to Grams.

4:05 p.m.

Dear Grams,

I don't know how to live my life without the Pop Crowd, cheerleading, partying, cheating, flirting with Tim and being fabulous. I also don't know how to go back to the Wisconsin farm girl Sadie nor did I want to.

SLM

At 4:10 p.m. my pen falls to the floor. I pick it up with my foot. Lucy tilts her head and gives me her best puppy dog eyes. I run my fingers through the hair on her ridge.

At 4:12 p.m. I tiptoe around my room wearing a crop top and short jean shorts my mom never found, whispering and pretending Tim Miller is there. I feel like a five-year old playing dress up.

Lucy grumbles in annoyance. Perhaps she's reporting back to Wyatt and Cindy.

'Oh you love me now, do you?' I pretend as I picture him grabbing me and pushing me against the wall kissing me profusely. What about today, I say?

'Al made me act mean to you, Sadie, baby, you're it,' he pulls my chin up and kisses me again.

4:25 p.m.

I open my laptop and Google ABA therapy, autism and educational therapy, reading a few blurbs about it. My cell chimes. I jump up from my bed.

Mom: Dinner at your door. Reality.

Me: Thanks, mom I pick up the plate with tuna wrap, sweet potato fries and a bottle of water sitting outside my door. I want to thank my mom in person but she's in her room now. I want to knock but I can't. I know she's not ready to talk.

5:45 p.m.

After dinner I wash the plate in the kitchen sink, dry it and put it away. After all, my dad taught me that much. I walk down the hall to my room and stop at the new picture my mom has enlarged. It has a picture of Grams smiling with a nice religious quote, 'We love strongly. We grieve strongly.'

What, are we Christians again?

I decide dress up playtime is over with a pretend Tim Miller and pull out my homework reminder binder, something the IEP team created for me to remember what homework is assigned. I start with Math. I read the directions over and over and finally understand it.

God, I hate school.

Math: Review pages 33-34 1-55 odds.

I actually know how to do the math, as it's a review from last year except the last problem. I throw my math book across the room because I cannot remember what was taught in class today. My thoughts go to Tim Miller. I think about his hotness and rewind our hookup session in my head. I pull my Xerox copy of my teacher's notes from math and try to make sense of it. I do my best. That's all anyone wants, right?

When I get to my homework for English: Read 1-20 of *Go Ask Alice*. I read the back of the book. It sounds interesting enough. Girl takes drugs. Or becomes addicted. Maybe death. Either way this book would have been helpful last year. I write a paragraph on it.

I think of Tim Miller again.

Chapter 19

GLENLIVET, RUM AND COFFEE

The warmth of the summer subsides and fall is in the air. Pumpkins start coming out as well as other Halloween décor. I go to school. I get worked, although, my teachers are more hands on and they work with me A LOT. I sit next to BFM at nutrition and talk a little (I don't think he likes me). I get called BITCH thirty times at volunteer hours as well as a mean ass stare down from Concha (I don't think she likes me either). I misunderstand my new Math and English homework at night so I make up shit for answers while filling in the real ones during homework check during class. I eat dinner in my room. (I don't think my parents like me.) Shower up. Bed.

Most evenings under my 234 fake stars, I lie in bed I think of Tim. He hasn't texted me anymore, although,

I never text him back. Even if I wanted to, my mom continues to check my phone nightly.

One evening, I watch the orange twinkling lights hanging outside my window sway with the fall winds and eat a sugar cookie shaped like a pumpkin from Gracie. When she gave it to me, she told me she washed her hands. I gave her a token, which meant she's progressing towards something behaviorally positive.

I feel a slight peace that my dad actually hung the lights outside my room allowing me the opportunity to enjoy fall and Halloween. It's one of his favorite holidays. I want to thank him but he is at work. My mom texts me that she's running late from visiting with some of Gram's old friends. I can tell she is panicking because it is the first time they have left me home alone at night in about three months. I binge watch *The Big Apple Cookoff*. I can still hear Grams' laughter during the parts where we'd both laugh. And, her name is still in the credits. A text chimes through.

Tim: Did you get my text?

WHAAAAT! I pinch myself. Playing dress up or reality?

Tim: Can we talk? I'm outside your window. It's about Chase.

He causes my heart to beat faster and it's only a text.

I hear a quiet knock on my slider and open it. Why I open it I have no idea? I don't want him to be here, but I'm slightly interested in what he has to say.

"I know you hate me, but I need to talk to you," he talks through the door. I see his silhouette through the pink curtain. I look down. I'm wearing VS boyfriend sweats and a black tank top. I powder my face and brush my hair. After all, I think about him a lot still. I not sure if I'm ready to put it behind me. I breathe in love, hate and disgust as I open the slider.

"Here goes nothing," I whisper.

He gives me this sullen look. He leans against the slider. It's most likely holding him up. He's wearing a black V neck manly shirt, slightly stretched across his broad chest.

Dang!

"Hi," Tim says.

I hold my hands behind my back. I press my lips together trying to prevent them from saying or doing unnecessary things like speaking or kissing.

"Look, Sades." He rubs his blond, shaved head, a nervous tic. It's something I've known about him. I can smell the Glenlivet. He is hammered.

I press my lips together harder. I may have to start my amount of sobriety days over just breathing in the air around him. This is actually reality. He is feeling bad. When has Tim Miller ever felt bad about anything in his life?

My body repulses at the smell and I back up. "You're drunk."

"Nah." His eyes are half open. "I forgive you."

"Huh?" I put my hands up.

"What you did with Chase. I forgive you." He takes my hands, pulling me back to him. I let him. It doesn't feel like how I wanted it to feel when I played dress up or how it felt when I was drunk the night Grams died.

"We weren't even together . . . you had a girlfriend," my voice cracks as I back up an inch, "And, Chase got the answer keys from someone. Why isn't anyone mad at him?"

He had some nerve.

"Look," he says. "Let's keep what you did with Chase on the down low. The sex in exchange for answer keys," he stumbles over his words.

"Tim, I never had sex with him," I plead.

"I forgive you," he says. "He could get into serious trouble with the answer keys though. Principal Dow was questioning some of us today. No one is talking."

"Wait what?" I question.

"Dow found a video of the person who has been breaking into his office."

I play dumb. "How is Chase getting the answer keys?"

"Just like everyone else is. Paying someone for them? I don't know. I never used them. I don't think Chase does either."

Wrong! He's paying someone to break in and get the answer keys, using them for his own studies and to manipulate me . . . I wonder who else he has manipulated?

"I forgive you though," he holds my face.

"Why? You and I weren't together." I remove his hands point blank. I'm repulsed.

"Yeah, but we had something . . ." he mumbles. He is blitzed. "No, you're drunk."

I push him away. "You never even came to visit me in the hospital. No one from the Pop Crowd did," I whisper.

He backs up. "It was hard, Sades . . .I had Allison pissed at me. Then we didn't know you were returning to school because we didn't know if you could go to school because of the learning disability."

My brow cocked. "Do you even know what I have? It's called Central Auditory Processing Disorder . . ." I stutter.

He laughs . . .

I feel my heart race.

He rubs his head again. "Ugh, sorry."

"GO!" I scream.

I'm so tired of them making fun of me.

I hear the garage door opening. He inches away.

"My parents will kill me, please go." I push him out the open slider. He fumbles but manages to get over the bamboo fence. I peek over and watch him walk to his truck.

I text Chase.

Sadie: Tim is drunk and driving . . . And, btw, you're pathetic. I release my pressed lips and air escapes.

"Sadie?" I hear my dad yell from the kitchen. I quickly delete all the text messages.

"Yes, I'm here, Dad." I yell. What the hell is my dad doing home? He's supposed to be at work.

I collapse on my bed and open my English book, wiping my tears quickly.

My dad looks at me and looks at the slider and says. "It's a little cold, don't you think?"

"Oh yeah, I'll close it. I didn't think you were coming home?"

"I'm home now and just so you know Sadie, I'm always home," he squares me in the eyes and shuts the door. "Close the slider."

"Just so you know I'm always home," I grumble under my breath. "We are up to twenty words, Dad, twenty words in twelve weeks."

I crawl in my bed thinking of my dad. I had to get it off my mind before I could process Tim. My dad and I, I remember he would get home from work at 7 a.m., my mom would be tired, so he'd take me to the park for the morning. He'd play Tickle Monster with me at the park. He taught me how to play soccer and SUP board and how to ride a bike. He taught me how to be kind and polite. Once I hit high school and Grams was involved, my mom and I lost sight of him. We had to be part of Grams' world because it was new and fabulous. He covered himself in work, gardening, his car, SUP boarding and bike riding. There's no blame except blame itself for our distance.

And, now Tim, as far as I can see nothing has changed with him, but I have changed.

The next day after school, I walk into Java Coffee.

I see Chase; he's drinking coffee with Betsy Grimes from school.

I walk back outside.

"Nice bike," she smiles at me as she walks to her VW bug.

"Are you taking photos of Betsy now?" I ask.

He bumps my shoulder. "Stop . . ." He looks down. "Did you forget the sun makes you tan?" he says seriously.

I don't even look at him.

"Sadie, C'mon." He smiles that perfect Chase Bynes smile.

I am quiet but then I explode, "I suspect you got my text about Tim."

"Yeah," he hesitates. "All handled.

"So he drinks and drives ALL the time and doesn't get caught . . ."

"Maybe he's a better driver than you are," he kids. I don't speak.

"Sadie," he follows to the side street where my bike is parked, "He told you about Principal Dow and the videotapes?"

I look at him.

"You can see someone in the videotapes, but it's hard to make out. They'll never figure it out," he assures me, "besides it's all stopped now."

"YUP!" I exaggerate my words.

"If this thing comes out, this thing you and I had, my life is destroyed, Sadie. No La Crosse scholarship. My dad's career." He stands in front of my bike.

I nod. "Chase, your dad is not running for president!"

"I know that, Sadie." He watches me undo the combo lock on my bike.

I roll my eyes.

"So the pictures of me are destroyed?" I ask.

"Yes," he mutters, looking away.

Why isn't he looking at me?

"Okay, so, let me get this straight. Al hates me because I kissed Tim, but they are back together for the millionth time." I hold my finger for number one. "Nic hates me because she thinks I slept with you all these years in exchange for answer keys you paid someone to break in and get, but they don't know that." I say in an octave a little higher than necessary, holding my finger for number two. "Tim forgives me for sleeping with you all these years, although, that's a damn lie." Number three.

"And, you never want me to reveal that you're gay and dating your dad's campaign manager who is in his thirties?"

"SHUT UP!" He grits his teeth, pushing my shoulder slightly.

I feel my mouth drop, "DON'T EVER TOUCH ME AGAIN OR I WILL KNOCK YOU OUT!!!"

I grit my teeth, gripping his shoulders as tightly as I can. "I'd rather be dealing with my learning disability, Grams death, the DUI, car crash, concussion, overnight hospitalization, mandatory volunteer hours, ongoing AA and, basically imprisonment at the MacPhearson house than ever hanging out with you AGAIN."

"Sadie . . ." he tries to touch me again.

I shake him off of me, "OFF," I scream this time and move my bike in between us. He finally backs away.

"You know what, Chase, out of everyone, I thought I could trust you the most." I grip my handle bars.

"It's just a lot happened with you with the Learning Disability thingy and we didn't know if you were going to a special school." Fire ignites my fingertips. "Tim said that too. A special school? How *did* you hear about the learning disability thingy and who is we?"

"Nicolette saw you coming out of the special education office when she was bringing the staff samples of her mom's new protein bars. We knew it wasn't extra credit," he says, as if it's like nothing big, like changing the toilet paper.

"And, they went to their minion leader," I say.

He nods. "And she's the one who called the cops to tell them you were driving drunk."

"HOLY . . ." I scream, "I swear. I sincerely hate her!" "Calm down." He grabs my arm. "Here."

He hands me a mini bottle of Malibu Rum. Didn't he hear me say I was in AA?

"No!" I throw it. "I mean I would have gotten in trouble anyway. The upsetting part is none of my 'so-called friends' checked on me."

He looks at me. Tears cover my eyes.

I wave him away. "I understand Al is not human, but you, Nic and Tim all went along with it? Our friendship meant nothing?"

"They were upset about us," Chase says.

"There was never an us. Just you, me and a camera." "I know," he says, "I was worried about you."

"I. AM. DONE." I swing my leg over the seat. "LEAVE!!!!!!!!!!!"

He vanishes. I look at the Malibu rum bottle on the ground and pick it up. One shot and all this stress will go buh bye.

"I don't think you want to do that," Jay appears with the Santa Ana winds, taking the bottle from my hand.

"Oh, thank you. I had a bad day and didn't even realize I was holding the bottle." I breathe while pulling my hair out of my sunglasses.

He's a head taller than me wearing black Ray Bans. I look up at him high in the orange and yellow autumn sponged sky. He's wearing blue board shorts, a long sleeved black shirt that says LA City Fire 9's Skid Row and black Reef sandals.

"You're welcome," he says, his voice low. He clears it.

"My dad works there." I point to his shirt, inevitably changing the subject.

"So does my bro," he reciprocates. "Josh, well, you met him."

"I seem to be running into your family . . . like a lot lately."

I block myself by folding my arms.

His head moves towards Java Coffee. "Don't take Concha serious. She can be Grumpy McGrumperson sometimes."

"I'm not . . . taking Miss Grumperson serious," I lie.

"Good. Wanna get a coffee and talk?" he asks, a little louder than before.

I shrug my shoulders. "Why not?"

The whole point of going to Java Coffee before was to get a coffee.

Friggin' Chase!

The next thing I know, I am sitting across from Jay at the coffee shop hiding behind a large, orange mug. I block myself again. I'm not sure why. The kettle on the tiny stove whistles and the Santa Ana blows customers in and out. I catch a glimpse of myself from a reflection on the stainless steel. I sit Indian style, wearing skinny blue jeans and a tight, short-sleeved green shirt that says, I love Camping, something I haven't worn since Wisconsin. My skin is pale and my blond hair is pulled to the side.

"Sorry your friends suck," he throws it out there . . . into the world; his opinion after I speak about them for twenty minutes.

I don't say anything.

"Blueberry muffin?" he pushes it across the table, staring at me. "You have to let the anger go when you're ready."

"No, thank you," I push it back, staring right back. "I don't eat carbs. And, I will let the anger go when I want."

"Oh right, you should probably think about losing some weight." He pops blueberry muffin in his mouth. And, there they are, more thoughts out in the air.

I feel my eyes widen. I laugh inside. I'm surprised at his lack of subtlety. I'm a little tired of people's bullshit anyways. I'm not angry. I just don't remember how to be nice again.

I blush. "On top of my learning disability issues."

He smiles, "on top of your drunk driving issues."

I twist my mouth back and forth. Not sure I care for the complete realness, but he is being a little sarcastic; I like it.

"On a serious note, please don't tell Mel or anyone I almost drank that bottle. My parents will send me to a boarding school. My probation officer and Judge Harmon will probably make me do mandatory hours until I turn thirty-five and my sponsor will probably make me, I don't know, start over and go to more AA meetings." My fingers rub my bare knee as I look down. I feel flushed.

"You have a drinking problem?" He sips his coffee.

My shoulders relax a little and I smile. "I used to drink a lot but ninety days sober." I put my hands up like I'm doing a scout's honor thing. "It was mandated by Judge Harmon. He wanted to make an example of me."

"It sucks it had to be you but maybe it's a good lesson for other teens." He licks the blueberry muffin crumbs off his lips.

"I am extremely happy to be the one to be made the example . . ." I say sarcastically, reaching for the blueberry muffin. He pushes it towards me.

"The blueberry muffin taste is overwhelmingly explosive in your mouth. One pop of the warm blueberry oozing with confidence makes you feel alive. Brace yourself." He smiles.

I chew, swallow and then say, "Hot damn."

He nods, chewing the last bite. "Hot damn is right, sista."

Calm your jets, Jay.

I flash my lashes and release a small smile. Maybe.

It's silent for a second. Maybe he senses my frustrations.

"I like this song," I point to the speaker, finding a buffer for the awkwardness I feel.

"*Back to Black*," he says.

"*Back to Black*," I repeat.

"Oh, so, you're not the Drake, Sia and Ed Sheeran fan?" he says.

"No."

"I hated hearing that over and over in Ceramics. All my faves are dead, including Amy Winehouse."

"Mine too," a text chimes through. "Oh crap, it's my mom.

I gotta go."

He gathers the trash, "I'll drive you."

"It's okay, I . . . I," I start to spew words.

"You like this coffee?" he smiles. "Me too. Stop trying to find things to comment on when you don't know what to say. I'm happy to drive you."

How did he know I was going to say, I like this coffee? Sober, I can't seem to make conversation anymore.

I suck the inside of my cheek. "I live a street over."

He smiles. "Well, I'm going that way. I'll follow you to the street over. Besides, you just had some carbs. You probably need to work it off, anyways."

I cock my head but don't speak.

"That's what I thought . . ." he says. "And Sadie, he's not worth going back to black." He follows me out. "No one from the Pop Crowd is."

"What does that mean?" I ask.

"Like whatever your weakness is, their bullying isn't worth you going back to drinking, black."

"Okay," I chirp, heading toward the door as he follows me out.

"Yeah," he says point blank. "They made fun of your math skills and reading skills like every day."

"I . . ." I start.

He's so opinionated.

"Okay, well, believe it or not." He watches my leg loop over my bike. "I can help you with school, too, so . . ."

"No thanks, I'm done asking for help from guys." I push off from the curb and off I go, leaving the orange, red, and yellow fall leaves in his face.

We aren't that tight, yo!

My hair blows in the wind, allowing it to be free. Allowing me to be free. Free from the criticism, the bullying, the lies, lack of support, the hate, the jealousy, and all that these people in the so-called Pop Crowd have done to me. I want to feel friendship again: a sober friendship, laughing, loving and kindness. As my tires crunch over the fall leaves, I brace myself for a change, a change in weather and friendships.

Chapter 20

MY PINKY PILLOWS

Luckily, I roll into my house before the sun sets. I hear the motor of Jay's old black car continue on. I barely said good-bye. I was so dramatic about my departure I couldn't look back. But, I will say, I've never had a guy follow me home. My mom and dad are eating Grams' famous brown rice pasta with spaghetti sauce, mushrooms and homemade meatballs at the kitchen table. It smells delicious and for once I don't want to escape to my room. Maybe it's because my breath doesn't smell like liquor.

My mom points to my plate that's already made with a foil over it and a bottle of water. I pick it up and say, "thank you . . ."

"Cell phone, please." My dad holds his hand out. I pull it out of my purse.

"Here."

My dad puts it in his pocket and looks at my mom like I didn't exist, continuing with his conversation. "So, anyways, the guy came out of nowhere and the fire truck.."

I disappear down the hall with my dinner as my self-worth deteriorates.

How long are they going to punish me—Wyatt and Cindy MacPhearson? Sitting on my bed, I savor each bite of spaghetti. The fresh Italian spices from the International Deli near Malibu and the grated parmesan cheese from the farmer's market make my belly happy and make me think of Grams, but my heart is not feeling the hugs and kisses. Maybe the fall wind blowing outside is getting to my head because my thoughts are racing about the bullying comment. Was it bullying or was I being naive?

I bury my head in my hundred pink pillows. "I HATE THEM AND THEIR FLAWLESS LIVES!" I scream. Black mascara smears all over my hundred pillows. "I HATE TIM!"

"Crap," I say to myself. "My pinkie pillows . . ." I start laughing deliriously, saying "my pinkie pillows." Now I'm standing up on my bed, jumping up to grab the pictures from the pink picture collage. Paper cuts each finger as I rapidly pull at the pictures of my former so-called friends. "My pinkie pillows." I rip their heads off. I rip their bodies in half. "My pinkie pillows," I say. I think about that Malibu rum. Jay took it or was it left on the ground? Jay was right. None of them were worth going back to black.

In AA, they say to surround yourself with positive things, so I pull my nightstand drawer open and put my favorite picture of Grams over my heart. The picture was taken at our old church in Wisconsin. I was in junior high. Grams and I stood on this medium-sized hay bale. She ended up jumping up towards me and I grabbed her holding her like a baby—all of 110 pounds of her. She wore a white romper with her hair short and had the widest grin. I had two French braids in my hair, braces and wore a black tank top and a long floral skirt. I couldn't stop laughing. Our relationship was something money couldn't buy.

The next morning, a knock sounds on my door. "Sades?"

My mom mumbles.

I sit up and rub my eyes. "Yeah."

She opens the door. "You're late . . . whoa."

"What time is it?" I sit up, turning on the light, glancing at my room in the mirrored closets. Black mascara has run down my cheeks. Pink pillow dust and stuffing is everywhere in my room. I'm wearing the same I Love Camping T-shirt from last night.

"It's 7:05 a.m.," she says, picking up a ripped picture of the Pop Crowd and I. Whoa, Sadie."

"Sorry, Mom. I got really upset." I'm not sure why I didn't rip those pictures up sooner.

"I see," she continues to gather ripped pictures. I look at her. "And, I couldn't sleep."

"I know Tim stopped by . . . Dad saw him," she starts. "We're not stupid, Sadie."

That's why I got the even colder than icy shoulder last night. I shrug my shoulders, pulling my long T-shirt over my underwear. "He knocked. What was I supposed to do? We're done anyway."

"He's making bad choices. You need to start making good ones." She pulls the white clothes out of my hamper.

I start gathering the ripped pillows.

"I'm done." Tears gather in her eyes as she throws the clothes in the laundry basket. "Your dad and I have tried to raise you right. And, it's like nothing is ever good enough or you are never happy or another lie appears."

For once in a long time I see the stress lines in my mom's face and the anger in her eyes. I know it's because of me.

"I'm sorry," I whisper.

She scrunches her face. "Look, I know it was hard hearing about your learning disability and Grams dying, but promise me you'll start making good decisions."

"I promise." My voice is soft and low.

"TOOT." My dog Lucy let's out a good push.

My mom almost cracks a smile.

I hide my laughter behind Lucy's head. "Feel better?" The dog grumbles and rolls over.

"This is all not going to matter in five years . . ." My mom continues, folding the laundry right side in. "That's what I keep telling myself. Do I need to home school you, Sadie?"

"Like *Little House on the Prairie*? Do you really want to be around me for days on end?"

"No!" She slams down the basket. I smile because it's dramatic.

"I need a little more time, Sadie," she says. "I want to smile with you again."

"I know. Grams would have liked the *Little House on the Prairie* comment," I say.

"Get your stuff ready. I'll drive you," my mom says. "Maybe after volunteer hours you can tell me why you ruined about one hundred pink pillows."

I swear I can almost hear her heart soften while listening to her. It makes my heart feel hugs and kisses, and I feel like there's more hope in continuing on with life. I turn on the water to the shower and let the black mascara melt off of me. The anger hasn't gone away but it's lessening.

That morning, I sit next to Jay at nutrition. I look at a picture of my room that I had taken of the carnage. One hundred torn pictures and pillows on the floor. I giggle.

He tries to ignore me, because he is almost finished with his hundredth sniper book.

I giggle harder and even let out a snort.

"Okay." He looks at me. "What is it?"

I show him still laughing.

He doesn't smile and asks, "How many pink pillows do you have, or, sorry, did you?"

"Too many pinkie pillows . . ."

"I don't picture you having pink . . ." he glares at me.

"Are you serious?" I glare back. "I'm Pinkalicious."

"Nah, you're some color, just not pink . . ."

"Oh," snotty Sadie kicks in. "Are you a colorist now?"

He's silent and looks back at his book.

"Why do you think you can say stuff like that to me?" I turn my body towards him. "Back to Black. You're not pink."

"Someone has to remind you of who you are and who you're not?" he says, closing his book.

The bell rings and we both stand up at the same time. Our shoulders touch. He apologizes. He's damn tall, like a foot taller or so.

"I know who I am," I grit my teeth.

His eyes squint and he grimaces. "Okay." His eyes are olive green colored with long curtain eyelashes. I remember noticing them last year. I want to dip the olives in my martini and shoot the whole thing.

"UGH," I grunt.

"Coming?" Orange opens the door of our classroom as I turn away from Jay fast, pacing down the hallway.

"Is that Jay?" she asks as I enter the class. I don't answer but give her a nod.

"Hmm, he looks skinnier this year," she says, closing the door behind her.

Mr. Lathan passes back math tests. I shake my head as I look at my grade.

Orange taps my shoulder "I thought you were better than me in math." She shows me her grade, 54 percent.

Mr. Lathan puts his finger over his mouth. "This is just a review."

"Nope, Orange, I suck at anything academic," I whisper.

She lets out a ha. "Me too."

I slip my test under my folder and pull out a pencil to start taking notes on today's lesson. It figures I can't get more than a 50 percent on my math tests. I don't know what Jay is talking about as far as colors, but right now I'm feeling blue. I look out the window. It starts to rain. I watch the raindrops gather together on the window, like a little lake. Tim at the lake last summer crosses my mind. I remember the picture I ripped up. The one of him standing on the dock wearing his blue O'Neill board shorts that hung ever so slightly off his beautiful six pack, hips and general beautifulness. Screw him and his perfect body. There was another picture of Nicolette, Allison and I sporting bikinis as we all threw out peace signs. God I really hated them, too. I didn't know it until now, but I've always hated them. But mostly, at this present time I hate myself.

After another sleepless night, I slap my cheeks and say, "Wake up."

216

Filing through my closet I noticed my black nail polish is almost gone. Maybe I should chip away at my clothes, too. Maybe I should remind myself of who I am or figure out who I am. Looking at my closet I had everything from shirts that showed my stomach, to shirts that went off my shoulders, ripped jeans, short shorts, really short skirts, stilettos, screw-me boots, and sandals. I hid this stuff from my mom when she went through it all. I look at the back of my closet to find the long floral skirt I wore in the picture Grams and I took at church one day in Wisconsin right before we moved to Mariposa Beach.

As I look in the full-length mirror in the bathroom at my naked body I am skinny, frail, pale and my freckles are coming back kind of like the Wisconsin Sadie. I dust off the skirt and pull a white tank top over my nude bra and simple black Havaianas sandals. I brush my hair and pull it up in a ponytail. I pull my makeup drawer open. The rainbow of eye shadows shines from the reflection of the artificial light in my bathroom. I paint the lighter powder onto my face and stop. I wipe it off with a tissue and look again.

"There she is," I whisper to myself, looking at the light freckles I've tried so desperately to hide.

A few minutes later, I'm cruising on my bike to Java Coffee a quarter of a mile from my home close. I need some fuel injection stronger than our Keurig machine. It's cold this morning. I huddle over my warm bagel and pumpkin spice latte, and sit on the cement outside of Period 0. I see Nicolette from the corner of my eye focusing back on my bagel.

Where's Orange when you need her?

"Hi." Nicolette stops in front of me.

"Hi, me?" I point to myself.

"Sadie, C'mon," she squares me. "You're the only one sitting here."

"Nic, you have ignored me for months." I stop, putting my hand out. "What do you want?"

"So, you ran into Chase at Coffee Bean?" she glares at me.

My brows furrow. "I did."

"Stay away from him," she orders.

"That won't be a problem." I sip my coffee.

"Chase and I are still dating." Nicolette shrugs.

"Did you hook up?"

"Oh yeah," I say. "We made love on the floor of Java Coffee." She looks terrified.

"Nicolette, I'm joking," I say.

"Okay, AND Allison wants to talk to you. Can she call you or maybe stop by?" she asks.

"What?" I look at her. "What in the hell does she have to ask me about? I don't owe her my breath. And what about you? Three years of friendship gone."

"Sadie, as far as I'm concerned I owe you nothing. And, this sarcastic humor isn't you." She tucks her phone in her back pocket.

"Maybe it is," I say. "Maybe you don't know me." I feel shaky.

Suddenly the fog of the day is getting clearer and the lives aren't looking so flawless. Nicolette has told me a million times she wants a body like mine. Also, she's always said Chase and I were more than friends because we would sit on each other's laps, hug each other, and put our arms around each other. If she only knew the guy she's in love with doesn't like women.

In English, Mr. Clark's gives a very descriptive lesson on how to write a poem. He asks us to write something about an object that represents us. I force my mind to wander to the last beautiful object I saw. I think of the chameleon Jay sculpted last year and all of the colors it included. Maybe the chameleon is me. I am the chameleon. I scribble, "I am a teenager with a chameleon soul." I stop and look at the words for a minute. The words pour out of me.

I put my pencil down and hand my paper to Mr. Clark. Talking to my tears, I plead with them to wait until I slip on my sunglasses, and they do. I let a few fall as I'm walking to sit with Jay.

At nutrition, I sit behind Building C again next to Jay. I'm hiding tears behind my sunglasses. Tears. I casually scrape them away with my left hand and then right. He finished the *American Sniper* book and is onto another one with Army guys on the front. I open my math book and scribble some answer to number eight. It's completely off. He leans his head on the locker, puffing his lips at me and shaking his head no. He takes his pencil and writes the problem out on a piece of paper in four simple steps without saying a word.

I don't make eye contact with him, but say, "thanks, I get it now."

He nods, darting his eyes back on his book. I close my book shut.

"What's up with the military books?" I ask, "don't you want to branch out on a romance novel or a sports novel?"

He smiles and then a raspy, voice escalates from his lips, "in my opinion, real heros don't have a name on the back of their jersey. They have their country's flag on the arm of their uniform."

"Amen," I yell out.

He laughs, "A good romance novel? I'm not a female." He shrugs, "I'm an overweight military book critic disguised as a senior." He then adds, "bah duh buh," like he has a set of drums on him.

"Was that a drum sound?" I ask. "Yeah, did it suck?" he chuckles.

I do the same noise. "It's been a while since I've laughed," I say softly.

He leans his head against the locker and those eyes peer back at me. "I know what you mean, Sadie," he says.

It is silent for a while. Sometimes I can't unlock, cut off the intense stare we have going. Does he want to say something to me? I know I'm wearing less makeup. Maybe he has opinion about that, as well.

I know what it is . . .

"OH MY GOD, I still have Joey's towel from that paddle boarding day," I say.

"Oh yeah, I forgot about that," he looks down, gathering his things as the bell rings, "Just bring it whenever. I'm sure I'll see you again."

"Okay," I concur.

"Later," He says, as I watch him walk towards the ROTC room, which is a portable building north of Building C. He has the same walk as his brother Josh.

I wave.

Later, at home, I lay on my stomach on my bed typing my outline for the writing prompt: "If We Were All Forced to Wear a Warning Label, What Would Yours Say"

My thoughts so far: Back Off! I'm short, BLOND and fierce!

Basically I got nothing. Thoughts move around my head like a carousel.

What does Allison have to talk to me about? Maybe it's a warning to stay away from Tim.

Was Jay really thinking about the towel?

I hate that he helped me with the math problem. Maybe if I could just see him to clear the air of some weird stare downs. I find Joey's pink towel in my bathroom. It smells like lavender. A knock sounds at the door.

"Hey." My mom pops her head in.

"Come in," I say.

She opens. "Just wanted to let you know I'm going to the store. Can you take Lucy out front to pee in a few minutes? I planted some new daisies, and I don't want her to get into in the backyard."

"Sure," I say with more exuberance than usual.

She smiles, "I'm gonna start dinner when I get home."

She looks back. "I'm Short. I'm Blond. I'm Fierce . . . really?" She reads my computer.

"My mind is a little unfocused at the moment," I rub my face.

"Take a break with Lucy in a few," she suggests. "Remember the special education staff said do your work in chunks of time."

"Okay," I agree.

"Chicken Marsala is at 6 p.m. Maybe you can sit with us tonight." She winks.

I feel a step in the right direction. I get through another hour of writing. Now I have CAUTION as my warning label.

Chapter 21

CRAZY TALK AND FLIER

I may explode if I don't take Lucy out to explode. Lucy paws the door open leading me to the small patch of grass on the front yard. I pull my thin, orange silk scarf over my shoulders. The clouds roll in. "Hurry up, Luce. We are in for another storm."

I see a familiar red Mercedes parked on the street under the palm tree.

"Hi." Allison gets out. She is wearing a short jean skirt and a mauve spaghetti-strapped tank top with black heels. It's chilly, and she looks like she could pass as a hooker.

Here we go!

I grab Lucy's collar and walk down the driveway. I'm surprised I'm giving Allison the time of day. My sweaty hands rub along Lucy's hair on her ridge.

"Jake, I'll be five minutes," she yells to the guy sitting in the car. "Is that your cousin?" I joke, remembering a lie she fed Tim about some racy text messages he found on her phone from a USC guy she hooked up with. At the time, she claimed her and her cousin were joking, but Tim was too drunk to realize her parents are both only children so she has zero cousins.

I say, "STILL SUPER CLASSY!"

She's calm as ever. In a natural voice she says, "Shut up, bitch! You're probably wondering why I'm here." She takes another step towards me as I meet her on the sidewalk.

I roll my eyes. "It may have crossed my mind."

"I don't appreciate your rudeness, Sadie, oh by sorry rudeness, I mean slight bitchiness." Allison plops on the curb crossing her ankles.

"I know what rude means, Al." I sit on the stone wall about three feet from her, positioning Lucy in between us.

"Could have fooled me!" She lights a cigarette handing me one.

I shake my head no. "We don't jive like that anymore."

"Really, are you one of Christ's children now?"

"No, it might be laced with something and then you'll probably have the cops on their way?" I shoot off like a cannon, shocking myself.

"Okay, you would have been in trouble regardless, Sadie. You drove into the side of a Mariposa Beach

Elementary School building intoxicated." Al puffs her cigarette and blows smoke on the red and pink roses behind her. "It's a shame that judge gave you so much . . ." she smirks.

"I know, I blame myself," I say, solidly, "Can you blow your smoke away from my mom's roses?"

Lucy growls.

"Shut up dog!" she mumbles. "You shut up!" I point to her.

"WOW WOW! Your mom's roses suck. And, I'm here to give you fashion advice first of all." Al looks down at my long, black skirt and light pink tank top. "What happened?"

"I have to volunteer at a school every day and have to stop dressing like a hooker." I look her up and down feeling my face get red. "You have one minute to say why you're here or I'll call the cops to drag your ass off my property."

My heart is racing.

"Okay, why are you such a bitch all of a sudden?" She puts her hand up like a stop sign.

I want to slap it down, pull her over to the gutter and beat her ass down.

I take a deep breath, thinking to myself, only a few more seconds. You are here to give me that same warning that Nicolette said about Chase, stay away from Tim. He came to me, Al.

"Anything happen with Tim?" Allison tilts her head with slight hesitation.

"No, crazy," I say. "Tim is a lying piece of shit . . ."

"I'm not crazy." She crosses her arms.

I smile, rolling my eyes blatantly at her. "You're pretty mad at the crazy comment, crazy."

Al stands in shock.

"I'm not under your spell anymore and I'm certainly not afraid of you anymore," I say. "And, it's a little disgusting the way you and Tim constantly cheat on each other. And, the way you have bullied me for three years."

"BULLIED??" Al screams. She is as red as the Skittles I was eating the day she broke Jay's chameleon. "I came here because I wanted to see if you touched him."

"No, just the night you caught us," I say.

"So you slept with him, too?" Al asks.

"And the bitch is back. Nope, we never slept together," I say and point at her. "You walked in on us . . ."

"Right, you're so pure now," Al says, pushing my shoulder.

I slap her hand away. "Don't touch me! No, I'm not saying that. All I know is he wanted me . . . like he always has." I push back with my words.

Al cackles. "RIGHT! He still thinks you're stupid . . . you're delusional. Are you sure he wasn't getting anything in return? Just like you never gave Chase favors in exchange for copies of the answer keys?"

"I don't have to answer that," I say, "And, he may think I'm stupid. And, I may think I'm stupid, but AT LEAST I'm hotter than you."

"HA." Al loads ammunition in her proverbial gun. "Sadie, you're such a piece of trash." She stomps on her cigarette. "WE ARE DONE."

"WAH," I pretend to whine like a baby. "THANK YOU JESUS!!!! NOW, GET OFF OF MY PROPERTY."

My mom pulls into the driveway in her Audi.

Jake gets out of the Al's Mercedes. I recognize him instantly as the guy who asked me if I wanted to party months ago. He's wearing ripped jeans and a wife beater fully sleeved with the same tiger tattoo. He points to me like he remembers and pulls down his sunglasses, winking at me. I wonder if he's looking for the same thing he was in Malibu. He opens the door for her, and she shimmies her way in. "You shouldn't lie about stuff, Sadie."

"Oh, okay, let me write that one down in my Secrets to Life Book written by SATAN," I reply. "Go, be a popular bitch . . . I want NOTHING to do with you ever again. And, good luck with that one, Jake."

My body is overtaken by laughter as I'm holding the scarf over my mouth.

I feel a wider than usual smile across my face as I walk into my house. I feel like a dozen balloons lifting in the air. I feel free.

My mom motions me into the kitchen, handing me the block of feta cheese to crumble. "I never liked her, you know, that Satan girl."

When I first starting hanging out with Allison, I was her little project. I was the Laura Ingalls dresser with a long French braid. I let her cut my hair, pierce my ears, dress me and cover me in makeup. She taught me how to talk sexy to hot guys, rudely to minions, ignore low lifes and be horrible to my parents. She gave me my first drink and my five hundredth drink, my first cigarette, e-cigarette, the first boy I kissed and my second, third, fourth one to follow. She told me it was all good, do it often and that everyone in her Pop Crowd did it. I believed her. All I wanted to do was belong.

The next Monday, I go to class and in my peripheral vision, I notice a flier. It is the photo Chase took of me with the skimpy black bikini on a snowy scene. I will work for test answers!

He didn't delete them.

"What is that?" Orange takes it from me.

Tears don't fill my eyes this time. My ears burn with anger. If I could pick my color right now, it would be crimson red. So, I bust out of English and run across the grass right into Allison's class. Orange follows me.

I walk right up to her, ready to rip her hair out. I pushed her hard. She falls to the carpet. Nicolette and some minions grab her. Orange stands behind me, breathing heavily like an ox might.

"Really?" I hold up a flier.

"It wasn't me,"

Allison shrieks nervously, looking at Orange. "I don't believe it for a second. You're severely troubled to be doing something like this." I inch closer to her face, "I almost wanna say CRAZY."

"You're a bitch liar." She stands up, inching closer to me, slightly pushing me back.

I feel a warm hand on my arm pulling me away. It's Jay. He puts his hands on my shoulders, backing me up, not taking his eyes off of mine. "It's not worth it."

Heavily breathing, I let him back me up, but my arms and right pointer finger are still in motion. "You're a bully and a liar and a cheater, but mostly you are a psychotic bitch!"

"Okay, that's good." Jay's hands grasp mine pushing me gently. He is still backing me toward the door but I continue, "And you . . ." I point to Chase. "I thought you deleted the pictures of me. You are hiding a secret that no one in this school knows . . . that could 'ruin your family image,'" I air quote.

Chase stands there confidently arms folded. "Yeah, well, at least I got laid for three years and I don't have to cheat my way through school."

Allison relaxes her shoulders, turning to her friends who burst into laughter.

Orange charges Allison but stops right in front of her.

Allison blocks her face. "Not my face, please."

Orange just laughs and says, "C'mon girl," to me.

At this point, Jay is still holding my hands trying to move me. I release my hands when Jay's expression changes. I turn to look at Tim in the doorway, glaring at me. I look at him. I don't see him like I did that night we kissed and the three years before that. His board shorts aren't hanging so sexily anymore.

Jay grabs my right hand and says, "let's go." He leads me to the door, but Tim's in the way.

"Excuse us," Jay's voice sounds normal like he's keeping his cool.

"She's all yours now," he whispers to Jay. He smells like Cabo Wabo on spring break. I feel Orange behind me. She has her hand on my right shoulder.

In an octave higher than I would have liked, Tim yells, "You're practically a prostitute."

Still holding my hand, Jay gets an inch away from Tim's face and says, "Yeah, well, at least she isn't a murderer."

"Truth!" Orange yells. What does that mean?

Jay towers over Tim with weight and height. Tim puts his hands up, walking inside as the teacher warns everyone to go back to their classes.

Jay still holds my hand as we all walk out of the classroom. I turn to face him.

"Thank you."

"Sure," he says. "Talk soon. Mr. Bleakman will drop kick me if I don't sit down in his class right now."

I nod as Orange and I walk to our classroom.

"You should have punched her," I say.

"Violence isn't the answer," she reads the caption of the poster on Mr. Clark's door.

I put my hand over my mouth laughing. I know it's not funny. A lot of us could have gotten expelled for what just went down, but my goodness was it funny and it felt liberating. And, there you have it—it is the end of the Pop Crowd for me and the start of something new.

Orange laughs too. "I don't know what went down with Chase or the DUI or whatever, but I'll do anything to embarrass any one person from the Pop Crowd . . ."

"Well, Orange, maybe one day I will tell you," I say.

She plops down next to me. "I'll be waiting on pins and needles . . . besides, my little sister loves you."

My hands are still shaking from wanting to murder Allison. I try taking deep breaths. "Wait, is your name Ariana? Are you Gracie's sister?"

She smiles. "Yeah, I'm Ariana Robbins." She extends her arm. "Nice to meet you."

"I didn't know your name . . ."

"It's okay, you're clueless to a lot of things. And, Gracie is much happier with you. Mama Chantel likes you, too. She's not always easy to please."

"Mama Chantel is so sweet," I say, "Gracie, I feel like she wants to murder me in my sleep . . ."

"Nah." She writes the writing prompt on the board.

"I didn't know you were sisters," I say.

"Yeah, we're both adopted . . . so." She shrugs and then proceeds to tell me her life story. "And we have three more siblings, not as crazy as Gracie but they're cool and from all over the world. Thank God for the two nannies because between my dad's OB GYN job and my mom's clothing line, Girl Scouts, soccer, horseback riding, piano, Chinese lessons, we are crazy . . ."

I nod. Who knew Orange was adopted, talkative and vulnerable all in the same thought?

"Sadie, the principal wants to see you," our English teacher gets off the phone.

Time to face the music.

"Good luck," Orange squeezes my hand.

Chapter 22

OLD FRIENDS AND NEW

The shaking hasn't stopped. I walk the cobblestone steps to the office and round the corner to the main office. I wish I could have Jay there with me. I plop down in the chair.

"Hi," Principal Dow says, motioning me to his office. Dr. Plumb, the school psychologist is there as well as the school nurse, Nurse Jackie. My dad walks in. He is in his full blue firefighter uniform.

I don't say anything. I want a shot.

Nurse Jackie hands Principal Dow the flier.

"What's this?" Principal Dow points to it.

"It's a picture someone took of me, a photographer I know. Some people at school got their hands on the photo." My voice is rocky as I rub the palm of my hands with my fingers looking at my dad.

"It's provocative, Sadie," Nurse Jackie makes her presence known.

Tell me about it. I'm the one in the photo.

"And, she's underage," my dad says.

Where's mom? She's nicer.

"The photographer is my age and we were messing around," I say casually, although, there was nothing casual going on. "It was a while back . . ."

I don't want to sell out Chase, even though I hate him. And, perhaps I don't understand what he is going through.

"Does he go to this school?" Dr. Plumb asks.

"Yes," I can't lie anymore.

"And, the quote, let's see here," Dr. Plumb grabs his glasses.

"I will work for test answers," I say.

"What the hell does that mean, Sadie?" my dad's voice raises. Principal Dow motions for my dad to calm down as I'm looking for a way out of the office. Maybe there's a secret door behind the bookshelf.

"We talked to about thirty students to figure out who was going into my vault during the night for the answers to tests scores." He points to the square steel safe behind him. "We left you out of it, because we know you have an IEP now and the legal stuff going on . . ."

"But . . ." I suggest.

"Do you know anything about this, Sadie?" Nurse Jackie's voice rings in my head.

"Please be honest, Sadie," Dr. Plumb says.

"People are messing with me because of all the stuff that went down last year," I say. "I now think it's considering bullying."

My dad closes his eyes. I bet he wishes the cute girl with braids would come back.

"That doesn't help me," Principal Dow says. "Who?" "Who?" I start, "Who?

"Who?" Principal Dow and Dr. Plumb say in unison.

My dad slams his hand down on the desk. "Let her answer."

I righteously say this tirade like I've earned it and everyone needs to back off. "I have a lot of people at this school who hate me for various reasons. One person hates me for kissing her ex-boyfriend at the time, but they are back together this year." I shrug. "One person hates me for a rumor of me hooking up with her boyfriend, which is not true. One person hates me, because he or she is confused on sexual identity. One person hates me because I'm skinnier than her or cuter than her. Some girls hate me because I was part of the Pop Crowd and really mean for three years. Most people in the AP classes hate me because they think I'm a low life with a learning disability. BUT most of all . . . Mariposa Beach High School and the city of Mariposa Beach for that matter hate me because I have a DUI and crashed into the side of an elementary school building and that does not settle well with most. So I would start with the last name A and finish off with Z." I stand up.

My dad smirks, taking my shaky hand. "Are we done here?"

I stand up and walk out.

"We'll get back to you," Principal Dow says.

My dad and I stand in the hallway.

"I gotta go back to work, but maybe we can talk tomorrow afternoon when you get home from school," he speaks while looking me in the eye.

He speaks.

"Okay," my voice is hoarse.

Back in English class, I tell no one what happened. I just sit down.

Orange turns to me and says, "Hey, do you think Jay could help me with my English essay?" She makes puppy dog eyes similar to Gracie's when she wants something.

"Jay?" I say, possessively.

"Yeah," she says. "My mom says if I have one more F on an English paper, she's taking my cell phone away."

"Oh yeah, I feel naked without mine," I say. "Yeah, I think so.

He's offered to help me. Come with me at nutrition today."

At nutrition, Orange hands Jay her essay. He reads over it as we all sit in silence working. It's our first time with the three of us studying together. I'm quiet. I'm not sure why. In my head, I am over the flier and onto something more real, Wyatt MacPhearson's forgiveness.

"Okay, Orange, I made a little key as to what the colors red, yellow and green mean. Just go through it and you'll understand," he hands it to her.

She takes it, "Just a few marks."

"You have good ideas. That's a good start," he points to highlighted pieces.

"Thank you," she says, "I will go over it."

I look at both of them.

"Jay, Orange," I say. "Thank you for helping me with Allison."

"It's fine." She throws her black Adidas backpack over her shoulder.

He nods. "As much as I would have loved to have seen a catfight . . . and watch you and Orange beat her down, I thought of the potential you both have."

"Potential?" We say in sync, looking at him.

"Yeah, potential." He looks at me. "You both are extremely witty, yeah, you may have some roadblocks with learning traditionally, but your ability to come back like you do, it shows you are intelligent."

"Thanks, Jay," Orange pats him on the back.

My legs fill with liquid and I am unable to move. Someone said I'm intelligent. I should go with it, naturally?

"And, you too, Sadie. If you ever get off your high horse and ask me to help you, I'd be more than willing . . ."

I roll my eyes at him and ask, "you're really that willing to help Orange and I?"

"If I feel you have potential," he replies.

Why does he really want to help me?

Orange chimes in, "I'll take it without any questions."

"See," he says.

Orange's cell rings so she answers it off to the side.

"And, by the way, you look better without all the rainbow crap on your face, Sadie." He presses his lips together, waiting for my response.

I couldn't think of a smartass comeback, so I just say, "thank you, question mark?"

I'm trying so hard not to be compatible with him.

"And, I know it's cold now, but if you guys have wetsuits and ever want to join me for Stand Up Paddle boarding, here's my cell number," he hands me and Orange a piece of paper.

"Okay." I take it.

"Maybe if you're lucky."

Jay cocks his head as he leaves for the ROTC room.

Orange looks at me. "I think you've blown it with the smartass comments. Maybe you should actually be nice to him," she suggests.

"Yeah, it's just been the week from hell . . . I hate being nice sometimes," I lie. "Besides, he can take it."

"I feel ya." We walk towards period 3. "My mom is always like, Orange, be pleasant, and I don't want to."

This girl is funny. Before the Pop Crowd, I could make people laugh. I could laugh. However, maybe the week from hell is really getting to me or maybe who I am is really is so far pushed down deep inside that it'll take several humorous attempts to remedy.

"Hey Orange . . ." I say. "For a mute girl, you talk an awful lot."

"Mama Chantel puts her hand over my mouth some nights just to shut me up," she says.

I catch a reflection of my smile in the classroom window. It's been a while since I've seen her.

Chapter 23

DOLPHINS AND PUMPKIN NECKLACES

The next day, later that afternoon before the sun hit the water, I text Jay to go SUP boarding but he had to babysit his nieces last minute. I need to blow off some major steam. I prance around my dad, clipping roses in the garden, wondering if I should ask him to go with me. I would have a ride and wouldn't have to carry my SUP board five blocks to the water.

I put on my bikini; winter wetsuit, booties and a cap since the water is a little chilly in October, hoping my dad would get the hint. I pull out the long, pink SUP and paddle, a purchase I was dying to have when I moved to Mariposa Beach. It was something I used only the summer before I started hanging out with the Pop Crowd.

"Hi." My dad pulls off his cowboy hat and garden gloves. "You going paddle boarding?"

"Um yeah." I look down at my wetsuit. "Do . . . you . . . want . . . to . . . come?"

"Well, I'll go with you," he says. "I wouldn't want you to have to ride your bike, holding your paddle board."

"I was going to walk holding my board," I say.

"Then maybe we can order a pizza and hand out candy to the trick or treaters," he replies.

"Oh yeah, it's Halloween," I say, wanting to let out a big sob. Typically, I should be at Allison's getting ready and pre-partying for her parents' huge Halloween party but this year is a little different.

I jump in his truck and we drive down to the beach. It is silent. Like the awkward silent where you're praying for a bird to hit the windshield or anything like . . . anything . . .

The waves are rough, but I have to get past the break in order to enjoy the peace and calm. My dad helps me. I stand up on the board, balancing my legs evenly in the center. My dad and I are silent as we stand there, enjoying the view of the beautiful city of Mariposa Beach palm trees, private docks and beautiful beach houses. I need a minute to process the almost catfight and expulsion the last few days. I think about all the horrible things I have done, and I think he knows that's what I'm thinking about. I bullied. I did favors for the answers to tests. I lied to my parents. I hooked up with my so-called best friend's boyfriend. I let people treat me like crap. I drank. I smoked. I humiliated myself. I lied to Nicolette.

Seconds into my thoughts, I feel something flipping under my board. Panicking I crouch down to maintain my balance. Sitting on my knees I grasp the strap on my board.

"It's just dolphins," my dad yells, twenty feet in back of me.

"Dolphins, plural?" I yell back, looking down to see at least ten bottlenose silvery gray dolphins swim next to my board jumping, squeaking and swimming.

"AWESOME," my dad yelps.

I look back at him. He's laughing so hard. I start to laugh, too.

It wasn't a bird on a windshield but it helps brake the ice.

About two hours later, we pull in the driveway still talking about our encounter with the majestic dolphins and laughing.

"You did good." My dad put his hand on my knee. "We should go again."

I gulp, trying to dismiss the tears and I point. "Um, the ghosts fell."

"Okay, I'll get them," he says. "Why don't you go in and see if your mom has candy to hand out?"

"Wait." He puts his hand on my leg. "I wanted to ask you . . . has this been going on for years, Sadie, the bullying?" my dad asks.

I'm surprised to hear my voice, calm and collected, "Well, with the Pop Crowd, they always made fun of me for my math skills, but Allison put everyone down. And, she did catch Tim and I, well, kissing so she's angry with me. I don't blame her."

"Still no one deserves this," my dad says.

I want to share all about Chase and the answers, but I best not go there. They hate me a little less now, and I don't want it to go the opposite way.

"And the photos? They were never nude?"

"No," I reply.

He opens the door. "Okay, stay away from the boy that took them."

"He's not my friend anymore."

"Okay." He slips his sunglasses in the visor. "I think your mom has some butternut squash, pumpkin bread and the apple cinnamon fries ready for dinner."

"Hhhhhmmmm apple cinnamon fries, my favorite," I say.

He smiles. I can feel my parents' hearts soften as we sit in a triangular shape on the front porch, handing out candy. It is the first time I really told them the truth. They are astonished about stuff Allison and her friends said. I am beginning to think that Jay and them are right about the bullying. The strand of orange lights twinkles. The ghosts sway. The air is crisp like the apple cinnamon fries I've been devouring. Kids collect their Halloween candy and dolphins continue to swim. It is the first time I feel like there's life outside of Mariposa Beach.

"Hi," I say lively, as four Felix girls dressed as Disney princesses walk up. "Well, aren't you beautiful?" I give them each a rubber ball and a life size candy bar.

"Hi Sadie," Joey says first and they all follow. "So beautiful!" My mom smiles from ear to ear.

"Thank you. I'm Joey, and this is Noah, Tyler and Billie. Our uncle Jay knows Sadie and wanted to say hello." The oldest girl covers her mouth so he can't see it and whispers. "I think he likes you."

My cheeks redden.

I see three adults dressed as princesses twenty feet behind the girls.

Jay and Josh wave. I wave back. "You can come up," my mom says.

"Oh, it's the Felix's." My dad stands up.

My dad walks down the driveway and the three men start talking. The girls, my mom and I follow.

"Hi Mel, this is my mom, Cindy," I say.

"Pleasure," she extends her arm.

"Your daughters are so beautiful, and they all said thank you," my mom says.

"What? My daughters?" She tickles all of them. "Thank you."

"You make a fine princess," I say to Mel, "but your husband and Jay make the best. Huh girls?"

The girls giggle. "That's why they are dressed like princesses."

My mom and I laugh.

"Yes, Uncle Jay and daddy lost a bet." Mel turns towards them. "They said mommy couldn't grow a pumpkin before Halloween, so now they owe three nights of babysitting, and dressing like princesses for Halloween."

The group laughs. She's funny.

My mom turns. "You really got a big one there."

I pair off with Jay. "Wow, red looks good on you, Pocahontas."

"I'm Mulan," he rebukes.

I giggle.

"You didn't want to dress up, Sadie?" He walks up one step as I walk down one step.

I'm wearing grey jeans and an off-the-shoulder purple T-shirt that says 'Yo.' "Not feeling very spirited this year."

He pulls out a long necklace with orange lights from the orange plastic pumpkin. "Here, this might help, may I?"

"Yea." My eyes blink as he takes the two steps closer, placing it on my neckline. His fingertips are warm brushing my collarbone.

Is he flirting? I've had guys flirt with me, but not like this. This is different. Maybe because it's not sleazy. He did have eye makeup on, but I could still see his olive green eyes and this time I didn't want to stop looking at them.

"Perfect Halloween spirit." He smiles as he backs up, waving a pretend wand in the air. "Bibbity bobbity boo."

I smile, thinking if I had a daughter I'd want my husband to treat her like Jay treats his nieces.

"Uncle Jay, wrong movie . . ." Joey yells. "And," she's says, impatiently with hands on her hips and all, "there's a haunted house down the way, and I need your hand . . ."

He puts his hands on his hips. "Okay."

"Go Mulan," I say.

"Bye," he says, "And, Happy Halloween."

I walk back over to my parents back to the triangular seating.

My dad sips his apple cider. "Now that there is some good people."

He is right. They remind me of people from Wisconsin. "What happened to his parents? Why does he live with Mel and Josh?" My mom asks.

"Josh told me his parents died within months of each other when he was fifteen," my dad says.

"Gosh, how sad," my mom says.

"Yes," I reply. I didn't know that.

"Well, they invited us to their church Sunday in Malibu. I think we should go," my mom says.

It's silent. My mom glares at my dad.

My dad nods profusely and says, "yes."

I click the Halloween pumpkin necklace on and let it light up my shirt about six times. It makes me smile. This necklace and sobriety remind me of who I used to be, a happy-go-lucky girl.

Chapter 24

PERCENTAGE AGAINST US

A few days later, after some girls try steal Gracie's Mickey Mouse erasers, Gracie finally calms down after a long talk about bullies. She rocks back and forth in her chair managing to write her name on her paper.

"Miss Sadie, what's 3 times 6?" she asks calmly.

I draw six circles with three dots in each one, "count by 3's"

"Thank you to the moon and back," she screams as she shoots her arm up in the air. This makes me giddy and wanted.

I feel my eyes close and try not to laugh watching her do as I say, "Perfect."

"You teach me good stuff, Miss Sadie, I love you," she babbles.

"And, I love you," My eyes water so I fixate on something glittery across the classroom.

I joyfully walk through the office door of the volunteer school. The office lady smiles at me as I walk back to Concha's office.

"Hi," I say, as Concha continues to fill out paperwork.

"Hi Sadie." She looks up from her computer, closing it slightly.

"Did you want to see me?"

"Yeah, I'm almost done here. I got the results of your written CPR test."

I gather my hands together, looking at the linoleum floor. My biggest fear is test results.

"It's right here somewhere." She continues sifting through papers. "Here we are."

"Okay," I reply back.

"Sadie, I understand you qualified for an IEP the end of last year, and this is a volunteer position, so," she shifts, "let's . . . um . . . let's go over this together."

Concha puts the test between us and says, "Number four, the most common obstruction is food, not dentures or tongue.

I look at her. "Okay, yeah, that makes sense."

She creases her lips.

"I understand it better when I hear and see it," I state, wiping my left eye with my pointer finger.

"Aw," she shifts in her seat.

We spend the next thirty minutes going over the entire CPR exam. I feel warm and clammy after it, which in turn makes me feel anxious. I feel stupid, in other words. I feel sometimes I can really get things and other times it's a foreign language.

"Okay, since it's mandatory volunteer and there's a certified teacher with you, I'll pass you and now you can continue to work with Gracie." She stands up. "But, keep studying though, Sadie. This stuff is important."

I shrug. "Okay."

"She actually likes you," she says, as I'm almost out the door, "but don't get too personal with her."

"Too personal?" I feel slightly back in the game of life with that rebuttal.

Her glasses lay low on her nose. "That's what I said."

I blow air threw my nose. She hates me but I try to ignore it.

After my volunteer shift, I jump on my bike. AM I EVER GOING TO GET IT? Will I ever recover from having a Central Auditory Processing Disorder?

I want my flask or a smoke in my mouth to numb the pain of my body. I settle for a smoke. I always keep a pack in my purse, just in case. Parking my bike on a lone rock in the park nearby, I light my cigarette. Blowing out, my silent therapy encompasses me. I'm embarrassed that I can't process simple things like the best reason to give the Heimlich. I replay my incident with Concha in my head. It feels like when my teachers would announce test results in front of the class or call out names of students who are staying back for recess because they don't get it. Or how many members of the Pop Crowd would use my intelligence as a target. I suck and blow to ease the pain.

"Hi," a familiar voice sounds on the other side of the rock.

I turn to see Orange dressed in all black, carrying her backpack.

She sits down next to me, helping herself to my smokes. "Feel free to have a smoke," I say.

She pulls out her English paper.

"A plus," I read it.

"It's the one Jay helped me with." She smiles. "First A plus ever."

"Wow, that's awesome," I say.

She takes it back, looking at it. "Yeah, it's a framer."

"Why aren't you hanging by yourself under a tree?" I joke. "It's fun to talk to you," she says. "What's wrong Sadie?

Orange asks. "Don't tell me for a second that Allison has gotten to you? That flier was wicked, but it's Allison Pratt. She's evil."

"NO WAY . . . the world moves on after the Pop Crowd . . . I just feel so dumb sometimes . . ." I start and then venture into the findings of the CPR test.

A few seconds later she suggests, "Wow, so science or math aren't your thing, Sadie."

"Not so much," I hit my cigarette until it's a butt.

"I got evaluated for a learning disability when I was seven and have had an IEP for ten years," she starts.

"ADHD?"

She giggles. "Yes, funny you guessed that one?"

"Well I mean you are known as Orange Crush," I say sarcastically.

"Yep."

I put out my cigarette in the dirt, "What do you want to be when you grow up, Orange?

She shakes her head. "Women's Wrestling." She smiles.

I throw my head down in laughter, "In Mariposa Beach?" "Sure," she jokes.

"Oh," I giggle.

"In all seriousness, I want to do something. I love cooking. I was reading about my learning disability and it said that 40 percent of kids with any disability don't graduate high school," she explains.

"I don't wanna work at McDonald's." I look at her.

"I don't either," she replies.

"Or be homeless?" I smile.

"Or sell oranges on the freeway" she replies.

"Or a prostitute?" I say back.

We giggle. I feel the energy between us. It feels electric. "Orange . . ." I say a few seconds later.

"Yeah," she lowers her sunglasses and looks at me with these beautiful brown eyes.

"Pinky promise me, we will graduate." I show her my baby pinky finger.

"I don't know, Sadie, up until a month ago, I hated you." She links her pinky with mine.

"A month ago, really?" I half smile.

She looks up at the sky and then sighs. "If you promise to find the Sadie that you are comfortable with. If it's the moody, bitchy Sadie you have been for three years, fine, but if it's the easy going, kind, hilarious Sadie that you really are, then I'm in."

"God, you are nothing I expected . . . Orange," I say honestly, surprising myself.

"And, you promise to snap out of it."

"Fine," I squeeze her pinky back.

She smiles. "Besides Jay is like uberly smart, right? Maybe he can help us pass."

I feel for the Halloween necklace under my sweat-shirt, "I think so."

She stands up, "I think he is like number one in our class.

You should let him help you. "

She pulls me and I say. "Where are we going?"

She turns around. "Let's get started. I am not going to end up like my real family and that A plus today tells me I have something."

We throw our cigarettes and ride our bikes to the Java Coffee, where we do our homework.

That night I lie in bed, thinking of my conversation with Orange. My bed equals sanctity. I analyze things in bed. Before I just pass out, I think of how my life would have been if they'd caught this learning disability a little earlier in my education. Maybe I wouldn't have been part of the Pop Crowd? Maybe I wouldn't have been hiding all the time or making excuses for dumb comments, bad grades or not understanding things sometimes? Maybe I would've tried harder in school? Maybe I wouldn't have a DUI at 17, a drinking and smoking problem? Maybe I wouldn't have given it up to the guys I did? Maybe I wouldn't have been such a bitch to so many people.

After a long weekend, a few days later at nutrition, I sit next to Jay. I feel comfortable today in my red stretchy pants and a long, black sweater with black boots. My hair is in a bun. I'm wearing zero makeup.

"Hey," he says, nonchalantly.

"Hey Mulan, I need to pass high school," I blurt out, "Can you help me, or do you have to fight in a war?"

"Now you want my help?" He's honest. "Well, this princess is all washed up."

"Fine, I'll do it on my own." I stand up.

GOD, WHY AM I BEING RUDE?

"Wait!" He stands up next to me. "I have ROTC practice until 3:30, 4:00 okay?"

"OKAY!" I annunciate.

He pulls his backpack over his shoulder, staring right at me.

"Girl, take it down a notch. You don't have to put on a show with me."

"I'm not . . ."

He lowers his sunglasses, which basically shuts me up. "Java Coffee?"

I nod, "Java Coffee is the only place the employees don't snicker at me."

"Orange, is it okay if she comes, too?"

He nods, "yea."

My face lights up like a Christmas tree. My shoulder bumps his as we turn opposite ways. I feel a tingle in my bare toes. If I'm being honest, the tingles in my toes are something I really cannot explain. I know it isn't the cold weather either.

I ride my pink cruiser down the street. It's November 2, and the city has already been decorated minus the main Christmas tree. The line of palm trees hold streams of white, red and green lights while huge metal bells hang from lampposts. I soak up the stunning lights.

At Java Coffee, I'm perched at my favorite round table in the corner, wearing black Lululemons, a long sleeved white thermal and bare feet with Uggs on the floor. I like this particular spot because it has a view of everyone who enters, in case an escape route is necessary. The temperature in Java Coffee is warm with all the ovens baking the chocolate chip candy cane cookies. The smell is overtaking my senses. I grab a cookie and a small hot chocolate.

"What's up?" He sits, as he points to my glasses. "I like the glasses." His hair is wet and slightly gelled. He's wearing a pair of blue jeans and a white, long sleeved shirt that says ROTC on it, as well as some Reef sandals. He looks thinner.

"Yeah, my eyes start to hurt . . .and I figured I would try to look smarter," I adjust them.

"And, you need to start loving yourself," he really says it.

"Loving myself?" I ask.

"The wearing the glasses comment to feel smarter. You are smart, Sadie." He says what he means and means what he says.

"Oh okay," I surrender, wrapping my arms around myself.

Now I'm making fun of him and he manages to say, "No, really."

"Okay," I push the chocolate chip candy cane cookie towards him.

"No, if we are going to do this and work together, you have to believe in yourself like I do," he says, biting his lip.

Stop presenting so much love and kindness and everything from your heart to your toes for me, Jay. I don't know how to be like you. I don't dare say my thoughts out loud.

"Jay, I've been in the low academic group for years and struggled tremendously," I feel my face tingling as I reveal. "Come to find I had a learning disability at 17 years old. School is hard and will always be. Sometimes I need to voice it."

"Okay, but if you're working with me you cannot say you're dumb. Rule number one."

"Math." Annoyed, I slide my book across the table.

He moves his body next to me as he begins with the chapter, explaining rays and half lines. I grunt a lot as he asks me to identify rays.

"Rule number two, the attitude gets checked AT THE DOOR," he says in a high-pitched voice.

I feel my eyelashes hit the lenses of my glasses and I cover my mouth, losing it to laughter when Jay snaps three times in the air like the spirited chef Manny on the *Big Apple Cookoff.*

"Sorry, Joey, Tyler and I watch *The Big Apple Cookoff* too much," he admits.

"Manny?" I suggest. "He's so funny."

"Yeah," he smiles, "I love that it's filmed in New York City."

"I know, it's such an amazing city. I wish I could have spent more time there . . ." I say.

He pauses.

"My Grams," I say, my voice scratchy. "We used to go every fall to visit Grams towards the end of her filming. She'd put us in the Big Apple Hotel, where they filmed the show. The show was funnier behind the scenes because of her." He listens attentively to me as I run my finger along the outside of the lid looking down.

"Your Grams, was one of the top funniest, nicest people I've ever had the pleasure of knowing," he adds.

She really was.

I stop for a moment and take a breath. "And the view from our hotel was a panoramic view of the city: buildings, cars, taxis and people. We visited the famous spots like Statue of Liberty and Empire State Building, but I never felt like I got enough of it. Once Gramps died and Grams found out she had cancer, we never went back . . ." my eyes are definitely watery at this point. The same pointer finger wipes a tear under my eye.

"It's okay to speak about them and feel sadness," he says. How does he know?

"I'm fine," I bark.

"Well." He sees my angst. "I want to seriously visit there one day," he says, changing the subject.

"Yeah," I agree. "Okay, so, I get the rays now. Here's the math review." I push the paper in front of him.

We mosey over the math review. He sits next to me, a good enough distance away, proudly watching my eyes get bigger with understanding and sadly watching me bite my lip when I am lost. Or maybe he's getting annoyed at the gutful giggles I'm producing when I get a little anxious. Every now and again, I look into his warm and inviting olive green eyes. Green, my current favorite color. The color almost bounces off my heart and hits me in the forehead. Wake up, Sadie, it's BIG FAT MEXICAN!

The crowd in Java Coffee lessens as the Santa Ana winds kick in and the clock turns 7 p.m..

"Well, that was a joy," I say.

"That's what I mean . . ." Jay packs up his books.

"I do feel better." I throw my book in a large pink tote.

"Stop being so positive," he jokes.

A text chimes on my cell.

It's my mom: Please be home by 7 p.m. and put your cell on the kitchen table. I'll be home from yoga by 8 p.m..

"You okay?"

"Yep!"

"Awe." He snaps.

I pause. Half of me wants to open up to him and half of me wants to be a bitch.

"Prison ward says I have to be home now," I say. "I should probably leave."

"Prison ward?" He cocks an eyebrow.

"My parents, they hate me still, " I say.

"Nah, they spent Halloween with you . . . seem nice," he suggests. His eyes follow some minions dressed in cheerleading uniforms, walking into Java Coffee. Betsy Grimes has a C.A. on her uniform; she took my spot. We hear snickering and giggling as he slowly pushes me to the escape door, opening it and motioning for me to follow.

"I put them in a BAD predicament," I say about my parents and then in the same breath motion back at the minions. "God, can't get away from the bitches."

"Those girls are followers. They wanted to be you and want to be Allison and Nicolette."

"Oh, they don't want to be me anymore, huh?" I ask.

He laughs. "Probably not."

I shift my body around, wanting to say something in my defense but decide against it. I take it as an insult but then I start to realize that he's simply being real. Jay is real. He is honest. It's something I haven't appreciated in a long time. Maybe if more people were real with me then I would know myself a little better.

"Awe crap." He looks down at my bike. The back tire is flat. "Right on," I say, as I pull out the pink push-pin stuck in my tire.

"I wonder who that could have been?" He left brow furrows.

"Could they stop being so cruel, as if the flier wasn't enough?"

"Black Nova." Jay points to the parking lot pushing my bike along. "My trunk is large, so it'll fit your bike. And you were cruel, too."

I was; this is true.

"Right, I'll never forget where I came from." I roll my eyes, slightly annoyed walking next to him. "Thank you for that."

"Anything for a friend, and, aside from the wording on the flier, whoever saw that picture of you at school was probably either a little jealous or . . . Uh," he bites his lower lip anxiously, not looking at me, "a little turned on . . ." he reveals.

The words hit me upside the head, stars and all.

"Well . . ." I shrug. "Good point, Jay."

He slowly opens my door without saying anything.

I throw my purse on the floorboard along with the provocative comment he made. I take a deep breath as he walks around to the driver's side. "Nice car."

He jumps in. "Thank you."

His jeans are tight from his upper thighs.

I look around. Nice black paint job, beautiful leather seats. If I didn't know better I'd say this car made Jay a pimp. Instead of calling him a pimp, I politely say, "my dad would appreciate this car."

"Why?"

"He's a car guy," I explain. "He had a bunch back in Wisconsin. Here, there's no room."

"Well, I restored it with my brother. He knows more than me, but I'm learning," he admits.

I nod. I picture Jay and his older brother working on the Nova in the garage. It's a nice picture.

"This is a dope song," I say, as his Pioneer speakers pulsate.

"Dope? Are people still using dope?" he jokes, cranking it up. Jack White's "Love Interruption" is on the radio. We both sing along and I am beginning to think sobriety is worth it.

Outside the window, I watch the sun melt into the ocean. The Christmas lights on Main Street flicker on. At Mariposa Beach, November 1 marks the start of the holiday season and decorations go up immediately. I love Christmas. I love Mariposa Beach at Christmas. There's a 30-foot Christmas tree decorated with mini surfboards in the middle of someone's front yard. Christmas time, that means almost four months I have been disassociated with the popular crowd. Almost 180 days sober. Almost half way done with my volunteer hours. My GPA is improving.

Chapter 25

MISUNDERSTANDINGS

The song is over. Berlin's "Take My Breath Away" filters through. I think of the movie Top Gun, one of my dad's favorite movies.

I hide my smile by looking away from him.

He puts on his blinker to turn into my street and parks his Nova under the streetlamp.

"Well, here you are." He points to my house. "Nice Christmas lights."

"Thanks," I look at the strand of Christmas lights hanging on my porch. "My dad was Clark Griswold in Wisconsin."

Jay's brows furrow.

"God, I sound like I'm obsessed with my dad." I slap the air. "It's complicated. We had a different relationship." I'm acting anxious because I don't know what he wants from me right now. He did help with me with my homework.

"It's okay. I don't mind hearing about your dad. Wyatt is nice," he replies in a low voice.

Silence.

"Oh screw it," I take a deep breath and scoot towards him, lifting up my shirt so he can feel my boobs on him.

He pulls me back by the shoulders. "Sadie, stop!"

I grab the back of his neck and almost pull his lips to mine.

Before they meet, he stops me. "WHOA, WHOA, WHOA, WHOA, WHOA. Sit over there." He points to the passenger seat.

I pull my shirt down quickly and sit where I'm told.

I wish I could tuck my head in my shell but instead I look down.

He moves towards me. "Sadie, look at me. I don't need anything but friendship in return."

I nod as tears roll down my cherry red cheeks. I feel humiliated.

His eyes are intense. "Was it the comment about you looking good in the flier because I seriously want to take that back."

I throw my thoughts around the Nova. "It's okay. I'm good. You good?"

"Who?" he asks, with a low, gruffly voice, head hanging low.

"What?" My voice is hoarse.

He smiles, "Uh, Sadie . . . who made you like this?" he looks at me.

"Like?"

"Like, if someone helps you with schoolwork, you owe them something? Who made you believe that?" He seems angry.

"Oh that?" I say sarcastically.

"Tim Miller? I will kill him." He pulls his cell out of the cup holder and scrolls through his contacts.

"No, no wait . . ." I pull his phone away, "God this is all so fubared."

"Yep, it is," he agrees.

He knows what it means.

"It was Chase," I say.

"Oh, standup guy number 2," he pounds the steering wheel. "His dad is too good to be true."

"Jay," I say loudly. "Let me explain . . . when I lived in Wisconsin, I was at a private school with individual help and did okay but everybody knew I was slower. At Mariposa High it was hard. Classes were bigger. The average was a lot higher than the school in Wisconsin. I started to struggle. I wanted so badly to be part of the Pop Crowd. I failed a few tests. Chase noticed and I sort of made a deal with him."

"What was the deal?" he asks as his fingers tap the steering wheel. He is angry.

My cheeks feel hot and tears are running down my cheeks. "Please don't tell anyone. He paid someone, I don't know who, to break into Principal Dow's office and vault to obtain the answer keys for the tests for all the teachers on campus . . . Oh my God, why am I telling you this?"

"It's okay," he says.

"He and I tried to have sex once but it didn't work . . ."

"Because he's gay?" Jay throws it out into the world.

"Yep," I gulp. "How did you?"

He cocks his head. "What? I'm observant."

"So . . ." I wipe my eyes. "In exchange for the answer keys . . . he wanted something. I let him take pictures of me because he said I was beyond photogenic. Always clothed. He wants to be a photographer and build up his portfolio. I know crazy, but he is really good. When I was diagnosed with the Central Auditory Processing Disorder, semi-hooked up with Tim and got into all the legal trouble, they disowned me, including Chase. When Chase's parents saw some text messages between him and this older male, he basically told them he had been sleeping with me for the past three years and I was his scapegoat. All the parents are close to Chase's parents. They told Al's, Nic's and Tim's and then they all found out."

His hands are on his head. "Wow, why don't you tell them all the truth?"

"It's not my place."

"Sadie, you're a good friend," Jay says.

"I know."

"Always clothed?" he interrupts.

"Maybe underwear and bra but they are really professional, kind of like Victoria's Secret . . ." I justify.

He is quiet.

"All I need is four kids," I laugh. And, the laughing
turns into an uncontrollable laugh and the laugh turns
into tears.

He is quiet.

"I'm not saying what I did was right," I start.

Jay goes quiet again.

Grams' Guy Fact: When a man is staring at you in
silence, he's listening to you.

"I was desperate!" I scream and with everything in
me, I scream it again, "I WAS DESPERATE!" I shake
my head and scream, crying.

He scoots closer, putting his huge arms around
me, "SH, SH, SH," he whispers. My head leans into his
chest. I smell his fresh man scent which is like a clean
sweat smell. He holds me in his arms and cups my head.

"I was desperate," I whisper. "No one can know. We
could get into a lot of trouble."

"I know." He holds me.

His arms are so long and thick around me. It's like
hugging a huge teddy bear that won't let go. I let him
hold me as I rest my head on his chest.

Grams' Guy Fact: When You are Laying Your Head
On A Guy's Chest, he has the world.

My secret has been revealed and he is still holding
me. It's silent except for my whimpering and light pit-

ter-patter of rain on the roof of his Nova. It feels comfortable. Five minutes goes by, six, seven.

"Why is it always raining when we hang?" His chin rests on the top of my head. "It's so fubared."

My belly shakes with laughter, as I shrug, looking up at him inches away from his face, still in his teddy bear embrace. He breathes out. It smells like mint and chocolate chip candy cane cookie. Eyes connect.

I remove myself from the embrace. Do I want to blow this up? "I'm sorry I was a bitch last year."

"And up until a few days ago as well?" His dimples sink through his cheeks. I am not sure if he's trying to hide a smile.

"Let a girl apologize . . ." I snap again like Manny from *The Big Apple Cookoff.*

"Why do you feel you have to tell me that?" He leans against the window of the Nova, folding his arms.

"Because . . ." I'm smiling now.

"Oh, I feel better now that you've explained," he chuckles. "Because now is the time to apologize," I start. "You know, step eight, making amends . . ."

"It's okay, Sadie." He touches my arm. "I never really cared what any one of you had to say. I actually never liked you until we talked at Chase's party."

I look at him and point to myself. "Me? You never liked me?"

"Yeah, I liked you when you first came to Mariposa Beach High School but then you got AL-I-FIED." He shakes his head no and chuckles a little. "I hate her."

"You really do, huh?"

"And I was BIG FAT MEX for a while, so that's always a good time."

"Ugh, that was Allison's wording," I say, leaning against the car door. "She really hates you, too."

"BFM wasn't my favorite, but it's motivating me to lose weight," he says, "And Allison can pound sand because that girl's a bitch."

I nod. "Huh, Tim used to say that all the time, not that I even care what he ever says AGAIN," I say with absolute confidence. "Why do you hate them so much?"

"Sadie," he says, "I need to tell you something. First of all, the thing with Chase is safe with me."

"Thanks." I look down.

My body is still and ears open for listening for what is about to come.

"In junior high, Tim, Chase, Allison, Orange, who was Ariana at the time, and a girl named Candace, my twin brother Jack and I were all friends. Well, the guys at least. I couldn't stand Allison back then but she was infatuated with Jack."

"Wait Candace. I saw her name with the Pop Crowd at Gracie's school," I say.

He nods.

"Oh my God, is this where you tell me what happened with your parents?" The words come out faster than I anticipated.

He playfully slaps my arm. "Tact, my friend, tact."

"Okay." I cover my hand with my mouth. "Sorry."

"It's okay." he smiles. "Anyway, Jack was the super skinny cool twin. He was the Tim Miller of the elementary school and middle school. He was smart, good looking and super cool but not an alcoholic or an asshole like Tim."

"Right!" I snap. Not sure why I snap.

He shakes his head and snaps back at me. "Anyways, he'd always have me come along to anything social, because I was his brother. So in middle school, a girl named Candace came to our school. She was beautiful." He stops and fidgets with his hands. "Looked a lot like you."

He thinks I'm beautiful. I mean he's eluded to it but this is the first mention of it.

I feel my head shake like one of those bobbly heads my dad used to have in his Mustang in Wisconsin.

He goes on. His body is at a 90-degree angle facing me. "Candace's dad was the inventor of the Drop Pounds Exercise machine. My brother loved her from the get go and they became a couple. Allison would not let up about wanting to be with Jack, so clearly she wanted to destroy Candace."

I clench my teeth. "That's how she rolls."

He continues, "Yeah, so Allison had a party where there were marijuana brownies. They all tried it, except Orange and I. Orange's mom is pretty strict. The party went on for hours. They were tripping. I stayed to make sure my brother was okay. Well, Candace starting seizing . . ."

"Was it laced?" I put my hand over my mouth, "OH MY GOD it was!"

"So, she basically lost all consciousness and they rushed her to the hospital. My brother and I rode with her in the ambulance. They tried to revive her but lost her, within minutes. Meanwhile, Jack was coming out of the high, but he wasn't that high."

"He said he remembered stuff. He remembered Candace taking a brownie and then Allison grabbed it from her and said this is the one you should have. Anyway, the toxicology report said that bath salts were included in the marijuana brownie. I told the police everything while they took me down to the station. They drug tested me. I was clean. They did the same to Orange and she was clean. Since it was Allison's house, they questioned her and her parents. She said Candace brought everything. Nicolette, Tim, and Chase all backed her up. Candace's parents pressed charges against Allison and her parents. Allison's dad is a famous litigator in downtown LA so he pretty much won the case."

"So everyone got off scott free?"

He nods. "Yes, that's why I hate all of them. They were all there. They didn't even show up for her funeral. And, then I saw them at school the next day. It was like nothing happened."

I put my hands on my head. "THAT'S INSANE! The court never took yours or Jack's statement or Orange's for that matter into consideration?"

He taps his finger on his lips like he's thinking hard. "Orange's mom was trying to adopt another child so there was something with that . . . you may want to ask her."

"My Aunt Concha, my mom's bossy older sister," he says. "I know her," I state.

"Yeah, we can't wait until I'm 18. Anyways, she has been in my life for the last fifteen years as a joint custodian with my older brother Josh. She tried to get a good lawyer for Jack, but they lost. They decided, well, my aunt decided to send him to a boarding school in Utah for the drugs. He's doing really well. He's been clean for three years. He's ready for college. Girls lined up," he says, rubbing his chin.

I sit for a second in silence pondering everything I've heard. The car is musky from our body heat. The rain has stopped. I feel slightly warm, so I roll down the window and say, "I need some air."

I pull off my off-the-shoulder sweater, leaving a tight, blue tank top underneath. The fresh rain air seeps in and cools me off.

I feel him looking at me and I kiddingly say; "I'm not trying to come onto you anymore."

He tilts his head back on the window with his eyes on me still. "Your eyes match your tank top."

Grams Guy Fact: When a guy stares at you that way, he thinks you are the most beautiful thing in the world.

I ignore it, "How did your parents die?"

He sighs. "This lovely story . . . My mom died delivering Jack and I. And, my dad was an Army Ranger." Jay breathes in. "He was trying to get out because my mom died and there was no one to parent us. But he got called on one last mission and died—landmine," his voice cracks, "So, when we were born, my brother Josh was fifteen—my parents had him when they were sixteen, Josh tried to handle us but he was too young . . ." His eyes look glossy and he clears it all with a big, "SO, we moved to Mariposa Beach to live with our aunt Concha, my mom's sister who is in the education field as you know. We had a nanny and lived decently . . . I mean you know . . . my grandpa from my dad's side is still alive and in near Camp Pendleton, so we'd go there for the weekends. Like I said my brother Josh was substantially older so as early as I remember we were always driving with him to grandpa's or meeting Mel. He basically raised us like my dad would. And, if he didn't know how, my grandpa would jump in. Perhaps maybe why I do ROTC and military-type things."

He pulls it together and sits up straight.

"That's a REALLY sad story." I intertwine my fingers in his. His big hand is warm and calloused, like my dad's. I squeeze like Grams would.

"Emotions don't usually get to me but you're asking and the way you're looking at me with your kind eyes is making me feel like you're sad for me, so I should be sad. Maybe Mel is right and I need to get emotions out here and there." His thoughts spoken out loud ping pong through the Nova.

"Thank you for sharing, and I'm really sorry," I say, "And, it's good to tell the truth, even if your voice is shaky."

"Yeah," his voice deepens and he's back to normal. "I know." He moves over next to me, not letting go of my hand. "Sadie, please don't cry. This is stupid!" he jokes.

"No, it's the water droplets from the palm tree." I put my head out the window.

"You remembered," he says.

"Barely, I was pretty hammered when a lot of bad things went down last year, but I just realized recently that you were at every event . . . so thank you," I'm trying not to look flustered by the fact that I almost want his hand back. I want the hand back because it fits perfectly in mine. That's enough for tonight. He's sensitive; I kind of like it.

I exit the Nova. He follows me up the driveway. Before I turn to walk up the steps to the front door, I stand before him. The muscles in my mouth are stale. It was a lot of talking.

"So, yeah, well," I clasp my hands behind my back.

His green eyes are low and vulnerable; staring deeply into mine . . . so deep it tips the surface of my soul. A chill runs through my body and I react.

"Are you cold?" he notices. "You should probably go before your mom . . ."

"Sades, it's been an hour," I hear my mom say, as she closes the bay window.

"It's been an hour?" I repeat.

"Sorry, Mrs. MacPhearson," Jay yells inside.

"Night. Maybe we can talk more about wanting to be in the Army."

He nods like a soldier would, "Night." He walks down the driveway and fires up his Nova.

And, there I am left in my driveway with the cold winter winds creeping through my body. I walk inside my house.

My mom lies on the couch watching *The Big Apple Cookoff* with a fire going and a fleece blanket over her and opens the blanket patting the couch. "That's the only boy I'll let you talk to."

I slip off my Uggs and enter the warmness of the fleece blanket and my mom's embrace.

Chapter 26

CHRISTMAS DECORATIONS

Falling asleep, I remember before my grandpa died when we lived in Wisconsin. We had a nice property, small farm with a few horses, hens, chickens, dogs, nice house, and a pool in the backyard. I played soccer in spring and hockey in winter. We went to church. I had real friends. My mom was happier. She went to Bible study. My dad wasn't so stressed about bringing in money. He'd restore old cars for fun. We didn't have materialistic things. Gramps and Grams were still alive. We'd play Rummy Cube. They were the glue that kept us together.

The next day the sun meanders into my room. My brain is awake but my eyes are heavy. I tossed and turned all night through the storm outside and the one in my head . . . What does Jay think of what I did? How can Allison and the Pop Crowd get away with what they did to Candace? How is he such a balanced person with all the tragedies he has been through?

My eyes open and I say "coffee." I look outside my window and the green grass on the front lawn is covered by a little frost. The lighter shade of green reminds me of the color of Jay's eyes, which peered at me all night in my dreams. Not sure if they were judgmental olive green or what. He seems to have been fine.

Perplexed, I watch the water slip off the birds of Paradise planted near my front window. Jay's dad and Candace will never see nature's beauty again.

> Dear Grams,
>
> I think of how I felt after you died. You had an amazing full life and although you battled cancer for a long time, you always told me you are lucky to have lived longer. Candace, on the other hand died at thirteen from drugs that were peer pressured on her. She didn't have a chance to experience high school, college/career or having a family. Did you ever meet her, or, are you with her now? And, Jay's parents? I hope you had a chance to meet them.
>
> Sadie

P.S. I've been sober for six months. Mel gave me a blue chip. I keep it in my wallet.

During my volunteer hours, I work with Gracie about not talking about her favorite Playboy bunnies of 97 at school. I picture myself busting up with laughter when she reveals their bra size but try to keep a straight face, asking her what she ate for dinner last night. I am slowly becoming envious of Gracie because she knows who she is and what she wants. She is intelligent, quirky, creative, and a lover of Playboy bunnies, anything Disney and refrigerators. I can't believe she forged her mom's signature and ordered the Playboy magazine using her mom's credit card all these years without her mom knowing.

After a long day, I shower and dress in a pair of green Yoga pants with a black oversized sweatshirt. Orange knocks on my door. She tells me Jay has to babysit again because he lost another bet to Mel. I laugh first, but then my heart drops. Why didn't he text me why he wasn't coming. I'm not sure what all of that means, but during the whole Shakespeare's *Midsummer Night's Dream* prep I keep focusing back on my thought bubble.

What are my feelings for Jay?

Orange and I prep. We highlight. We laugh. We tackle the next chapter, which helps me understand. Jay has laid things out perfectly for me: how to answer multiple choice and long answer essays. I feel stupid about my approach in the past. I glance at the microwave. It's 9:30 p.m. No text from Jay. My thoughts are unstable.

"How's Gracie doing?" Orange asks.

"What?" I say.

"You just looked at the time on the kitchen microwave and then your cell phone." She sips her candy cane hot chocolate, spinning slightly on the bar stool at the island in the middle of our kitchen.

"Gracie is hilarious and doing well." I sip mine, spinning on the other one. "I think Jay is taking space."

"Because of the Chase thing?" She wipes her mouth with a Christmas napkin.

"Yeah." I tell her the whole thing, too.

"Gotcha," she says. "Well, it is a hard thing to grasp. Jay is pretty pure though."

I ask, "pure?"

"Oh don't go there with me." She points to herself. "You know he's still a virgin."

"So," I say.

"So, he may feel weird about the whole thing," she says. "And, you did press your boobs against him. He may even like you."

"No," Goosebumps appear on my arms. I shut the small window in the kitchen.

"You two are kidding yourselves," she says, as her cell rings.

"What does that mean?" I lock the window shut. "Gosh, it's cold this winter."

Just then my dad busts through the door, wearing his uniform with a bomber jacket over it and holding a box of cookies from Diddy Riese Cookies in Westwood. "Oh sorry, am I interrupting anything?"

"No, we were studying," I say, taking the box as I lick my lips. "This is Orange, Ariana."

"Wyatt MacPhearson." My dad shakes her hand and pulls a glass bottle of whole milk out of the fridge.

"Dad, this is Gracie's sister," I give him more information. "Yep, Gracie, the one who ordered the Playboy magazine from Amazon," she laughs.

"Gracie is a fun topic of conversation at our dinner table." He opens the cookies and reaches for three glasses.

I smell the candy chocolate chip, oatmeal raisin walnut, peanut butter and white chocolate macadamia nut. I let Orange pick first and then I go for the white chocolate macadamia nut.

"Jay is missing out," Orange chews her peanut butter cookie. Why did she bring him up? What were my feelings for him?

My dad smiles. He knows what Orange is trying to do. "We do love the Felix's."

"Hi." My mom walks into the kitchen in her Santa Claus pajamas, "I smelled the cookies from all the way down the hall. Oh, you got the box of a dozen?"

"I was at the credit union down there," my dad says.

My mom hugs Orange. "Hi, Mrs. MacPhearson." Orange smiles.

"Call me Cindy." She dives into the box, pulling out the candy chocolate chip cookie and takes a bite. "Hhhhmmm!"

"Right!" Orange's eyes widen.

"Hhhhhmmm," we all say and then we giggle. My parents catch the laughter and we all mimic, "Hhhhmmm."

It was weird to think Orange may have been my first friend in Mariposa Beach to have actually come in my house. Allison and Nicolette would honk and wait in their cars or we'd hang out at their houses because their parents worked all the time.

"Orange, what do you have planned tonight?" My dad shifts his stance, holding milk in one hand, dipping his cookie in.

"I'm supposed to be home in twenty minutes," Orange says.

"Well, we were going to decorate for Christmas . . . do you want to join us?"

"Sure, my mom will want to talk to you, if that's okay." She pulls out her phone.

"I wouldn't have it any other way." My dad smiles widely.

I chew my cookie to distract myself from wanting to cry because he's actually asking one of my friends to participate in something with him. Decorating the tree was something we did for years. We'd chop down the tree, grooming the pine needles appropriately and then play Christmas music while decorating and drinking hot chocolate. Since we moved to Mariposa Beach . . .

"By the way, are these your mom's yoga pants?" He tugs on my leg.

"No," I reply.

"Oh, well they look cute on you."

He wrinkles his nose. "Thank you," I turn to follow him, mouthing OH MY G to Orange. She slaps me softly on my shoulder and we follow him into the living room.

My dad scoots the tree to the middle of the room and asks me, "Centered?"

I balance my body like I'm on a balance beam and answer, "Centered."

My dad looks at me smiling. It's almost like a maybe you're my sweet, little girl and I'm sorry we lost touch smile. Besides the fact, I let one little air of forgiveness out of my body. He can never find out about Chase. I find the Songs of the Seasons channel on my television and pull the tinsel decorating our six-foot fake tree. My dad pulls ornaments out one by one showing each one to Orange and asking me if I remember them? Orange graciously smiles at each ornament.

"Thank you for being here, Orange," I say.

"I wouldn't want to be anywhere else," she retorts putting her arm around me. "Well maybe on a date with Josh Felix."

I giggle. Orange is slowly becoming my best friend.

"My oh my." My mom walks in. "Let me get some more hot chocolate in the works . . . oh and the camera."

"Funny." I roll my eyes, draping more tinsel on the tree. My dad walks in the kitchen to grab the big bags. I see something shining in the corner of my eye. I pick it up. It's the angel I made out of paper plates and pipe cleaners. The picture is what made me blink. It was me in eighth grade with pigtails, braces and glasses. I put my thumb over my face to wipe off the dirt. I remember that day. Grams, mom and I were crafting while dad was working on something manly. I wanted to make something for my parents for Christmas, so I was 13 and made an angel. The next fall I started high school and everything went to hell in a handbasket.

"She always looks so photogenic." Orange smiles as she's helping my dad put up the string of popcorn.

"Beautiful then, too." My mom pulls my braid, putting her chin on my shoulder.

I put my hand on her cheek. "Thank you. I love you, mom."

"I love you, too, sweetie," she whispers. "Oh and honey, I guess Jay told Mel how much I love Poinsettas and how they remind me of New York City and Grams. She had Jay bring some over from her garden today." She points to the glass vase full of beautiful seasonal poinsettias.

"Wow," I say.

My mom walks over to smell them.

"See, you and Jay are kidding yourselves." Orange nudges me.

I pick up the tinsel, throwing it at my mom and Orange's head. I need a distraction.

My mom pulls it off, throwing it back in my face. "Merry Christmas to you, too."

My mom cranks up Gayla Peevey's "I Want A Hippopotamus For Christmas" while handing Orange and I more hot chocolate with marshmallows coming off the top of the rim in Santa mugs. She is smiling as she hands my dad one. I smile back at her while inhaling three marshmallows in my mouth. They drop into my stomach and make my heart feel warm.

It is midnight. The sheets feel cold. I love cold sheets. I read over the text messages from Jay and I earlier as I tap my lower lip. Jay says I tap or bite my lower lip when I'm trying desperately to figure something out.

Jay: I forgot to tell you that I have to work tomorrow after school but study the notes. You should do fantastically on the test. Heavily review 1-20 on the review sheet and reread pages 112-200 highlighting with a red, yellow and green highlighters like I showed you.

Sadie: K

Jay: K? Hello Chenzy!

Sadie: Sorry, I will fantastically look over the notes. Thank you!

Jay: K

Sadie: LOL! Wait, you missed cookies from Diddy Riese Cookies.

Jay: Poop emoji. Hey, see you in the New Year. I have a midterm during nutrition and we are off to Utah to visit Jack. Snowboard emoji

Sadie: Have fun Jay.

Jay: Thank you, Merry Christmas Sadie. And, Merry Christmas to you, too, Cindy and Wyatt.

I giggle because he knows my parents will read that in the morning. That's all I have energy for as my eyes dose off. We haven't really been alone since the interesting night where we revealed a lot and made a lot of physical contact. I want to know where he is at, but studying for finals, trying to figure how to improve working with Gracie and hanging with my parents and Orange have sucked up a lot of time.

I roll out of bed, eyes dart on the clock, open my English book, read, study, study while getting dressed, go to school and take an exam.

Four hours later, I find my legs shaking as the English teacher passes the tests back.

"So," I say, tucking a piece of hair behind my ear and flattening out my short candy cane patterned skirt nervously. I am about to clasp my fingers together when someone finally speaks.

"Great job," he says.

I raise my eyebrows. "The bell will ring in five minutes. Hurry, I have to go to my volunteer hours."

"Wow." He smiles at me, handing me my test.

"What?" I smile at him. "One hundred percent?"

"Yes," he jumps in. "*Midsummer Night's Dream*, check. Hey Sadie, I'd like for you to enter the Show and Tell contest. This chameleon soul poem is good and I

know you had Ceramics last year so you can pop in anytime and work on a piece to match your essay."

"I'll consider it," I say nicely. "Congrats!" Orange
taps my shoulder.

"Thank you," I smile from ear to ear. I take a picture of the test and send it to Orange, my parents, Jay
and Mel. They all send me nice text messages back.
Mel reminds me that she'll be in Utah but will have her
phone on anytime, if I need it. I haven't thought about
drinking in over a month.

My day is perfect. Orange drives me to volunteer
because it's freezing outside. On the way, we hold our
100% tests showing them to other drivers and pedestri-
ans. We are dying of laughter. In fact, that's all Orange
and I ever do is laugh. We laugh so much our stomachs
hurt. It feels good. I wave goodbye to Orange.

Today is my last day volunteering before winter
vacation. I have mixed feelings. I am a little spent from
the two days before but I will miss that spirited, little
girl. I sign in to volunteer when Concha catches my
attention. "I need to give you your evaluation."

I follow her into her office and sit down, plopping
my tote on my lap.

She hands it to me, "I marked you're meeting standards being that you're a mandatory volunteer."

That sounds weird to me but I nod.

"Review it and sign it by the end of the day." She
stands up.

Later in the classroom, Grace was not in the mood to do her writing after a morning of Christmas parties hence the pencil and paper being thrown around. And, I was still confused on why I was receiving meeting standards on my evaluation. It was the bare minimum. I would get accolades all the time from the staff and Mama Chantel. Was Concha being was rude because she wasn't invited to Utah with the family and she might be taking it out on me? I try to focus on the 100% on my test I had just received. Not wanting my flask at all.

I give Grace a token for picking up her pencil. Honestly, I am rewarding her for breathing at this point.

"Good Gracie." I hand her another token. She smiles and slaps me across the face.

I softly hold her wrist and set it down nicely saying, "Don't hit Miss Sadie, no."

She puts her head down, laughs and goes for it again.

At this point I make eye contact with the teacher and she calls Concha. I'm annoyed because I never needed Concha. I am literally in charge of the hardest kid in school and can handle it. I guess being friends with Allison paid off.

Concha stomps into the classroom and bitches my name, "Sadie."

Grace puts her head down on the table and cries.

"Oh really," I say. "Gracie, Miss Sadie is not mad."

"I want Santa to bring me a Playboy calendar, but mama said no." Tears roll down her cheeks. "She said Santa doesn't bring adult toys to kids."

I look at Concha, who begrudgingly half smiles.

I purse my lips and breathe in to hold back my laughter. "I'm sorry," I say to her. "Maybe you can tell me what else you want from Santa? Is there a new refrigerator out?

I'm learning a lot from Grace: every Playboy bunny from the time I was born until now, how Disneyland was created, a little too much about refrigerators and how they run and most importantly, patience. Patience like I never knew existed down deep in the core of me. Patience I will probably need to have once I am a mom. Since I started working with Grace, I used the token system to get her to do simple things like put her school supplies in her box on her desk, write down her homework assignments in her agenda book, wash her hands after using the bathroom, and raise her hand in class. And, I used the same token system to get her to do some harder tasks like greet adults and peers appropriately, help her start conversations that weren't in her favor (not about Playboy bunnies, refrigerators or Disney). For every five tokens she received, she got a five minute break on her iPad looking at refrigerators for sale online or playing Mickey Mouse Clubhouse.

It was funny because I think everyone in life has a token system. Me for example, the old Sadie would do things I was uncomfortable with like dress sexy, wear makeup, drink, smoke and be a bitch to all, and I would get the one thing I strived for—attention from Tim or the Pop Crowd. And now, I want to prove myself by getting good grades and more than meeting standards on work evaluations.

Grace jets out of the class and I grab our jackets, following her because the air is brisk. My God, this kid is the worst sometimes. She's really testing my patience.

Concha walks me to the yard as Grace runs and jumps on the jungle gym screaming, "I want Kendra, Holly and Bridget."

I giggle.

Concha crosses her arms, standing next to me.

I turn to her and share, even though she probably hates me. "Grace was like Miss Sadie, do you like Hugh Heffner? I said not as much as you, Gracie. She said, yes you do Sadie, you just don't know it. He's the ultimate ladies man."

She's doesn't respond. An awkward silence permeates around us. I wish for a bird to hit the windshield or multiple dolphins swimming around us or something.

The bell rings. Thank you Lord! It's 2:35. I see Gracie's mom and wave to her, "Have a nice break, Sadie, I left a little Christmas present for you in your teacher box."

"Okay, thank you and Merry Christmas!!!" I yell.

I block the sun with my hand, looking back at Concha.

She lowers her sunglasses. "Sadie, I think maybe you should finish your hours somewhere else . . . maybe this isn't the right fit."

"Oh." I turn to Concha, feeling hurt. "What am I doing wrong? Officer Sob said I've been doing great and everything is fine here. I know Mama Chantel loves me."

"Yes, but it seems . . ."

I interrupt her, "Why am I only receiving meeting standards on my evaluation?"

"Well . . . I think . . ." Concha starts.

I interrupt her again and face her. "This has nothing to do with Gracie. You know darn well that I'm exceeding standards but you won't write that. This is about your family."

She sticks her finger in my face. "Stay away from Jay. He's too good for you. Maybe you can stay."

I gulp and walk away from her and move my legs as quickly as possible to the classroom to gather my things from my teacher box. I try not to cry or analyze what the hell just happened until I pull out the five Christmas cards and gifts from Gracie's mom, a few teachers and the principal.

And, so maybe now I'd like a shot. I settle for a smoke at the park on my bike ride home. Thoughts appear one by one crushing my soul. Why is Concha doing this? Will anyone believe my side? What will Gracie do without me? We have come so far. What will Officer Sob and the judge think if I'm simply meeting standards? I want to prove myself. What will my parents and Jay think if I'm assigned another student at a different school? Should I tell Jay? Is Jay really too good for me?

I call Officer Sob and let him know what Concha said. He tells me he's heard nothing but good things about me from the school staff and that he will call Concha after the winter break is over to see if she wants me to switch. He reminds me I shouldn't have any relationships going on in AA. I tell Officer Sob Jay and I are simply friends. I toy with texting Jay but I know he's gone to Utah.

Chapter 27

CHRISTMAS BREAK CATCHUP

It has been a good three months since I have talked to Tim, Chase or anyone from the Pop Crowd at school. First reason being, I hate them! I knew if I hadn't done that I might have been tempted to reunite with any one of them if they'd given me an inch. To avoid the Pop Crowd at school, I know what to do. I slip into period zero two minutes before class starts, avoid halls A and B during nutrition and park my bike on the East end of the school.

Orange is my focus now. Maybe I need to break away from Jay since Concha and Officer Sob are warning me now. I don't want to jeopardize my future or working with Grace. But, Jay is helping me with my schoolwork. The way he stares at me makes me think it may be more for him. I try to use the winter break as space from him and the decision.

Over winter break, instead of going to snow skiing in Aspen or Mammoth, we decided to stay home. My mom, dad and I were planning to make Gram's Christmas dinner (roasted chicken, homemade macaroni and cheese and a side dish of brussel sprouts, bacon and dates, homemade sage bread) for the homeless, wrap presents for the less fortunate kids and Christmas Carol in the old folk's home. It's fine with me because the snow isn't my favorite thing. And, there is something about kicking it at home on Christmas that makes it magical.

One evening, Orange, Mama Chantel, and her husband Rashid and Orange's four siblings stop over. Neal is fourteen, Shirone is twelve, Gracie is nine, and Angel is eight. My parents and I are sitting by the fire drinking hot cocoa and wrapping toys for the less fortunate children in Los Angeles when they arrive. They join us in wrapping. Amy Winehouse's version of "O Christmas Tree" echoes in my ears and every now and again I catch Orange and I singing the same parts.

Gracie sits right next to me and it makes me want to cry the thought of losing her. The adults exchange their favorite Midwestern state Christmas pastimes while Orange, Gracie and their siblings and I sit knee to knee, giggling. When I catch a glimpse of my mom smiling at my dad's big claim to fame Clark Griswold story, it makes me want the same thing.

Orange's mom is so nice, proper and sophisticated in her designer wear. No wonder Orange wants to impress her. Her dad is Middle Eastern and extremely funny, probably where she gets her sense of humor from. I've met both Chantel and Rashid separately as they have both dropped off Gracie periodically throughout the year.

They both tell me how much they've enjoyed what I've done for Gracie. I want to stay working with her. I want the satisfaction of doing the right thing and staying away from Jay. I look down at my cell. A text from Jay: MERRYCHRISTMAS!

I ignore it even though every ounce of me wants to text him the craziest Merry Christmas emoji'd out text message.

Orange has a last-minute business trip to New York City with her mom to speak with Stretch about a spring line. I envy her. I want to be the one going to the NYC. But, my dad surprises my mom and I with a three-day trip to Disneyland where we make some new families memories. We ride rollercoasters, eat chocolate ice cream Mickey ears and enjoy the new Frozen show. When I get home, I find some time to SUP with my dad, I repaint my room and added some different accent pillows, catch up on *The Big Apple Cookoff* with my mom and research some new ways to work with Gracie.

On the Saturday before the Monday we return to school from winter break, I plan to meet Orange at Java Coffee. The red Christmas cups are gone and it makes me blue having to wait another year to see them. But, the winter flavored berry teas are here with the blue coffee cups covered with polar bears doing all sorts of silly things. When you're sober, you find glee in little things. I sit Indian-style, wearing black jeans, Uggs and a long kimono with a blue tank top taking in the berry scent to my winter berry tea. Orange walks in.

She looks different. She took all of the orange out of her hair and it is now 100% chocolate and straightened. She has makeup on and wears jeans and a long sweater with some black Chucks. It has been a week since I've seen her.

"You look so good," I say, warming my hands with my tea, "and your hair, it's great. What's his name?"

"Tito, but he's gay. More importantly, I'm in love with her."

I throw my head back in laughter, "So this is your lesbian look?"

"No, I'm straight as all get out. The NYC. I'm in love . . ."

"Oh yeah! A lot of hustle bustle, but I remember feeling an energy like no other place had."

She slams her hand down on the turquoise green coffee table. "I'm going to move there."

"You should," My hand slams on top of hers.

She smiles. "I will, so how was your break?"

"Good," I shrug. "We stayed around town for Christmas, went to Disneyland and just farted around."

"Farted around?"

"Yeah, my mom says it a lot." I realize it's silly. "Did you have any farting contests?" she laughs.

I laugh. I love Orange because I can have these silly conversations with her and not have to be a certain way. I can be myself.

Jay walks up. "Should I go back and come back in?"

I freeze. Who invited him?

"No, Sadie was just saying she had some serious farting contests over the break," Orange reveals.

His cheeks turn red. "I'm going to order a coffee."

"Grande Drip for Jay," the barista dressed in a light blue apron and blue hair yells.

"That's yours," I point to the barista.

"Okay." He mimics me, sidestepping around the people huddling against the fire to play checkers. He has a more fitting white shirt on and it looks like he lost some weight. I don't know if it is that his dark skin looks amazing in white or if his white shirt looks amazing on his dark skin? All I know is Orange is feeling the same vibe. We just stare at him.

"Why did you invite him?" I mumble under my silk, light blue scarf.

"A little bit rainy and chilly out today, no?" He settles next to Orange, looking at me and then her.

Orange and I snap out of our trance and reply, "Yes," at the same time.

"Yeah, yeah, yeah," I say, holding my arms. "Brrrr."

Orange laughs. "What she means to say is you look good, Jay. Have you lost weight?"

I slap her across the shoulder. "Okay, yes, that's what I meant to say."

His cheeks cherry a little. "Thanks. I did a lot of snowboarding."

I need to tell him about what Concha said.

"Did you have a good trip? How's Jack?" I frontload him with questions.

"He's good. We had a good time," he says.

"Well, I have to lose a little weight so I can join the Army after graduation," he says.

"Army, so you're serious?" I can't hide the disappointment in my voice. Why am I disappointed?

"Yeah."

"What about college or the fire academy?" I ask.

"I thought you had some scholarship money for your grades?" Orange asks.

He starts to roll up his sleeves. His arms are more defined.

"Well, I figured I'd continue with what my dad started and you know my brother Josh was in the Army. He said it was a great foundation. I'm going to take some online classes in my spare time," he replies.

I nod. "If that's what you want?"

"You guys know how much I love military intelligence books." He brings his coffee to his lips, blowing on it in a weird, unbelievably attractive way, which makes me not able to speak.

"Yeah." Orange nods as she grasps my knee.

"Orange is going to move to NYC," I blurt. They both nod.

I sink in my chair and tune out of their conversation of what to do after college. I don't know what my plan is. I know I'm not smart enough to go to a four-year college. Nonetheless I have to get a grip on some feelings I might have intertwined with the Concha and Officer Sob opinions that I have not shared with anyone.

"I will get a little money for college, too," Orange says. Snapping back, I look at her. "My dad just told me the other day that the money he had saved for college he spent on DUI expenses."

Orange shrugs. "Well at least it will be off your record when you're eighteen."

"Yes, but college is a positive thing," I say.

Orange and Jay look at each other.

"You think I'm spoiled?" I look at each of them.

"I just think you're lucky, Sadie." Jay smiles, placing his hand on mine. "But it's not a negative thing. We're all lucky."

"Yeah," Orange agrees. "You've worked really hard this year."

"And, I didn't before . . ." I trail off in my own head.

"I know."

"Yeah, I mean you were partying like it was 1999 and got into a lot of trouble at school and with the law," Jay starts. "Maybe your father doesn't feel like you've proven everything there is to prove."

My shoulders back. "That's a strong statement." It makes me want to work harder.

Orange is quiet.

Jay proceeds. "Wyatt is a highly respectable dude."

"I'm sure it's a lot to take in. You give and give and give and all your kid does is take, take, take," Orange says maturely. "I shouldn't be talking. I don't even know my parents . . . I've lived with my adoptive mom since I was super little."

It feels like my heart is on the table in the middle of us and they all keep stabbing it with their wooden Java Coffee stirrers and straws.

"I agree." Jay stabs his stirrer in my heart. "And, parents can only try so much but at some point, eighteen, it's up to the adult."

"It's a good thing I'm only seventeen and in my parents care," I spout out.

Asshole.

Is he acting like this because I didn't text back Merry Effin Christmas. Did Concha say something to him?

"I'm changing the subject because Sadie is annoyed." Orange looks at me and licks whipped cream off her top lip.

I breathe in the only oxygen left in Java Coffee.

"So when I was at the airport flying to New York, I saw Principal Dow at the airport. He was with his pretty pregnant wife and their little boy Shane. So cute! Anyways, Mama Chantel knows him from Malibu High School I guess. Did you know his father was murdered?"

The mood shifts from cutting tension with a stirrer stick to a lot less tension.

"No?" Jay shakes his head in denial.

"Grams said something about that once," I stated, "but I'm not sure what happened."

"Well," she says sipping her coffee. "His dad was a police officer in L.A. His mom was a principal. He had a couple brothers a lot younger. I guess his dad was followed home from work by this guy on LSD and murdered in his home. Bryan, Principal Dow took his dad's gun and killed the guy. I guess he was like eighteen years old or something."

"Holy crap." I feel my mouth open.

"That's insane!" Jay agrees, "That's gotta do some serious damage to one's soul."

"Right, he seems so civilized," Orange says.

"He seems tired . . ." I say remembering him yawning a lot at IEP meetings.

"It's because of all the crap he has to deal with . . ." Jays snarls.

I watch Orange look at Jay and then me. She criss crosses her hands in the middle of us and says, "TV timeout guys . . ."

"I have to go," he grabs his jacket and he's out like the wintery chill.

"What's up with him?" I bark.

Later, Orange and I sit on my bed, looking at jobs in New York City on my laptop. It seems so natural, sitting on my bed with her. She let me put on my rock and roll music.

"What the hell was Jay's problem today?" Orange asks. "He seemed so icy."

"Like I said, he's taking space," I say, looking up from my laptop.

"Knowing him, there's more to the story. Talk to him . . ." she says, as I flip through the New York magazines Grams left.

"Hey," she bumps me. "Are you okay with the whole you're lucky and need to prove stuff comments?"

I nod, "I have a lot to prove . . . to my parents, my parole officer, Concha, my teachers, students at Mariposa Beach High School and pretty much everyone in the community."

She nudges me. "You've come such a long way that you have a little to go." She inches her pointer finger and thumb apart.

I don't know what I did to deserve her friendship— Ariana, Orange.

"Orange," I say uncomfortably. "How come you aren't wearing your pearl bracelet with a heart? You took it off around Christmas. I know it has something to do with Candace and I've never asked you . . . I just didn't want to pry." My eyes meet hers.

She sighs. "Okay, no time like the present," she says, "Kindergarten through third grade I was a loner and mute."

I lay back on my pillows.

Orange leans against my pillows, too. "My mom said I could spend the night, by the way."

It reminds me of how Grams used to lay back when we'd have our pillow talks.

I clap with excitement.

She puts her hand on mine, giving a please calm down, Sadie touch. "So Candace moved here like a fourth grade. She was a lot like you: pretty, smart, and really funny. So, she was like super good friends with Jay and Jack. She started dating Jack and immediately moved to the Pop Crowd. She brought me with her. We were best friends. She would listen to some of the stuff Allison and Nicolette would say and I would tell her no, so that's probably why they hate me . . ." She waves both hands. "But I'd rather eat my shit and die than ever worry why they hate me..."

"Lovely!" I smile as I play with the string on my new olive green pillows my mom and I bought at Bed, Bath and Beyond over the break.

"So before she died from an overdose of bath salts in a pot brownie, she was my best friend. That night she gave me a real pearl bracelet with a silver heart and said we will always be best friends." She touches her empty wrist. "That four-year anniversary was a few days ago, so I decided to stop depressing myself and put it in my jewelry box for safe keeping."

"She was that special to you?" I ask.

"She was my best friend for a few years, but maybe I've feeling a new friendship now?" She pulls the string of the green pillow trying not to look at me.

"Like me??" I jump on the bed trying to add some humor to the seriousness.

She rolls over on her back, cracking up at me. "Well, now, it's you."

I lay on my back next to her, linking my arm with hers.

"But shortly after, Mama Chantel adopted Gracie, who I have to admit is one of my best friends as well."

"Mine, too," I agree.

"Sometimes things just are meant to be. Around the time Candace died, my family was trying to adopt a little boy, and I had to have a perfect clean record so the adoption agency would clear us again. I was clean but my parents had to pay Allison's parents a lot of money to keep my name out of it. But it didn't work out with the adoption and we just heard the little boy ended up dying of cancer, so we would have had to go through that . . ." She sniffles.

It takes everything in that moment not to want to scoop her up in my arms and hold her as long as she needs, so I settle on the linked arms and tell her, "it's okay."

"You know, Sadie, I literally hated you when you moved here. You looked so much like Candace it reminded me of her. Then when you started hanging with the Pop Crowd, that made me hate you even more." Her eyes are wide as she looks at me.

"Oh, you too . . ." I say.

"And then Allison gave that kid money to pants me," she says. "All because my mom wouldn't allow her to work at fashion week in Mariposa Beach after Allison hosted the party that Candace died at."

"OH!" A light bulb appears.

"I know . . . I . . ." she stutters, "And, I didn't hate you as much after that," she starts.

I tilt my head and look at her, "Why?"

"Because when everyone was standing around, looking at my bare ass, you were the one who looked stressed and upset about it. I think at one point you even walked over and tried to help me, but Allison pulled you away."

"Oh yeah, what a winner I was, Orange," I say.

"HEY!" She yanks my arm with hers. "I said I hated you a little less . . ."

I turn my head and cover myself with a pillow laughing. She hides her laughter behind her pillow and that moment makes me believe that friendship is forever. After a while, Orange and I sit in silence looking at the fake stars on my ceiling. I make wishes on the fake stars. I wish to always remember this moment.

After her eyes close, I throw a big fleece white blanket over her and pull off her black combat boots. In the corner, I listen to Officer Sob's voicemail. He says he spoke to Concha and I will be starting with Gracie tomorrow and finishing out the school year. I set my cell down on the nightstand and crawl into bed next to Orange sleeping softly. Rubbing my forehead with the palms, should I let Concha get to me? School starts tomorrow and all I know at this point is I'm excited to see Gracie again.

I need a mini vacation from my thoughts, so I stalk some people on Facebook using my cell phone, which my parents haven't yet confiscated this evening. I find Kate and Sarah. Kate had dyed her hair black and is a rocker in a band. In most of the pictures she wears black. I remember my mom saying something about her brother's addiction. Sarah has a profuse amount of Bible verses on her posts. I have this memory of Kate, Sarah and I with braids in our hair sitting on a hay bale and that's where the memory stayed. Where would I have fit in? Looking at the most recent pictures of Tim on Facebook, he isn't as attractive as I remembered. He's gained a little weight. I look at Chase's Facebook. He's still drinking and lying. I look at Allison's page. She has it blocked like she is too pretty to be looked at. I roll my eyes. Nicolette's page is full. Every three days, she posts stuff like, #hittintheslopeswithAl, #pre-game-tailgating, #chickflickwithmybesties. Fake Facebooker! And, Betsy Grimes is set at private. There was a message on instant message sent December 26. I click on it, which makes it active . . .

Tim: Hey, I know you hate me but I think of you all the time.

Sadie: I think of you, too, but in a slashing horror kind of way . . . delete delete delete I didn't reply.

I text Jay instead. Orange is right. I need to talk to him.

Sadie: Jay.

Jay: Sadie, whad up?

Sadie: just saying hi.

Jay: what are you doing? Watching *Big Apple Cookoff*?

Sadie: NO! Orange is sleeping over. She's asleep

Jay: Sorry I couldn't stay longer. Josh and I lost another bet to Mel and now we have three more nights of babysitting while she goes out to dinner, sees a movie with friends and goes shopping in LA.

Sadie: LOL! What bet?

Jay: She is trying to be more domesticated, so she bet us she could cook two weeks in a row (14 days) without budging. Did we like the meals? Eh!

Sadie: Thanks for the clarification that 14 days is two weeks. Mel is funny.

Jay: Well, you haven't seen your math tutor in two weeks. Mel is great.

Sadie: I know, and I know.

Jay: See you at school, know it all. Maybe we can talk more at school.

Sadie: Okay . . .

Jay: NIGHT SADIE, SWEET DREAMS

Chapter 28

THE NOMINATION AND POSITIVE TALK

The first day back from the break, Mr. Clark sends me to Principal Dow's office to retrieve the iPads for the class to use as research. I hear familiar voices as I'm waiting for the secretary to get his attention in order to get the gosh dang iPads and jam.

And, one by one, they filter out of his office and into the waiting room where I'm sitting: Betsy, Chase, Nicolette, Tim and Allison. They all look a little older since I haven't really seen them in person in a few months.

Betsy glares at me, saying nothing. I do the same.

Chase smiles with his eyes. Zero response from me.

Nicolette looks the other way with a nasty, "hhh-hhmmmm pppphhh."

Tim's eyes widen and he tries to lock his eyes with mine, but my eyes wander to Allison's. I remember the private Facebook message.

And, Allison, she speaks, "Hi Sadie."

"Hi," my voice sounds croaky. I clear it.

What in God's green Earth were they talking to him about? Principal Dow stands behind her. He is dressed in a new suit.

He looks more rested. Maybe because his son is older now.

He smiles proudly, "The iPads, yes, c'mon in Sadie."

I walk into his office catching a glimpse of myself in his full-length mirror wondering what the Pop Crowd just saw. My hair is up in a huge, messy bun with my eyelashes painted with light mascara. I'm wearing pink skinny jeans, black Converses and a flowery long-sleeved silk top.

His office looks different. His desk is still a rectangular wooden desk in the middle of the office, but he has painted the walls light yellow and added a professional painted mural of flowers on the wall. His shelves are monstrously covered in La Crosse trophies from Minnesota State University, teacher of the year awards and his framed degrees. I notice on his desk in a baby size picture frame, the size of my hand is a picture of him, his wife and his son Shane.

"Did your wife have the twins yet?" My eyes explore his office.

"Not yet . . . she's waiting at home . . . any day now." He bends over, fiddling for the iPads in a cardboard box sitting next to the vault where all the answer keys are present, except it's wide open and there's nothing in there. "Here." He passes me the box.

"Thanks," I take it, trying to juggle the extreme heaviness.

"Do you need me to get Freddie to help you carry that to the class?" he asks.

"Ummm," I contemplate.

"Yes, it's okay." He grabs his walkie talkie. "Freddie, can you come to my office and help Sadie MacPhearson carry a box?"

He turns the corner, rolling a dolly in and pulling the box on it. "Hi."

"Bye." I wave to Principal Dow. He must have known I cheated last year, why didn't he ever confront me about it?

"Hey, thank you Sadie for helping out," he says, jumping back into his leather desk chair and tickling the keys of his brand new shiny Mac desktop. Freddie and I walk in silence besides the sound of the dolly, rattling over cobblestones.

I hear a female voice over his radio, "Hey Freddie, don't worry about it, the locksmith is going to change the lock."

"Roger," he says, pressing down the button.

We make it to Mrs. Clark's class.

"Are you still getting students breaking in?" I ask.

"Yeah . . ." he replies, picking up the box for me and eyeing me suspiciously.

Who is Chase paying now? I wonder.

A little while later, I see Chase. His tongue is down Nicolette's throat. She might have needed some extra encouragement because he looked at something or me too long.

I mumble, "How does he pretend to kiss her? We are all chameleons."

At nutrition, I'm the first to one to Building C. I pull out my strawberry yogurt and shake my premixed Cold Brew from Java Coffee. Jay plops next to me. It feels strange, like he almost doesn't want to be there because he immediately opens his military book without saying much. It's like that night where we divulged everything was blown up like a bomb. BOOM! I close my eyes, wishing I could spontaneously combust.

"Something weird is going on with the vault in Principal Dow's room," I say point blank.

"Seriously?" Orange appears.

Thank you, Jesus! Someone else is here. I tell them about the occurrence.

"Oh cow," he says. Orange nods her head.

"Yeah." I look at him. "Oh cow? Are you a 100 years old?"

He smiles and reveals, "it's something Mel has trained Josh to say because he brings fire station talk home."

"My dad cusses a little, too," my eyes shift to his.

I need to stop connecting to him.

"So is the case of the stolen answer keys still open?" Jay asks, as he takes Orange's math test. He looks at the grade and gives her a thumbs up.

"I don't know why I was never got called in to Principal Dow's office again," I reply. "The writing was on the wall."

That afternoon, I walk into the main office of Mariposa Beach Elementary School to sign in for volunteer hours. I see Concha working at her desk. She doesn't acknowledge me. SHOCKER! I sprint to Gracie's classroom as she smiles from ear to ear when I tap her shoulder and asks, "How did the homeless people like Grams' Christmas dish?"

Tears envelop my eyes as I realize she is asking me a question about me, which is not something kids with her level of Autism are often capable of. Plus, this conversation took place two weeks ago so the fact that she remembered was amazing.

I swipe the tears fast. "They liked it just fine, Gracie."

She smiles and turns back to her math seatwork. And, at this moment in time I need Gracie in my life. She needs me and nothing else really matters.

Sunday night I meet Jay at the Juice Farm, a trendy juice press place with a black and white checkered floor and red leather booths. He wanted a juice instead of coffee so I agreed. He had been busy all week training the new ROTC helper so I hadn't seen much of him in order to *talk more* as indicated in his text message to me. My stomach feels like it flips over itself when I park my bike. I have a weird feeling.

"Hey." He stands up for a hug. He looks nice in his jeans and black sweatshirt.

"Hi." I embrace his hug. It's a tight teddy bear embrace I feel I can get lost emotionally in. I want more hugs from him. I release myself.

"Orange is not coming," I say, sitting down pensively, handing him his fresh press juice in a tiny glass milk bottle. "She has to help her mom with something."

"It'll just be me and you then." He smiles. "Let's get started, and thank you."

I open my math book. It has been three weeks since we've worked together. I've missed his ability to laugh at my jokes. We work on math for forty-five minutes straight. I do well. There's an awkward vibe still.

He sips his Cherry Tart drink, "Well, I think your math test should go well."

"Thank you," I pause. "Are we okay?" I have to ask. I still wonder if Concha has told him to stay away? The speaker all of a sudden blasts "Don't Wanna Fight," by Alabama Shakes.

"What?" He gets up and sits next to me. "I can't hear you," he says over the music and shuffling of people wearing winter boots walking into Juice Farm.

"I said thank you," I say.

"And, you said are we okay?" he adds.

"Why did you ask me if you heard me . . . God, my dad does that," I laugh.

His face turns a shade of white.

I laugh. "You don't have to get all weird."

He points to Chase, Nicolette, Betsy, Tim and Allison walking in together.

"Oh my God, we have to leave," I mouth to him. We are slammed in a two-person booth in the corner.

"Trust me?" he takes off his baseball cap and black sweatshirt, handing them to me like I'm a famous person trying to hide and he's my bodyguard. I quickly slip them on.

"I do, but they are sitting right by the door. It's inevitable."

"Inevitable?" He looks at me. "You've been studying your words."

He turns me facing toward him, wraps his hands around my waist, pulling the hood over the baseball cap and slams my cheek into his chest, hiding my face as we walk toward the door.

"Hi slut," Allison says.

Jay opens the door and yells, "Shut up, bitch!"

I laugh.

"At least we tried," he says.

He holds me all the way to the parking lot. The light of the street lamp catches his eyes: olive green, sexy, low lids. He looks at me an extra-long second.

He finally speaks, his hands still on my waist, "sorry."

"It's okay," I whisper. "It sort of feels nice to be hugged by a man besides my dad . . ."

"A man?" he asks.

My head nods. A raindrop splashes on his forehead.

"Really, it's raining again when we're together without Orange, weird?" A drop splashes on my cheek. "I have to ride home in the rain."

"Don't be silly," he says. "Get in and I'll get your bike and drive you home."

I jump in the front seat of his Nova, watching him grab my bike. It looks like people are dropping buckets of water from the clouds.

"Holy holy." He opens the driver's door, jumping in.

"You're soaking wet," I say.

He pulls off his sweatshirt, wearing nothing but a tight white undershirt and jeans.

His arms are big and more defined.

I gulp, trying to relax a little. Is he becoming more attractive or am I becoming more desperate for human touch? It has been six months since Tim and I kissed, and he was the very last boy I kissed.

Get these thoughts out of my head!!!

I chose Gracie already. "I live up the street. Let's go there until the rain subsides, and then I'll drive you home," he says.

"Okay," I text my mom exactly what I'm doing. She texts back to say stay off the road.

The White Stripes, "Seven Nation Army" filters through the speakers. We sing along.

"Good song." He lowers the volume when it's over.

"Yep, thank you for defending me," I say.

"Hmmm." He looks at me for a quick second, then his eyes focus back on the road.

"I thought she was being extra friendly the other day because Principal Dow was there," I say.

"Duh," he says, an octave lower. "She's a bitch."

"Yeah," I say.

"Five months of this place and we're off. I'm going the Army. Mel and Josh are moving to Westlake Village. Mel has been asked to be on the board for MADD, Mothers Against Drunk Driving," he says.

"My mom should be the president!" I joke.

"Ha," he says. "I think we all need some time away from Concha."

My favorite person. I should probably tell him right now what Concha said to me. I feel like it's unfair not to share.

"Wow, that's great you're all out of here," I say with a reluctant heart.

What are my plans? Is he really leaving?

His fierce black Nova turns the corner to a well lit gorgeous set of track homes that rest on the top of the largest hill in Mariposa Beach. "How about you? What are your plans?"

"Not sure . . ." I reply. "Maybe makeup artist?"

"Why don't you consider a career in special education?" He suggests, punching in a gate code to the gated community on the tippy top.

He smiles. I'm not sure why he's smiling, but I know it's the same reason why I'm not smiling because I'm simply not amused on the subject. He is silent.

"Stop with the positive talk. I have to do something simple," I say.

Chapter 29

MEN'S UNDERWEAR

He pulls in the driveway of a two-story Mediterranean-style home. He gets out and opens my door and takes my hand guiding me in the house through the storm.

I stand there dripping wet shivering.

We shuffle in, taking our shoes and socks off.

"Oh my gosh. I'm soaked." I shiver again, looking at my jeans.

"Okay, hang on." He runs upstairs, coming back with some clothes. "Bathroom right there. There's a towel under the sink to dry yourself. Here's some clothes. I'll throw yours in the dryer."

I walk into the beautifully decorated bathroom, setting the clothes on the sink. It's painted an avocado green with a daisy border. I take in the different colored daisies; the brightness and warmth it makes me feel. I'm shivering as I change into his blue fire cadet sweats. It all smells like lavender. Some black boxer briefs fall on the ground. I slip them on really quick with his gray fire cadet sweats. Maybe I'll win him over with my humor. Or, at least get him out of the funk he's been in.

"Um." I peek my head out of the bathroom. I see him standing in the kitchen. He's wearing grey sweats with no shirt on.

I notice his arms again. His stomach is thinner. He is pulling tea bags from a box.

"Hey Jay."

"Yeah," he yells from the kitchen, grabbing his black long sleeve thermal and throwing it on.

Damn!

"I've got the boxer briefs on," I prance in the kitchen and pull the elastic on my sweats, showing them underneath.

He puts his hand over his mouth. "They must have got thrown in there. Sorry I grabbed whatever folded clothes Mel put on my bed."

"Oh, I thought you meant to give me these?" I smile.

He pretends to punch my stomach, "Keep them. I don't want your poop stains on them anyway."

I hold my stomach as I'm keeling over with laughter. For a moment it's all that is encompassing my brain.

He laughs a little more and then says a little later. "Tea? It's decaffeinated."

"Sure." I take the clear glass mug, sipping it as I shiver.

"Come in here. I started a fire." He motions to the leather L shaped couch. I sit down and he throws me a big, snuggly blanket.

"Mel and Josh took the girls to Disneyland." His eyes laser beam mine.

I draw in a breath. "Fun! We are alone?"

"Not sure why I told you that," He sits relatively close to me pulling the blanket on his bare feet and over mine.

"I don't know either." I bring my mug up to my lips, sipping it.

Is he hiding from me as much as I'm hiding from him? We still need to talk more.

I move side to side as I get comfortable. "Adjusting to the briefs?"

"Yes," I say, holding my tea steady.

He covers his eyes. "Will you let me know when you're done picking . . ."

"I'm done," I say, as I'm still pulling the fabric out. He grins.

"Sadie," he finally says, "I don't want you to feel like I'm short with my replies when we talk about anything that happens with the Pop Crowd. I could really care less about them, but if it's important to you, then I want to listen better . . ."

"She's not worth any conversation," I start. "God, I should have never walked into Allison's spinning web."

"Obviously," he says, "before she spoke to me or Jack, I was like this girl is too gangly for me. Her poems suck anyways."

"What?" I ask.

"Well she is too thin and gangly. When she crouches down, she's like a praying mantis," he does an example.

I giggle.

He rests his head on the couch, facing me. "But, the big thing is I've had English with her for four years now, and her poems are horrible. Not that mine are any better but hers don't even rhyme. And, sometimes, she doesn't get the literature we read."

I duck my head with laughter and say, "Dude, seriously?"

"Yeah, like this one time there was a scene that required inferential thinking..."

"Non-literal."

"Non-literal, Sadie girl," he says in a thick voice, "You're ready to graduate . . ."

I grin, putting my hand on his forearm, "I have a good tutor."

He looks down at my hand. I remove it.

My heart feels hugs and kisses.

"I'm feeling more and more confident about myself and I'm wearing men's underwear, so what happened with Al?" I say.

He smiles at me, "So, in the story we were reading, there's a scene where the lit candle falls over and starts a mini fire burning a famous painting but the text just says the wind knocks the candle over, right, so Allison was like how'd the famous painting get burnt?"

"Wow, a little more literal."

"Definitely better in math and science." He nods. "And, Tim, he and I were partners in Bio Chem last year. He was horrible. I did everything."

"You don't have to say that stuff to make me feel better."

"It's true though," he says. "I asked him to hand me the beaker and he handed me a petri dish."

"Even I know the difference . . ." I roll my eyes. "Dumb ass."

He chuckles, "they aren't as smart and perfect as you or everyone thinks."

"Last year I didn't know that, but now I do," I start to say. "Well, I think you're perfect the way you are." He bites his lip nervously.

I chew on the inside of my cheek. God he makes my heart beat really fast!

"Thank you, Jay," I break the stare and look at the beautiful Wyland's portrait of two "Kissing Dolphins" above their fire place, "Beautiful painting."

He looks up at it and back at me nodding, "Kissing Dolphins."

I was hoping he wouldn't say that word. I focus on the painting and say, "they seem to be perfect."

"The dolphins?" he asks.

"Mel and Josh," I correct him, smiling at him.

"It took some time, but they are amazing now." He glances one more time at the portrait.

"Is that what you want?" I ask him.

"Yeah," he says in a low voice.

I give him my best fake smile.

I'm feeling the slight spark Orange was talking about. Enough to make my cheeks blush.

"Everybody wants to be happy . . ." he says.

I let my head fall dramatically. "But, what do you want?"

"Whoa, is your head okay?" He moves it up.

I give him my most serious look. "I'm trying to get to know you better, Jay."

"I know," he says back in a serious tone.

"Okay, here's what I know," I say, "You're Jay. You're in all AP classes. Your SAT scores were nearly perfect. You're a lover of military books. You're very funny. You're generous with your time. You're a great teacher/mentor. Awesome family. Fantastic uncle."

He held out one hand and waved for more compliments with the other. "Stop."

I laugh. "Last year, you looked different than you do now."

"And, how do I look now?" he asks in a low, husky voice.

"Um . . . you lost some pounds," I respond naturally.

He nods, "Pounds, huh?

"Yeah, and we're friends this year . . ." I sip the last of my tea and set it down on the coffee table.

"I mean at least I think so . . . your Aunt Concha did say for me to stay away," I say randomly switching the conversation. I need to not talk about how he looks now or what he wants in life. Maybe I am becoming better at sober conversations.

He waves. "She told me. I told her to eff off. She's harmless."

"Oh well she doesn't seem harmless to me. My entire future is in her hands," I object.

He squares me, "I promise, she would never do anything to hurt my people. She's a bit over protective with my feelings because of what happened with Candace."

I take it in for a second, "your people?"

"Yep."

"I think I was your people a long time ago. I think you lied to me when you said you didn't like me until Chase's party," I say it aloud.

His cheeks redden. "Sorry," I say instantly.

"It's okay," he puts his hand on my knee. I feel a tingle in my upper thigh, "You reminded me of Candace."

I take his hand, "And you wanted to save me."

He squeezes my hand. He's nervous. Our eyes zero in on each other.

My hands are just as shaky.

Damn, it doesn't matter what we talk about we always go back to touching each other in some way.

I'm officially nervous. He is holding my hand. What the HELL is going on with us?

I want to bring it up to my lips and kiss it. And, now I'm the opposite of conversationalist, I am tongue tied like I really officially was when I was five.

"Thank you," his voice is low. "Before the break, sorry for acting weird," he rubs my hand with his thumb.

"I'm surprised you even talk to me after I came onto you."

"That didn't bother me . . ." He smirks.

"What, you're Sadie MacPhearson."

I slap him as he smiles. He seems so innocent like he wouldn't like that I pressed my boobs on him.

I didn't think I was attractive anymore.

The mood shifts and I nod. "We cleared the Concha thing. She won't be messing with your people," I say.

He nods.

"So was it like the amount of guys I've kissed that bothered you, because I never even talked to you about that, and I know there's a lot of rumors . . ." I throw it out there, "And, sorry for not texting you Merry Christmas back."

He shakes his head no. "None of that either."

"Chase?" I shrug. "And the answer keys because I will never cheat again."

"No." He laughs.

I awkwardly laugh.

"Everyone has something they aren't proud of . . ." he says.

"Well, what is it then, Jay? If it's not the many sins I committed and told you about, then why were you acting weird after that night?"

He doesn't answer. The storm passes.

My cell chimes.

Mom: Can you try to make it home during the break of the storm?

Thank God for my mom. I love distractions. We drive back to my house listening to Led Zeppelin's "Tangerine." He seems fine. Back to normal with me? We had a moment, a spark. Probably more than one. Why was he acting weird after that one night?

I air drum on the right parts. He starts singing along with me. I notice his arms are more and more defined as he steers the wheel of his Nova.

We sit in the car, acting out the guitar session for the rest of the song.

"Favorite band by far," I say with confidence. "My dad used to play these songs all the time."

"There's still time . . ." he says.

I furrow my brow.

"What for? My dad and I?"

"Yes," he says.

I pull my tote over my shoulder and open the door.

He pokes his brows at me as he sings, "Sing my song." I nod, giving him a wave.

"Thank you."

His long eyelashes meet on his right eye. "You got it. Good night, Sadie."

324

"And, Jay, I'll never take off these underwear."

He laughs.

I exit his Nova, run to my house and enter my nice, warm bed.

I set the phone down on my nightstand, take a sip of water and thank God for bringing Jay into my life.

For the next few days, I wake up and think of Jay. The truth is I wasn't attracted to him until I knew his humor, charm and soul. But then I think he is kind of easy on the eyes. I try to count to get him off my mind. I try singing songs to get him off my mind. I try writing I need to get Jay off my mind in my diary.

Jay: To answer your question of what I want. A chick I love who is happy, independent, and loves the same things I do. I don't care what my career is as long as I'm a blue collar worker/civil servant because then I won't work a day in my life. Oh, and, some rugrats!

Chapter 30

THE NOMINATION

When I get to our spot behind building C, a thought appears in my mind. This spot we hang at is the most secluded spot on campus and the most beautiful.

Grams would have loved it. There's an ever-changing garden in front of us and the colors of the spring flowers are lovely. The Lantana flowers have grown in purple, yellow and red. The bluish purplish Morning Glories, pink and yellow Poppies, and white Callalillies have grown in about five feet from our cemented spot. I take it in a bit and revel in the colors thinking about my chameleon soul poem. Jay and Orange are in a heavy conversation about apostrophes, so it's a good excuse to be quiet. And, when they finally ask why I'm quiet, I say

I'm having a Grams thought. It's so nice being honest with friends.

Seconds later, I pull out my science test that I scrunch in my folder on my way out of class. I'm completely pissed about it and want to kick in the morning glories in all their glory pushing out lovely thoughts of Grams. I know Jay can explain it to me in laymen's terms and I'll get it, but I cannot keep letting him help me because he smells extremely manly and I can't get the smell away.

His voice sounds especially raspy today like he has a cold and I want him to whisper sweet nothings in my ear, even if he says the word poop. He's wearing a sweatshirt, but I know what's underneath, one more pound lost, and soon this guy is going to be more defined. He's wearing sunglasses, but I know what color his eyes are.

"Sadie?" he says, dipping his sunglasses at me.

"Huh, what?" I snap myself back into place. "You okay?"

"Yeah," I lie, as I back away, getting a whiff of his sweaty, salty, musky, work in the yard, build a fire, man scent.

He pulls down his sunglasses, winking at me. "Okay, well, I just wanted to tell you some people were talking about the vault with the answer keys today in English."

"Really?" I wave in the air. "Eh . . ."

"I heard your name in the conversation . . ." he places his hand on my leg. It still gives me the same warm feeling inside.

Orange looks up from her cell.

"Shit," my head collapses in my lap as I place my hand on top on his.

"I gotta go to ROTC," Jay rubs his hand with mine. "It's going to be okay. Can I drive you to volunteer today in case you're too upset to ride your bike?"

"Um," I say, "I'm good."

The loud speaker vibrates, "Sadie MacPhearson to the office . . ."

I close my eyes. "Here we go."

"You should just go to his office and clear the air. He deserves to know," Jay is still holding my hand, stroking it for comfort.

"C'mon Sades. I'll walk you," Orange links her arm with mine.

"Call me later." Jay releases his hand from mine.

Orange walks me to the office giving me the pep talk of honesty. I should have been honest back in October when he asked me.

"I'll tell Mr. Clark where you are," she says. "See you at class." She squeezes my hand.

I sit down on the bench at the waiting room. It feels like tiny ants are crawling under my skin. My eyes pull up to everyone that walks in. Orange hovers outside a little.

"Get over yourself," I hear her scream.

"Hi," Nicolette sticks her head in the waiting room.

"Oh, my favorite ex-BFF," I mumble, scooting all the way the to the opposite side of the bench.

"Huh?" she smiles.

"NOTHING," I annunciate as clear as possible.

"Sadie, I have to talk to you." She flies next to me, speaking in a low voice.

I roll my eyes. "Okay."

The secretary rounds the corner and takes an inventory of us. "Okay, Sadie, you are here, I'll let you know when Principal Dow is ready . . . we have a few more people showing up." She winks. What the . . . ?

"How long have you known about Chase?" Nicolette asks.

"Known what?" I smirk.

"Sadie . . . I . . ." She pops a sugar-free mint in her mouth to hide the cigarette breath. "After almost nine months of dating Chase, he couldn't, you know, get it up . . . so I questioned it. He said I'm not pretty enough. Later, I find some pretty intense text messages from someone on his cell so I called the number. He's gay."

"SH!" I say. "Lower your voice."

"I realize that was my only beef with you, so, I guess I'm sorry for that . . ." the volume of her voice doesn't change.

"Oh you guess you're sorry . . . well, thanks," I say in a sar-castic tone.

She ignores it. "So, he just took all those pictures of you in exchange for the answer keys? That was your deal?"

"It's kind of none your business," I remark.

"Wow, I mean you're pretty . . . but . . ." she replies looking down at her cell phone. "The question now is, who did he get the answer keys from?"

I shrug. I don't want to give her anything.

"Sadie, Principal Dow will see you now . . ." his secretary walks out.

I stand up, pulling my tote over my shoulder.

She pulls my arm. "When you moved here, I thought, wow, a different, pure, genuine friend. And, then well you were killed my Mariposa Beach teenage society."

"No, my soul was killed by you, Allison, Tim and Chase. Mariposa Beach teenage society is doing just fine." I pull my arm away and walk into his office.

"Sadie," my mom walks in wearing a light pink Juicy Couture outfit with her hair pulled up in a ponytail. My dad is in his firefighter uniform.

"Uh hi," I say.

"Hi sweetie," my mom says in a cheery voice.

My dad kisses my cheek.

Principal Dow motions for us to come in. He is dressed in a pair of nice slacks today and a Tommy Bahama polo shirt. My heart beats like a gymnast's on a high bar.

"So, Sadie I called your parents last week to tell them about this meeting. I want to share the good news with you and your parents in person. It's a tradition. I have like five minutes to share this with you and then I need to go because my wife is in labor," he says.

"No . . . no...go," we all say.

"How exciting . . ." my mom says sweetly.

He smiles. "I'm going to pack my things up as I tell you this.

Sadie, the poem you wrote, 'The Teenager with the Chameleon Soul,' in Mr. Clark's class has won for the Show and Tell poem award."

"What?" I say shocked and point to myself. "Me?"

"Yes, the seniors voted on it," he replies, pulling two notebooks out of his desk shoving them in his Michael Kors leather man purse. "It's a prestigious award here at Mariposa Beach, mom and dad."

My mom's jaw needs help being put back in place, and my dad wraps his arms around me.

My mom joins him as we all jump around in a circle.

"We will announce you won the poetry portion of the Show and Tell award at the graduation. Then you will read your poem."

"In front of everyone?" I ask feeling my stomach churn already.

My parents are still jumping for joy.

"Yes, and you're going to do great. Can I go now?" he says, smiling at us.

"GO!" we all scream.

"We all scream for ice cream!" My dad jumps and screams like a little girl.

I text Orange and Jay the good news and make my way to see Gracie for volunteer hours. Concha ignores me daily since our talk around Christmas. I used to dread the volunteer hours, but I move around Concha and soak in time with Gracie. I look forward to learning about her every day. She is one of the smartest, funniest, off beat kids I know and I take it in. I take it all in. The thought of reading aloud to my entire graduation class and their families and friends gets pushed down.

The months of February and March come and go at school. The warm fronts melt away the cold winter, although, never officially icy in the beach city but chilly. I watch the frost melt off my beach cruiser wheels every morning. I am still determined to show my parents I have it in me to ride my beach cruiser until the end.

The IEP helps. I am able to take tests in a small group with more time. I am given more time for classroom assignments. Other people take notes for me. I do better. Jay continues to work with me on the basics of reading, writing and math.

And as far as Tim goes, I never think of him, not once since he sent me a Facebook message. I guess Allison doesn't know about the love proclamation, but they are probably together with a large-breasted Betsy Grimes and Jake with a tiger tattoo in the way. Chase and Nicolette are friends and Chase's gay secret isn't known about at school. I don't even think Tim and Allison know. They all continue to keep the secret of Candace, and the more fake they are, the more sickening it is to watch. The more and more I think about it, I want out of Mariposa Beach as soon as possible.

Jay has transferred out of all of Allison's classes. He literally told the guidance counselor he wanted to beat her face in after she called me a slut at Juice Farm.

I do, however, enjoy every second I have with Jay and Orange. I know Jay has major goals of joining the Army and I haven't heard back from colleges to know where I am headed, so I've backed off on my feelings for him. Platonic is safe. Not to mention dating is against the rules of AA as I have been reminded. I make sure Orange is at everything we do together in case there is another vulnerable moment like when he held me in his Nova and every moment since the first day I met him. I can't mess up the time and effort I've put in for volunteer hours with Gracie and AA.

That evening, I feel the blast of sugar dive into my mouth as I watch Jay get out of his Nova and walk to my front door. The Happy Easter decorations in light pink, blue and yellow dye cuts sway in the wind and bonk Jay in the head. He furrows his brow in annoyance.

I giggle.

"Nice cookie, well done Gracie," I shove the duck-shaped cookie in my mouth and make my way to the door. I'll have to tell her this later when I see her. Before I answer the door, I wipe the crumbs off my face. I brush my hair, pull my ripped jeans up and flatten down my pink Grateful Dead T-shirt. I open the door.

"Hey," he says, holding two meatball sandwiches from Lunch Box. His full, brown hair is slicked back, and his green eyes pierce mine. He's got on blue jeans and a white collared shirt.

"So, Orange texted me on the way to Lunch Box and said she's out for dinner. Mama Chantel wanted to take her to a special dinner."

"Flake," I say. "That's okay. Come on in."

He walks in, brushing my hand with his. I think I'm officially attracted to him. I have been for a long time, actually.

"Thanks for the meatball sandwiches. I bought some root beer." I walk him through my living room and to the kitchen. My parents are at the neighbor's house for dinner.

I slip them a quick text that it is just Jay and I. I don't want there to be any surprises.

We sit across from each other at the table. I'm not afraid to eat my entire sandwich in front of him. He congratulates me on finishing the ceramic for the Show and Tell award. He tells me about ROTC. I tell him about Gracie. Then there is a long silence. The one I was afraid of. The one I was hoping to crawl under the carpet for.

"So, I never saw the completed chameleon." He wipes his mouth with a napkin.

"Oh, come on." I jump up, sort of regretting my quick response without thinking.

He is going to be in my room. This is why we always meet in a public place like Java Coffee or Juice Farm. But Orange insisted on them coming over.

He gathers the napkins, tin foil and plates quickly.

"Jay, come on," I say, anxiously. Before I change my mind about you coming into my room, I think.

He finishes throwing out the garbage. "I don't want your parents to come home and see the trash. You're walking on thin ice . . ." he jokes.

"They won't be home for hours," I say, closing my eyes after I say it.

He stops in his tracks. "You're not sure why you said that."

I just start walking, gulping. He follows me around the corner of the living room and down the hall to my room. I feel his eyes on me. My room, which is now painted light blue with accents of light green and intricately painted flowers of all sorts: Daisies, Morning Glories and Roses. I have blown-up pictures of my parents and I, and one of Orange, Jay and I, and one of Grams and I over my bed. My iPod is playing Mazzy Star's "Fade Into You."

"So this is Sadie MacPhearson's bedroom, huh?" He opens his arms out, spinning around. "I'm taking it in the coconut smell." He motions to the Wild Island Girl coconut lotion on the dresser and inhales deeply.

I watch him as I point to the iPod, "I swear I didn't cue the music."

"Sure." He does a little dance shuffle with his feet. He's cute.

I smack his stomach. It feels harder. He pulls my hand close to his chest, sort of in an arm grip in a playful, fun way. I bust my way out of it and my forehead ends up against his chest. I can't look up and meet his eyes. I won't look up and meet his eyes. He is the epitome of goodness and a main reason I still have faith in fellow teenagers. I just don't want to thank him in the wrong way by starting something I don't remember ever doing or finishing before.

Breathe in and out!

He puts his arms around my waist. I feel his fingers interlock above on my lower spine. His breath is shallow as he whispers the words of the song in my ear. I rest my head against his chest, hoping he is not like the rest.

"It would be a little strange if Orange was here," he says, our bodies still close under the dim light from my fan.

"Nah, I do this with all my friends," my voice seems to echo against his chest.

We both giggle.

"Why can't you look at me?" he asks sweetly.

"I've never done this," my voice vibrates on his chest.

"What?" he cups my cheek with his hand trying to meet my eyes, "Sadie."

I open my eyes, peeping up slightly at him.

"There you go . . . those are some sparkly blue eyes," he says in a sultry voice, looking the foot-length distance down. "What haven't you done?"

"I've never danced or have been held by a guy I like without having alcohol in my system," I say.

"I'm not trying to get with you, Sadie," he replies, "I just feel the need to hold you."

"Okay," I take a deep breath.

"It's not like I'm not attracted," he admits, "Most times I can't resist you, but I force myself to."

I breathe out a sigh, breaking myself loose from the embrace and plop on my bed.

"What am I doing?" I hear my thoughts aloud. "I don't know how to do this."

"Sadie," he sits next to me, looking at my shelf with the chameleon on it. "Oh there it is."

"Yep," I say in a low voice. We look at the mostly olive green chameleon with specks of pink, red, blue, orange, purple and yellow.

It's almost the size of a basketball. "I think it's a little better than your chameleon was."

"I think so. It's beautiful . . ." He holds my hand as I feel his eyes on me. I want to take a shot and make out. " . . . Like you . . . hey, I tried to tell you the other day . . ."

I break away and stand up, leaning against my dresser. He needs to stop following me around my room. "When you said nothing I did in the past bothered you. How could it not, Jay? I was an alcoholic, a cheater, and a slut. How does this thing happen? Maybe Concha is right."

He remains on my bed, rubbing his forehead. "Let's see you were meshing with the wrong crowd. You chose alcohol to ease the stress of thinking there was something wrong academically and with you. Your dad was at work a lot and completely checked out. You and your mom were intrigued by the lifestyle Grams had. And, then your mom was occupied by your dying Grams." He spits words out like an old school sprinkler watering the grass.

I want to say I don't deserve you, Jay. But instead I look at Grams and I in the blown up picture above my bed. "I . . . what do I do Grams?"

He turns his body to look at it. "She was really cool. When I was working that white party with her, she asked me if I knew you. I, of course, got blushy in the face. She was like yeah my granddaughter has the effect on most people. We had a pretty long conversation about you."

My arms fold. I feel my body shutting down 5, 4, 3, 2, 1 and I ask hastily, "About what?"

He gets flushed like he can feel my tension and speaks, "She told me everything about you . . . she told me she was dying . . .she told me she trusted me to watch over you after she died." He walks towards me.

"So I'm just a charity case?" I say insecurely, smelling his musky scent combined with my coconut pear lotion as he walks closer.

"I knew that was coming . . ." he stops. "No, you're not."

"Or, do I look so much like Candace? You actually want to save me this time," the words hit him like an AK-47 kick back.

What's my problem?

"Happy Easter," he says, throwing a small white box on my bed and walking out of my room.

I bite my lower lip. "What's this?"

I take it, open it up and pull out a small, silver necklace with a SUP boarder charm. My eyes get teary. I want to go get him and apologize but I know he needs some air.

"Wow, I love it." I clasp the shiny necklace around my neck and pull myself up to look at it in the mirror. I try to not to make eye contact with girl in the mirror. She doesn't deserve this. I don't deserve this. I need a shot like more than I've ever needed one. My parents have gotten rid of all the alcohol in the house.

Someone help me.

Chapter 31

MYSTERIOUS GUY IN THE BASEBALL CAP

I should call Mel but she is most likely at home with Jay. I pull up the private message from Tim on Facebook, typing a little something back. I found my someone to help me.

Twenty minutes later, I walk into Tim's room, smelling the Glenlivet in the room, NO! NO! NO! My insides scream. Coming over here is a mistake.

"What's up?" I hear his devilish yet familiar voice as he sways. His eyes are bloodshot and his skin is red. His room is huge and painted black, kind of like the tiny black speckles in his eyes. On the wall, he has a custom light blue surfboard that says Timmy, which reminds me that he had a childhood once. He props himself up.

He's still gorgeous but I seem to have lost my Glenlivet goggles.

"Where are your parents?" I ask.

"My dad and his secretary are living downstairs while I get the entire upstairs. My mom is at rehab for the seventh time." He opens his window and lights a cigarette.

CLASSY!

"Nothing's changed." My stomach is queasy. "Don't end up like them."

"NOPE! Let's do a shot." He pats the bed. "It's been a while, huh?"

"It's been 301 days," I recall. "On 301, 300, 299, 298, 297, 215 . . . I needed a simple beer, 191 I wanted a glass of wine. On 180, I needed a straight shot of Malibu rum . . .

"Well, you need something," he says, proudly pouring a shot of Glenlivet.

"SHIT," I feel the urge to take it and shoot it. I hold it in my hand, looking at it as I stand there in the middle of his room. The guy I thought about for so long.

What's one shot? Would I want eight more? I wouldn't have to feel the insecurity of having a man touch me.

"I believe you now . . ." He shoots his down the hatch. "I know he's gay."

I have to call Mel.

"Tim," I dry heave, watching him shoot his. I set the full shot glass down. I feel for my cell in my back pocket and try to find Mel's number in my contacts.

Sadie: I need help. Mel: Where are you?
Sadie: Tim Miller's house, 34 Strand Avenue.
Mel: Okay, leave and wait for me outside. Ten minutes.

"How could anyone not want to sleep with someone that looks like you for three years, taking those hot pictures?" He stands up and pulls me to him, trying to kiss me.

"Please, you're going to make me sick," I yell.

He grabs my wrist and presses himself against me, trying to kiss me. "Sadie, I love you. It's always been you."

Tears pour down my cheeks. "I've changed Tim."

"Well, you look like the same girl I once knew." He looks at me.

"GET OFF!" I scream, breaking away from him and running out of his house. I jump on my bike, feeling my adrenaline. It's late. My parents think I'm with Jay. I can't tell them. My stomach hurts. I see Mel's suburban round the corner. Thank you Mel!

My eyes flutter open as Mel turns on the light in the little cry room at the church with the old steeple. It's 9 p.m. and it's time for an AA meeting. She and I are the only ones there when we arrive. It's good timing for a meeting.

"Speak." She sits, crossing her legs and folding her hands.

I rise from the chair with undeniable fear and my black combat boots sound like Clydesdale horses taking their time. "My name is Sadie. I'm seventeen years old, and I'm an alcoholic." I smile at her, feeling silly.

"Hi Sadie," says an older gentleman dressed in blue jeans and a long flannel shirt. His face is hidden under a baseball cap.

My voice is shaky but never mind the shakiness, if I'm speaking the truth. "I had my first drink when I was thirteen years old. It was from a $100 bottle of wine. I wanted so badly to fit into this group, so I did exactly what they did. I wanted to be like the leader and date the guy she was dating. I wanted to be as beautiful as them, smart as them and rich as them. They made me over to look like them."

Mel moves her head, "continue."

"They helped me cheat my way through school, so I could keep up with them. I became popular with the guys. You know what it's like to mess around with guys starting at fifteen years old? It's too young. All of these things wouldn't have gone on without the help of alcohol. The sad thing was I became addicted, chemically dependent. My mornings would start out with coffee but I would always pour a flask of something from my parents liquor stash." I breathe out and for the first time in a long time, I'm coming out with it. I'm divulging. I'm verbally vomiting. I feel like vomiting.

The older gentleman with a Dodgers baseball cap smiles at me and nods his head to continue. His face is familiar, but I still can't see his eyes.

"And, then some really bad shit happened. My grandmother died. I was diagnosed with a Central Auditory Processing Disorder, which basically means I hate reading, writing and math, don't get it and can't listen to simple directions. Low confidence. High drinking factor. High school graduation rate has gone way down for kids with learning disabilities in this country." I make more what I think are jokes.

"I was the one who crashed into the side of an elementary school building . . .thank God I didn't kill anyone or myself." My voice cracks, and I let the water works appear. "And, my parents, thank God they like me now, but for months they didn't speak to me. I'm surprised they speak to me now. I wouldn't speak to me now," I have to throw in a joke.

Mel brushes her pointer finger under her eye.

"I don't know where to go from here. I think I deserve another chance," I sit down, "I've been 301 days sober." My hand raises.

The old guy stands up, pulling his baseball cap off. It's Principal Dow. "Good for you, Sadie."

What? I breathe in uneasily.

He's wearing a one-year bronze chip with a chain attached to it.

Mel stands up and walks over, wrapping her arms around me. "You deserve a second chance."

I want to believe her.

Mel drives me home. She pulls in my driveway. I don't know how to thank her, so I just say thank you.

She puts her soft hand on mine. "You did good. Someone did it for me. Remember Sadie; you should probably avoid a relationship in the first year of sobriety. It's against the rules."

I know. I've heard.

Oh God, did Concha get to her, too?

I see my eyes glisten in the rearview mirror as I think of Jay.

I screwed up. We screwed up. How did I let him get so close?

She puts her hand on mine, "I can feel you have something with Jay. I knew it when you paddle boarded with us last year. But, it's not fair to you or Jay. You have a few more months to feel grounded and then maybe . . ."

I let a tear roll down my cheek and drown my soul, "I agree."

"Oh honey." She wipes my cheek. "I had to do it with Josh.

I made myself be friends with him for a year. You have to be comfortable with yourself." She points to my heart.

I squeeze her and thank her again. My parents are still at the neighbors' house.

When I get in my bed, I flip my pillow to the cold side after relieving my headache with two Tylenol PMs and a glass of water. I get a text.

Jay: Are you okay? Sadie: Thanks to Mel.
Jay: Good.
Sadie: Sorry for the comment about Candace.
Jay: Apology accepted.
Sadie: Friends?
Jay: Absolutely. I promise.

How I wish that I could be with him. I royally screwed that one up. The Tylenol PM hits me and I'm fast asleep.

Chapter 32

FUTURE TALK

During the months of April and May, the mornings, before school, Jay, Orange and I SUP board. We'd go to various spots and do yoga moves on the boards. We sometimes do it again in the evenings. During nutrition, we have Jay look at our papers and tests, tell jokes and talk about how we will be friends forever. I soak in flowers during this time trying to forget my more than friends feelings for Jay. At volunteering, Gracie riles me up and spits me out but I enjoy the few moments of achieving goals and finishing what I started. I go to an AA meeting weekly but I don't ever see Principal Dow. My parents and I hang out more. We spend most afternoons cleaning the house and gardening because now it's on the market. They want to sell the house and buy a condo wherever I decide to go after graduation.

The last few weeks of school are hot. I get home from volunteer, we SUP board and then Orange makes us something healthy to eat as we study for our finals and dip our feet in the Jacuzzi at my house. We talk about plans for next year and our future. My mom likes them both. Well she loved Jay initially, forever and always. The pounds literally shred off of Orange and Jay. Both look different. I pack down my Jay thoughts in the deep of my soul because I don't want to ruin practically everything positive in my life. I don't want to Tim-ify the situation.

We complete our finals Friday morning. I manage to get Bs on all of them. I do volunteer with Gracie. Today marks 365 days of sobriety. Mel buys me a bronze chip and bouquet of Daisies. That afternoon, we take Jay's family suburban and SUP board for hours.

At 5:30 ish, we end up back at my house. Orange piddles around with my mom in the kitchen as Jay sits on the side of the Jacuzzi dangling his feet in the water. I'm under the wood patio cover, holding the ivy and he is sitting on the other side getting a blast of the afternoon sun on his olive green board shorts and white Quiksilver shirt. I want him to speak and I want to say something funny like, 'aren't you getting hot? Take off your shirt and then tell me.'

"So, Gracie was all over the candy and kept trying to hide it in her cleavage." I wrap up the story about her. "But she doesn't have any."

Jay laughs.

"That's my favorite story."

I gaze off into the clear, blue sky. "Ah, I sure will miss her."

"I'm sure . . . she will probably miss you, too," he retorts. We are silent, dangling our feet in the water and peeking at each other like two sea otters.

I try not to be alone with him too much. I think he feels the same way. The AA thingy is a huge reason. Then we are all out of here in a few days and going our separate ways. These are factors reminding me to keep my distance, but a magnet is pulling me. My mom and Orange walk out of the kitchen door and towards us with a plate of white bread egg salad sandwiches and corn chips. Grams used to love sandwiches. Jay and I both take a napkin and our portion of what we want.

"Orange." I bite into the best egg salad sandwich I've ever tasted.

"Right!" Jay chimes in. Now, he's shirtless: big arms, flat stomach, brown skin. I've never seen him like this. The sun is beating massively on him. I wear sunglasses to make sure I'm not staring too hard.

HOT DAMN!

Orange's eyes get bigger. I shake my head.

"It's all healthy, too." Orange carries on, scooting out of the sun towards me. "I made it with plain Greek yogurt."

"From the dill from my garden," my mom adds, sitting next to me on the deck of the Jacuzzi.

"Sorry Mrs. MacPhearson, but I couldn't pass it up." Orange smiles.

"Call me Cindy and, it's okay. I'm truly happy for you getting into culinary school in New York," she says, popping a corn chip in her mouth. "Grams would be proud."

She really would have liked Orange.

"I just had to work hard this year and get through school." Orange slides over towards me in the shade.

"You did it, Orange," I say, patting her back.

"Congratulations to all of you for completing your finals and high school," my mom says. Orange, my mom and I squeal. Jay smiles.

"And, to Sadie for a year . . ."Jay clinks his sandwich against mine.

Everyone hoots and hollers. I feel proud.

"Now I just need to find a roommate." Orange nudges me.

My mom pulls out three envelopes from her jean shorts pocket.

"We have four very important pieces of mail to open. Well one is our new insurance payment but these three are for Sadie."

She slips her feet in the water. "Gosh, it's hot out here."

You're telling me?

She hands me the envelopes: FIDM (Fashion Institute Merchandising of Design), Brooklyn Junior College and San Diego Junior College. FIDM is a school in LA for fashion designers in any realm of clothing, interior design or jewelry. Brooklyn JC has a general education curriculum with a specialization in kids with special needs and automated transfer to NYU's education school. I also applied to San Diego Junior College because I've always wanted to live in San Diego.

"Yes," Orange says. "So let me start with saying Sadie got 200 more points on her SATs this round, and I'm so happy for her."

"Drum roll," I say.

Everyone does his or her best version of a drum roll. It sounds similar to the one on *National Lampoon's Christmas Vacation.*

"C'mon Los Angeles!" I say, as my mom says, "C'mon Brooklyn!"

I sneer at my mom. "Their teaching program is too hard academically. I can't hack it. I barely passed high school."

"I got into San Diego junior college and FIDM." I shrug my shoulders.

"Great," my mom says.

Orange frowns. "Poop," she says.

"Yes, AND," Jay adds.

"And, Brooklyn JC," I say, setting the envelopes on the deck. Orange claps, almost knocking over the plate snacks into the Jacuzzi.

Jay laughs. He moves the plate away from her. "It's okay, Orange."

"I know, go where you want, Sades?" Orange jumps in. I smile back genuinely.

"I heard Nicolette got that scholarship for UC San Diego for academics," my mom says.

Out of all of them, I cared about her the most.

"Really?" I say, "Are they all going to move to Mariposa Beach number 2, Playa De Rico?"

My mom shrugs innocently. "I ran into her mom at the farmers market and that's what she said."

"I overheard about that, too." Jay jumps into the conversation just as he jumps in the Jacuzzi. "She was telling a few other people."

"Really," I say snottily.

"I'm not one to crush someone's dreams, so that's why I didn't say anything to you," he says. "That's if you choose San Diego."

I nod, chewing my sandwich and swallowing quickly. "I mean it would have been okay if we had gone to schools right next to each other."

I stand up, bend over and pull out coconut water for myself out of the mini wine cooler fridge under the patio cover. "Anyone want a water or coconut water?"

My mom fixes my bikini bottoms so the material is on my butt. I shoe her away as I pull off my turquoise spaghetti strap tank top revealing my yellow triangle top and bottoms. "I'm going to go in anyways . . ."

Jay bites his thumb as his eyes watch me slip into the cool Jacuzzi. He's hiding behind his black Ray bans, too. "Get in, Orange."

She is his buffer, too.

"I have to go in a bit," she says. Go? Like leave me here with Jay?

"BUT, SD is big, but Playa del Rico is right in the middle," Orange says.

My mom shakes her head in agreement.

"Well she hurt you massively, so there's no need to be friends," Jay suggests.

"Yes," my mom says, looking over at Jay.

"Are you sold on doing fashion?" Orange asks. "Because I think you're pretty damn good with Gracie, and my social worker has a connection with Autism Speaks in New York City."

"Mel does, too," Jay throws it in there.

"NYC is pricey," I ignore her, changing the subject.

Everyone nods.

"We could kick out the renters from the Battery Park apartment," my mom suggests. "We probably need to replace a few things. Utilities would be expensive, but the apartment is paid for."

In middle school, I remember going there when Grams was filming. It's on the seventh floor of an old brick apartment building in Battery Park, about 1,300 square feet with two bedrooms, two baths, a small kitchen and a small living room but a bigger outside porch.

Orange's face lights up. I change the subject.

"Jay, you're going to be in Georgia?" I ask in a non-chalant manner trying to play it cool, getting waters for everyone and fidding with the Jacuzzi's temperature control knob. In all honesty I am panicking because I don't want to be left alone with Jay. "Mind if I turn up the heat?"

My mom and Orange smile, leaning into each other. It's like they know.

"No." His dimples appear. I kind of want to swim in them today. "Fort Benning, Georgia, right outside of Columbus is the training for four months and then I don't know where," he says. "I think Orange has a point though."

I turn it up to 90 degrees and glide my hands across the water, looking down. "You have to be good in school in order to get your degree in special education or edu-cational therapy and I . . ."

"Can't do it because you're not smart enough? Seriously, this again, Sades?" Jay's olive greens peer at me.

"Fashion is the new black and I want to do that," I tell myself.

"You have a gift working with kids with special needs . . . maybe you could help someone like you would have wanted to be helped?" He moves his hand along the water, splashing me.

I splash him back.

"Okay, I don't want to sit next to the person being flirted with." My mom scoots away from me.

Silence and heat overtake the spa. The vibe and energy is lost for a second until my mom says, "God help me."

Orange says, "Seriously right?"

They have both said you can cut the tension between Jay and I with a knife.

"Brooklyn JC has a good teaching school, right," my mom finally says, "And, you know Grams always wanted you to go there for college."

"Yeah, but New York is big and scary!" I say.

"No." Orange splashes back. "New York, big and amazing, full of opportunities galore, cultured, good experiences, good food, killer music anytime, anywhere."

"Orange will be there," my mom says again, looking at Orange.

Orange smiles. "Sadie, I'm not going to get excited, but I would die if we moved there together. Die in a good way . . . Like I'd absolutely love it."

My mom nods. "Grams would have loved that you chose NYC."

She nods, looking over at me.

I squeeze her hand. "You already said that, but before you leave to pick up Jane at the airport, tell me why?"

I'm letting Jay know she's leaving, too.

"You know Grams was the essence of New York when we lived there. She and my dad raised me there. And, then we would go back and forth to the condo to film *The Big Apple Cookoff*. She would've still lived there if it weren't for Wyatt taking me to Wisconsin and then my father passing. But I was born and raised in this old apartment in Battery Park, which is super trendy now. New York was spectacular in the winter, just breathtaking, snowy and twinkle lights everywhere, people always walking, dressed in fur coats. And, in the summertime, block parties, water balloon fights and dance parties. Fall ferry rides and the most gorgeous colored leaves. And, then South Hampton on the weekend . . . I would die to live there again . . ." My mom shakes her head and tries to lower herself back to earth.

I smile sweetly at her, swimming closer to her. "I bet you've got a lot of good memories."

Tears swell her eyes. "Yeah."

I take her hand. "It's okay. It'll get easier."

She sort of backs up but lets the tears flow.

I get out and wrap my wet arms around her and she lets me.

"It's a Cindy sandwich," Jay says, piling on with Orange, too.

Everyone laughs and breaks apart. My mom excuses herself.

"She hasn't cried like that since the funeral," I say.

"She needed a good cry, and I really have to get to my night class to take my final, later," Orange says. "Who's Jane?"

"A friend of my parents from Wisconsin. She's like an aunt to me and is coming for the graduation," I reply.

"Cool, okay, wish me luck," she replies, slipping on her sandals and heading out the back gate.

"LUCK," we both yell.

Great, Jay think of something quick . . . no alone time for us.

It's too hard. The tension is rising. I haven't been alone with him since around Easter.

Chapter 33

THE WRIST KISS

Jay and I sit on opposite sides of the Jacuzzi. There's an entire five feet between us, among other things. A quick glide and I could be in his arms. I'm slightly annoyed that he thinks he can bark his opinion about my intelligence level although positive. He has no idea how hard school is for me.

The wind blows a palm tree leaf into the spa so that's now between us too.

He pulls the leaf out. "What?"

"What?" I say.

"Are you okay?" he laughs nervously.

"Yeah, I'm just a little irritated." My hands dip in the water. "Why?" he gulps.

"Because you seriously need to stop meddling." I inch towards him.

"Meddling?" He backs up, hitting the edge of the Jacuzzi.

"Telling everyone that you think I'm smart." I find myself about two feet away.

"Really." he splashes me.

I splash him. He splashes me for like thirty seconds straight.

"Okay." I put my hands up, surrendering.

We are standing, facing each other like a head and a half apart. In this moment, without a doubt in my mind, I know Jay is my first love. I'm not sure if I will ever tell him or show him but when I look in his olive greens I see a very deep, wonderful soul that I want to always and forever be a part of.

As I'm realizing, I breathe in heavily, "I'm never going to be college material. I may as well do something more fitting, like fashion or hair or makeup."

He grabs my shoulders and shakes me slightly. "You're simply amazing with Gracie. I can hear the passion in your voice when you talk about her and how you could help her. I know it would make you happy to go into that field."

"I can't do school . . . without you," I whimper.

"Come here," he pulls me into his bare, warm chest. My body feels little in his big giant teddy bear embrace but oh so warm. It's two pieces of the puzzle fitting together perfectly. My breasts press to his chest and he breathes out.

I look up at him, my head just below his chin. "Can't you tutor me from the base?"

He laughs, pushing my shoulders back while making eye contact. "Sadie, I taught you well: all the little tricks for reading comprehension, writing, and math. Strive to be the best version of yourself."

I inhale, holding my breath as I look up in his eyes. "Thank you for basically getting me through high school . . . but now that it's over."

"My pleasure." He moves his wet fingers along the backs of my arms.

He continues to stroke the backs of my arms as I put my hand on his warm, soft chest. We are silent. Lucy barks.

I snap at her, "be quiet."

He smiles, "So your year of sobriety is up . . . so . . . if you wanted to do . . . this." He closes his eyes and opens them again.

"This vibe." I brush my hand along his cheek.

"Yes," he sighs sliding his hand around the back of my neck. "God, like a major vibe."

His cell phone rings, and he jumps back a foot letting go. I collect myself and move to the other side of the Jacuzzi.

"Hi Principal Dow, yes, I can come early." It looks like a vein is about to pop in his forehead. He presses END and says, "I really have to go and practice my speech for tomorrow." He jumps out of the spa, lightning bolt fast. "Jack is in town, too."

"Okay." I smile at him watching him flutter. "Can I come by later?" He dries his body off.

"I don't know," I say in a serious tone.

"I promise not to say that Autism Speaks and Brooklyn JC will probably be the turning point of your life and the best thing that ever happens to you!" He puts on his white Quiksilver T-shirt.

I want to say you're the best thing that ever happened to me, but I don't.

I pull myself up to sit on the side of the Jacuzzi.

"Promise?"

"Hell yeah." He walks over to me, bends down face to face to me, pulling my right wrist up and landing a solid kiss with his soft, full, wet, mango lip balm scented lips. I'm branded now as I look down at my slim wrist. "Walk me out?"

"Yes." I hold my wrist as I use the steps to walk out of the Jacuzzi.

I follow him out the side gate, deliberately wearing my bikini only. I stand before him on the driveway. He uses both hands to pull my hair back over my shoulders, bringing my head to his chest. He kisses the top of my head. Um, this guy knows how to touch me. I want to kiss beautiful lips but not like this. "You should go," I point to his Nova.

He lets go, doing a once over. "And leave you?"

I push him away, grinning. "Go."

A few hours later, Jane is over and we order a pizza and salad. She mostly talks about her job, kids and new boyfriend. My parents take her out to a wine bar and I stay home. I lay on my bed wearing a pair of turquoise shorts and a long black V-neck T-shirt. I still smell the mango lip balm on my wrist and want it to last forever. I thought it was different that he kissed my wrist but I realize it's sensual. Maybe he wants to go slow. I want to. Mazzy Star's "Fade into You" comes on.

I scribble a pros and cons list for New York City:

PROs	CONs
New Adventures	Distance from Family
Closer to Jay	
Orange	
Culture	
Music	
Food	
Opportunities	
Good Education	

At 9:33 p.m., I check my cell.

Jay: Hey vibe girl, Jack, Josh and I are hanging. Sorry . . . I really want to come over . . . like you wouldn't believe.
Sadie: LOL! I understand, vibe boy.
Jay: Good night, Sades.

I set my phone on my nightstand. I try to understand or even make sense of what happened. Starting something with him is useless though. He is off to Georgia after graduation.

Evening comes, and he doesn't stop by. I wrestle with my body pillow all night thinking about his dimples that I want to stroke with my fingers, eyes I want to stare at, his white teeth pulling on my stomach, his raspy voice singing songs in my ear and his big teddy bear arms wrapped around mine.

It's the Sunday before our graduation, I decide to hit up Java Coffee for a stronger than usual coffee in order to solidify my Show and Tell poem for graduation.

"Hey Sades." Chase walks up to my table, wearing a pair of rainbow-colored board shorts, a tight, white T-shirt and Havaianas. How fitting.

"Hi." I string together a smile. "Beach day?"

"Yeah," he replies. "We're meeting at ten. You should come."

"When pigs fly," I say.

He taps his foot. "Okay, for what it's worth, Nic, Al and Tim know about me."

"I know they know . . ." I reply.

"They don't really talk to me anymore. I think they're all moving to Playa De Rico. I got into UCLA on an academic and La Crosse scholarship, so I'll be going there. Betsy is joining me," he says.

I tap my pencil like I even care and then say, "Tim should go to rehab. And, is Betsy your new prodigy?"

I feel like he needs a hug, but I'm not giving him one.

He looks down. "She's the one that got in trouble for cheating. She wasn't as careful. She has to do a month of cleaning at the school and was expelled for a few days. It should have been you though."

THESE. PEOPLE. ARE. CRAZY. This is Chase Bynes: wealthy, beautiful, smart, manipulative, super shady and selfish. Take it or leave it.

"It should have been you." I feel my body get hot with anger. "And, she still wants to be your friend?"

I think I know why Principal Dow didn't pin it on me.

"Hhhhhhhmmmmm kay," he sits down. "My parents don't know. They probably think I'm bisexual, but I'm waiting until I get that first year's tuition paid before I tell them. That'll be right around re-election time for my dad. What's up with that DIY hottie?" he adds.

I assume he's talking about Jay.

"Jay. Lost some weight . . . looks like Jack now. Friggin' smart," he suggests.

I nod. "Yes, he's a nice guy too."

"You guys banging?"

"Banging?" I almost laugh. "NO!"

He laughs. "Just kidding, however, if you are, I'm not sure why he was hooking up with Betsy last night after graduation rehearsal."

"What?" I slam my pencil down. My heart does not feel hugs and kisses.

"Yeah, she had a little after rehearsal graduation party. Jack and Jay stopped by for a bit. Tim, Al and Nicolette weren't allowed to come in, but I was there. Betsy was on Jay's jock."

WHAT? My inside voice screams. So, he is like every other guy out there.

"Are you sure it was Jay?" I stutter and shift in my seat nervously.

"Yeah, wow." He smiles. "I didn't think you were banging?"

"We're just friends." I roll my eyes at him.

"Come to the beach with me," Chase says. "I'm going to Johnny's house with some Hollywooders and a ton of single hot guys."

"I don't think so," I say immediately.

"Sadie, I know we had our differences, but I literally love you more than words can say and I so miss our friendship. We could start over and be the besties we once were." He's not even looking at me but scrolling through his phone as Betsy walks up wearing a yellow romper and holding two ice coffees.

"Tell Sades what happened with Jay," he commands.

"Hey Sades," her voice is high. "Oh yeah Jay and I kissed." God, I am such an idiot. And, now thoughts, emotions, words are spinning above my head and I can't do anything to stop them but have a drink.

"Really?"

"Yeah, he's hot now . . ." she remarks.

"I'm bored, let's go," Chase says.

A text message appears.

Jay: I'm out for SUP boarding. Valedictorian speech.
Orange: I'm packing up my life today. Flight after graduation Monday.
Me: Losers!
I individually text Jay: I thought we were going to talk.
Jay: Sorry. Later for sure.

I look at Chase as the proverbial dark cloud moves in and say, "I'm in. I don't drink anymore but I need a male distraction."

"Fantastic, I'll drive," he says. "Well, unless you want to ride your beach cruiser . . ."

We hop in Chase's brand new graduation gift, a brand new cherry red convertible Mustang and zip our way to Pacific Coast Highway through mounds of beach traffic. The beach air smells salty and I almost miss it already, even though I'm still not sure I'm going to choose to live in New York City.

The tradition is Mariposa Beach High School beaches it the day before graduation, so I see a lot of students from our school in their expensive cars, driving along passing drinks back and forth and listening to their genre of music.

He smiles at me, fiddling with his Pandora and finding the song, "Gasolina" by Daddy Yankee. "It's good to have you back."

I watch myself fakely half smile in his mirror. I should talk to Jay.

Betsy hands me the third water bottle of Jack and Diet Coke. I have no idea what I'm doing with him, but I need a drink to help ease my mind. I hold it in my hand, bringing it to my lips and stop. I think about my bronze chip and the hard work I've put into my sobriety.

I pull the drink away from my mouth and put it back in the drink holder. I recognize the red Mercedes next to us, which is stopped in still traffic. Nicolette and Tim step out, too.

"No." I want it. I want to escape.

"Great," Chase says sarcastically.

Allison steps out.

"Well if it isn't Sadie the ghost." She rests her arms on the car door, wearing nothing but a triangle bikini top and really short jean shorts. "And, Chase, the gay guy."

Chase turns his head away, lighting up a cigarette.

"Screw you." I turn away as quickly as possible.

"How are you?" she asks.

"Don't talk to me," I say.

She looks at my drink. "I thought you weren't drinking."

"I'm not," I hand her the drink. "Here."

She takes it. "Two things: stay away from Tim. I know you were like at his house a few months ago," she states.

"Al, relax!" Tim leans against her BMW next to Nic who won't step any closer to Chase's car.

"LIKE I'M ALL DONE, I don't like him any-more . . . haven't for months. He needs rehab, too." I point to him, needing a cigarette. I grab a cigarette from my tote and light it up.

"I am done with him, too," Betsy says from the backseat.

Tim mutters something under his breath.

I take out my cell and text Orange with shaky fingers.

Sadie: Orange, are you free to pick me up? I'm stuck on PCH.

"Drop out of the Show and Tell award," she says when I look up.

"NO!" I scream, blowing my smoke out on her face.

She blows her smoke out on me, "Drop out or I will tell Principal Dow it was you who cheated all those years. You're not the best at public speaking. It'll ease the nerves. And, your resume will still be good enough for McDonald's. Is that where you plan to work?"

"I highly doubt he will out me," I stand firmly.

"It's done," Betsy says.

"Or, maybe, your dad's fire fighter buddies will want to see all of the sexy pictures you took with Chase?" she threatens.

I close my eyes. "They're not nude . . . you really would, too, huh? Why?"

"Because Nicolette and I were second in line for the best friend poem. I need to spice up my resume a little if I want to get an internship at my parents' law firm . . . let the board know I'm friendly." She tilts her head back, cackling in the air like an evil queen in a Disney movie.

"No, I can't . . ." My hands are sweaty. "You have taken everything from me."

"Back off, Allison." Nicolette pulls her shoulder back. "It's over."

FINALLY!

I feel a presence. "Back off, that's not fair to ask . . ." Allison says.

"Jay," I say. He is followed by Orange, and his twin Jack who looks identical to him.

I put out my cigarette and open the car door. Did he hook up with Betsy or not? I want to know.

"Oh yeah." Allison stands up, looking at everyone. "Hi Jack," she says in her cute baby voice with Tim and Nicolette behind her.

"Those pictures are mine," Chase says. "I will never share them with you."

"Allison, BACK OFF," Jack says, "Or, I'll tell the world what really happened on the night of Candace's death."

She shakes her head. "You're crazy. What are you doing here anyways?"

"Rescuing Sadie," Jack smiles.

"Let's go, Sades," Jay holds out his hand. I take it even though I'm not sure. I look at Tim; he looks down at the ground. He is mortified. But holding Jay's hand in this moment is worth the pain this group of people caused me.

I turn around and look at Allison. She's covering her face. "For what it's worth Allison, no matter what you do in life, there will always be consequences," Orange says.

"Oh screw you, Orange Crush," she yells.

Jay, Jack, Orange and I jump into Jay's Nova. Jay and I sit in the front seat. His hand is on my leg. We watch a California Highway Patrol officer take her water bottle full of Jack and Diet Coke and smell it. She says it's not hers. Nonetheless, maybe she finally got what she deserved. He spins the Nova around and goes the opposite way of traffic.

"By the way, this is Jack," Jay says.

I look at Jack. "Nice to meet you."

I find Orange's leg and yell. "Thank you."

She winks. "Anytime. You didn't drink, right?"

"No . . ." I say.

She gives me thumbs up.

Chapter 34

THE ARCH OF LOVE—TAKE 2

We decide to go to Sea Breeze Restaurant for lunch. It's a nice restaurant on the beach with windows open and overlooks the ocean. We all order iced tea, and chips and salsa. I'm quiet while Jack and Orange do most of the talking. Orange is laughing and enjoying herself. I'm glad he came for me, but I want to know what happened with Betsy.

"Sadie, can we talk outside?" he finally asks. I look at him.

"Yes."

He sighs. "Sorry, excuse us."

"I'll just be here . . ." Orange smiles. "I'll text you when the food is here."

Tears form in my eyes, and my heart drops as he pulls me outside the side door to talk.

I lean against the wall, folding my arms. "What's up?"

"Um, same to you." He stands, tall as ever. He hasn't shrunk.

Nothing's changed with that. His arms are folded too.

I take in any air I can.

"What happened with Betsy?"

"She started to kiss me and I backed off," he says. "I worked on my valedictorian speech, picked up Jack from the airport and we ran into Betsy at Juice Farm. She invited us over, so we went. It was stupid. I wanted to be with you."

I nod. "Okay."

"She's not my type. I was having a conversation with her about what happened with Principal Dow and the answer keys."

I uncross my arms. "I know. Chase told me today," I reply.

"Yeah, she was the one breaking in to get the answer keys for Chase all these years."

"I feel bad about not admitting I was cheating but I think Principal Dow didn't want me to," I suggest.

"Stop, you have suffered enough this year," he says.

"God, those people." My phone dings. "Food is here."

"Okay, so I felt really bad and basically she cried . . . then tried to kiss me," he says really fast.

"Okay, " I put my hands up. "Okay . . . okay . . . okay."

He interlocks his fingers with mine, forcing me to look up in his olive greens. "Nothing with Tim?"

"No."

"More about the vibe we got going on . . .I would rather kiss you. I think it about it all the time. Like the first time I met you at the beach where we played soccer, in Ceramics like all last year, behind building C everyday this year, SUP boarding, in Chase's tree house, at the tunnel at the park, in my Nova, in your room and Jacuzzi . . . And every single night when I lay in my bed, thinking about those blue, sparkly eyes that remind me of the color of the ocean . . . that no matter where I am in life I will always think of them."

He releases his hands and pulls me to his chest cupping my cheek with his warm hand. His forehead is wrinkled. Maybe he thinks he said too much.

"Oh crap, hey lovers, if you want to eat dinner before we SUP board, please let's come eat . . ." Orange pops her head out.

We separate. We are both grinning from ear to ear as he holds his hand out for me to put mine in.

"To be continued . . ." he laughs.

About an hour and a half later, we're prepping our SUP boards for one last run. It's still very hot out, so we don't wear our wetsuits. Jay has light blue board shorts on. I'm sporting my gold triangle top bikini and tiny, white board shorts.

"Sadie." Jack smacks my SUP board to get my attention. He's hot but Jay is hotter.

"Jack," I reply, as I pull my hair up in a ponytail. "Thank you for making my brother happy." He winks.

"I'm happy to have met him," I say.

We are in the ocean a few hundred yards out. It's even clearer than the first day we ever went SUP boarding together. We push our paddles through the water, increasing speed. The water splashes on me every so often. It's refreshing on my overheated body. We all laugh and sing intensely to Radiohead's "Creep." Orange and Jack fight for the finish line, scooting along at a decent speed. I'm following Jay on my SUP board. He leads me to the Arch of Love. We stop to admire.

He gives me that look like he just realized what love is.

"Sadie." He stops. I paddle over and sit on my board. My heart pulsates out of my chest. Does he want to kiss my other wrist now? He pulls my board to his as our boards are now touching. He ties our boards together by the leashes. "Come here."

I crawl carefully on his board balancing and sitting Indian-style across from him sober and a little bashful. He scoots to me pulling my chin up with his calloused hand, and I cock my head. His olive greens and my blue sparklies match up and our lips meet with a distinctive "smooch." His lips taste like mango lip balm and salty ocean air and water. It's better than anything else I've tasted on my lips. His lips are like pillows I want to lay on forever.

"I've waited so long to kiss you," he screams out. "I just kissed Sadie MacPhearson."

Covering my mouth, I guffaw at him. His eyes are low and vulnerable as he holds the back of my neck and pulls me in for another soft smooch but this time he inserts his tongue as do I. The kiss is like soft snow-flakes in a snowstorm that I could easily explain to my grandchildren.

"So, you kind of like me, huh?" My hand is on his neck.

He puts his hands on my waist. His board is a little wobbly, so we even ourselves out in order to balance it. I just wanted to touch him a little so I can remember how he feels. You know, when I'm in my next life. Our lips meet again. This time, I wrap my legs around him sitting on the board straddling him as he softly kisses me. It's a softness, sweetness, gentleness I've never known.

"Hhhhmmmm." He breaks away. "So, I think I might like you a little bit," he says, softly.

I'm still straddling him. I brush his cheek with my hand. "Ever since the last time we came here," I add.

His eyes are heavy with ecstasy. He pulls me and kisses me, so strong I devour it.

"Oh Sadie," he whispers, "You should be kissed right."

He runs his hands through my long hair. I cup his dimpled cheeks letting his teddy bear embrace take over. The water laps against the board. The sun shines in the horizon. Moss is on the rocks. The Arch of Love is above us. Everything is in it's place and we are, too.

"Well, I didn't expect that from Big Fat Mexican." I smile.

"Nor I from Snotty Bitch," he says back.

I laugh, biting my lower lip. "Touché."

He backs up. "You're my favorite first kiss..."

"You're my favorite first kiss . . ." I say back.

He wraps his arms around me, kissing my head. "I will always remember your smell—coconut and beach waves. So good! I want to cap it."

I kiss his lips again. I can't get enough. Orange and Jack coast over to us.

"Sorry, we're lucky in love," I say to them.

Oh my God I just said I love him.

Jay squeezes my hand. "Yes we are."

We take another hour to Stand Up Paddle board in the ocean. Jay grins everytime I look at him.

Jack drops Orange off and then me, "I'm going to get some gas. Jay, why don't you walk Sadie inside? I'll be back in ten minutes," he winks.

Jay walks me to my front door holding my hand with his kung fu grip. He has his light blue board shorts on only, "here," he takes my key and unlocks the door.

He opens the front door. I walk in and throw my things on the floor, pulling him inside the house, pushing him against the front door I've just shut. I just want to feel his strong body against mine. Now for the land kiss. His hands creep from my backside, graze my bare stomach and cup my face, pulling me in deeper. The kisses are long, sensual, passionate and loving. He is breathing as heavily as I am.

He flips me around and pushes me against the wall with a large clock on it. The clock ticks and tocks as he kisses my neck, my ears and my stomach.

"I love you." His hands run along the skin on my back.

"I know," I reply, with his mouth on mine, "I love you, too."

As he kisses my neck and my face, he says, "So confident . . . okay, so . . ."

My body aches for his kisses. He runs his fingers along the bottom of my bikini top and he pulls me up kissing my stomach. "I am leaving tomorrow after graduation . . ." kiss . . . "So I have this gift for you. We'll say bye again tomorrow," he says.

"Tomorrow?" I pull him off my stomach.

He's panting. "I told you I had to leave for Georgia tomorrow night." He slides me down so we are both standing.

Reality hits me.

"Sadie, this is incredible timing."

"What, how is this incredible timing?" My eyes become watery.

Jay pulls me into his chest. My favorite spot to be and says, "because we have it as a memory . . . and if it's a strong memory, we'll want it to happen again."

Jack honks.

"We have to pick up our grandfather from Camp Pendleton right now." He kisses my lips and says, "I love you."

"I love you, too." I say back letting him walk out the front door.

I think about what he says as I taste salt from the ocean on my lips. I want to string the pieces of salt, sand and follow him out the door but I let him go. I think about life in Mariposa Beach without Orange and Jay. I have to leave. In fact, I have to be somewhere that doesn't remind me of the beach or Jay. I don't know if I can do it without him.

Chapter 35

EVERYONE MAKES MISTAKES

The next morning, before the ceremony, the granite kitchen table is filled with croissants, fruit, coffee, bacon, hard-boiled eggs and freshly squeezed orange juice.

My mom has already started on prepping dinner. When I ask her to join us, she says she's already eaten. My dad opens up the back door to feel the morning breeze. I sit across from my parents' friend Jane who's in Los Angeles for a summer teacher conference and said she'd love to attend the graduation. She is a shorter, meek-looking lady who is a teacher at the old middle school I went to in Madison, Wisconsin.

"So . . . that was the last four years for me," I finish telling her all of the crap I went through as I steal one last bacon slice.

"It's over today...my dad has already put the house on the market," My dad pops another piece of bacon into his mouth.

"I bet those Wisconsinites don't have anything on me," I say.

Jane smiles as she wipes her mouth with a napkin. "Actually, Katie, the punk rock, wear all black kind of girl is doing good.

She's going to college somewhere in upstate New York . . ."

"Great," I say.

"And, Sarah? Is she running the youth ministry at church," I kid.

"That's the interesting part. Her dad was the pastor of our church and he left. Later, I found out that Sarah became addicted to heroin," she explains.

"Sarah's a junkie?" My dad pours himself another cup of black coffee.

"Hhhhmmm, she had this boyfriend who introduced her to it," Jane says, nodding, "It's so terrible."

"Wow!" My mom says.

"Dude," I reply. "Bet you're lucky you have me as a daughter? I'm only addicted to alcohol." I look at both of my parents standing up and doing a little wacky dance. My dad sets his coffee down and pokes my stomach with his fingers. I giggle like I used to when I was a little girl. Jane laughs. We have come really far.

"But seriously, is Sarah getting any help?" I add. Jane nods, "I think she's in rehab."

"Get ready," my mom says.

The water droplets and coconut smelling soap erase Jay's salty mango scent from yesterday. My mind races, thinking of the intensity between us and the silly text messages all night long. I turn the water to cold.

My thoughts shift to Sarah. Maybe it was okay that I left. Maybe it would have been worse for me in Wisconsin. Graduation day feels a bit like the last day before I moved to Mariposa Beach. I'm excited to be done. I'm nervous for something new. Where . . . still to be determined.

I dry off, blow dry my hair and put on some makeup. I opt for the turquoise camisole dress with short, brown heels. I take a picture and text it to Jay.

Jay: DAMN! How can I leave that?

Sadie: We're pressing the pause button on us, that's all!

Jay: There's a good quote that my grandpa told Jack and I last night, it's unknown but I thought it was perfect for us, "Before you settle down, heal yourself, find yourself, know yourself, correct yourself, see yourself, love yourself, be yourself and respect yourself."

Sadie: God willing.

Jay: God willing.

My dad offers to drive me to school, but I want to have one last nostalgic ride on the watermelon pink beach cruiser. My poor bike has seen its share of the seasons this year. I park it, lock it and slip onto the plastic chair on the football lawn. I pull my gown out of my backpack and throw my sunglasses on ready for the emotional ride I'm about to endure.

"I'm friggin' here," Orange says, wearing a long, orange cotton dress with a blue coral belt and hair blown out. "I have relatives staying with us for the graduation and the bathroom was occupied . . . busy morning . . ."

"You look beautiful," I say.

"How was the kiss?" She reaches for a hug.

"So good . . ." I slump in my chair.

She shakes her head. "Jack and I watched it..."

"Weird." I bring my sunglasses to my nose.

"Well, a part of it, then we thought this is weird," she says. I laugh.

She lowers her sunglasses to meet my gaze. "I'm so extremely happy for you and Jay."

"He leaves after graduation."

"I know," she squeezes me.

And, in that moment with my precious BFF, I know my adventure with Orange has to continue.

Principal Dow speaks into the microphone, "Testing . . ."

"Hey Orange," I say softly into her ear. "Have you ever heard of Battery Park?"

She squeals. "Are you serious?"

I shake my head yes. I think I just made my decision then and there.

She yells, "AWESOME!"

I pull her to sit back down. "Calm down."

"Hello families and friends! Welcome to the 2017 graduation. I'm Principal Dow . . ." The crowd roars.

"Before I start with this speech, I would like to introduce the first winner of the Show and Tell poem award. This is a poem about trying to fit and I have a special spot for this girl . . . Sadie MacPhearson."

Attention Sadie!

The girl with the learning disability?

I stand up from my seat, shaking with laughter, tears and total fear to stand up in front of the entire high school. Orange wails with encouragement. I walk up to the podium, looking at both groups: my fellow classmates, and the families and friends. My hands shake and they're clammy as they uncrumple the paper. I see my dad. He smiles proudly.

I adjust the microphone, "My Grams, Annie Styles once told me, you'll know the people that feed your soul because you'll feel good after spending time with them. Nonetheless, thank you for picking my poem. And, remember stick to who are in your soul. This is for all the young people out there. Be yourself. Don't change for anyone," My eyes meet olive greens and I'm lowering my anxiety level . . . 5,4,3,2,1.

Jay shouts, "GO SADIE!"

The crowd roars. My eyes soar across the two groups as I shake with laughter.

"And, now the poem . . ." I try to sound confident.

The Teenager with a Chameleon Soul:

I don't like all people,
But I'd give one moment to feel the
popularity,
With this confliction, I am red.
Some people don't like me,
But they would give anything to be me,
With this contrast, I am blue.
I love him,
But he's not the one,
With this incompatibility,
I am purple.
I love carbs,
But I love my skinny body,
With this differentiation,
I am orange.
I love money,
But it has ruined relationships,
With this inconsistency, I am green.
I love drinking,
But I never want an ounce of alcohol
again,
With this worry, I am black.
I hate schoolwork,
But I really want to be somebody,
With this diverge, I am pink.
I love my parents,
But I want irresponsible parents,
With this friction, I am silver.
I mostly hate myself right now,

But I will always love myself,
With this dissonance, I am gold.

I fold my paper and put it by my side.
The noise overtakes my ears.
People are standing and clapping.
Principal Dow hands me a paper to read. I read it,
"It's my pleasure to introduce Jay Felix, our valedictorian. This young gentleman has received straight
As in all subjects including AP classes. He missed 100
points on his SATs. He's president of ROTC. He's a
good mentor, a good friend. He got fourteen scholar-
ships to various schools in California. He also got into
Yale and Stanford. All of which he turned down to go
to the Army. To serve his country like his brother, father
and grandfather did . . . my one and only, Jay."

Chills appear and tears water.

The crowd roars. He walks up and he pulls my ear
to his mouth, "Good job, future Mrs. Felix."

My heart skips a few beats.

Jay walks up there, confidently behind the podium
clearing his throat. "Has it ever occurred to you that
Graduation day is a bit like looking into a kaleido-
scope? It's full of pictures jumbled together all of which
together make up your life. There are the images of your
growing years with your family and friends. Then there
are the pictures of your student activities, the classmates
you met and, finally, the wonderful excitement of today
your graduation day. The pictures of your future are very

vague because, of course, none of us knows what the future holds. I had many of these memories and none of them at the same time. My memories will be ROTC, AP classes but mostly sitting behind Building C, Java Coffee and SUP boarding . . ." He smiles at me. He continues on with his speech and then Principal Dow is back behind him and the podium.

"Today, though, as mature and newly qualified adults, we recognize that without that back-up we could not have succeeded. So today I know my fellow students would like to join me in saying how much we appreciate all those who have helped make this day possible."

I think about my parents, Orange, Jay and Grams.

"From now on you will be taking your talents and beliefs with you wherever you go. If you have learned anything it is that you have to be adaptable, ready to take chances and go different routes. These days we have to be ready to update our knowledge, add to our skills and be ready to cope with change . . ." Jay continues. "Whatever we do or wherever we go, we won't forget today."

I clap for him.

"And now," Principal Dow says, "For the names."

He goes through the list of around one hundred and fifty names. I hide behind my Kate Spade sunglasses, crying when it's my turn. My emotions are uncontrollable as Orange squeezes my hand.

"Presenting the graduating class!"

Our hats explode in the air. I almost can't believe I graduated high school.

I lean into Orange. "I'll never forget this."

She squeezes my hand back.

Minutes later, Jay, Orange and I are hugging and smiling as Orange's parents, her siblings, my parents, my aunt and uncle, Jay's grandpa, Mel, Josh and the kids, Aunt Concha and Jack stand around us in a huge circle, taking pictures from all angles.

"My cheeks hurt," I say.

"Over here, Uncle Jay," Joey yells. Mel and Josh are laughing at her.

"One for the old man, Jay." Jay's grandpa smiles.

"Orange, I want one with you and your siblings," Mama Chantel says.

Jay and I still have our arms around each other. He turns to look at me inches away.

"Really quick, I have something for you," I pull out my chameleon from my tote I showed him in my room a while back. "It's to replace the one Allison broke."

He takes it and smiles from ear to ear looking at me. "Thank you. It'll remind me of you."

"What?"

Oh my God, does he want to kiss me in front of all these people? He does. He wants to kiss me and I want to kiss him.

I push my lips on his. We kiss.

Our circle roars with laughter. I hear "finally" and "I knew it," and "Whew hew!"

"Now that's a good couple." Principal Dow walks by, grabbing our arms.

"Thanks for everything," I say in his ear. "And, I mean everything."

"You're going to do great things," he says back to me. "Just keep up the good work." He winks.

"Thanks, Principal Dow," I reach for a hug. He gives me a quick, tight one.

"Good luck, Jay." He shakes Jay's hand.

"Thank you."

He moves onto the next crowd.

"Does the kiss mean she'll be our aunt one day?" Joey asks.

"Maybe," we both say. We both look at her. Jay's looking at me with twinkly eyes.

"I meant what I said, but, now, I gotta go," he says, still holding me. "We're driving to LAX." I say bye to Josh, Jack, his grandpa and the girls. Concha has her arms folded off to the side. I don't think she liked the kiss but hopefully she will sign me off on my volunteer hours.

"Call me when you land in New York City. I have a good sponsor for you," Mel squeezes my arm, "Jay, we'll be waiting by the car."

"Okay Mel, text me your new address in Westlake Village," I yell after her.

Jay wraps his big teddy bear arms around my short, skinny body.

"I know. It's hard to say good-bye," I quickly say, "but, I love you."

"I love you, too." He kisses me once more, slipping a gold box in my hand. "Open this after 7:30 p.m. I'm going to call from a random number like 8:00. Now go be gold."

"Thank you." I say. Jay turns around and walks away. He turns back to look at me. I blow him a kiss. He blows one back at me. I catch it on my wrist. The same wrist he first kissed me on. I watch him walk away. My heart feels empty.

"Okay, I have to finish packing and after Gracie's school picnic, we're going down to LAX." Orange gives me a hug so we are out, too. "Text me later. We will figure out details."

"I love you more than I can express," I bawl.

This is too much.

I look at my parents and Jane. "I have to do a few things: get stuff out of my locker and then I have to swing by Gracie's school for the last of my volunteer hours. Can you get the barbecue started and I'll be home in like two hours?"

They nod profusely and scurry away with the crowd.

A few minutes later, I'm gathering my things by my locker. I see the Pop Crowd divided on the quad: Chase and Betsy and the minions off to one side and Allison, Tim and Nicolette on the other side. I think about what Mel said last week at the AA meeting.

Step eight: Making Amends. With the For Sale sign up on our house, we are gone within a month.

I walk over to the quad that I haven't set foot on for almost a year. Standing next to Chase and Betsy, I cup my hands around my mouth, "Guys," I call out trying to get all of them to come to me. Tim, Allison and Nicolette take a few steps towards me. "Um, step eight in the AA program is making amends. And, the fact that we're moving out of state, I realize I'm never going to see you guys again . . ."

I see a sea of bitchy smirks but I shrug my shoulders and continue.

"So . . . Nicolette . . . I'm sorry if I ever laughed at fat jokes directed towards you. You're beautiful the way you are," I cup her shoulder with my hand.

Her lips quiver and eyes water.

I point to Chase. "Chase, I'm sorry if I pressured you . . . be who you want to be."

He stands, arms folded. His face is solaced. His identity is still not out to the entire public.

"Betsy, Avery, Lace, Eden, Lucas, Carter . . . I'm sorry if I ever made fun of you or treated you less than you deserve . . ." I look at all of them, the people I used to call minions, standing there with eyes on me, "You're all amazing people."

They're all quiet. I see a few smiles as an encouragement to move on.

I stand in front of Al and make sure she's looking at me. "Al, I'm sorry I kissed your boyfriend." I stop and wait.

Her arms fold and her head bobs. WAIT FOR IT! No bitchy comment back.

"And, Tim." My gaze meets his arctic eyes hopefully for the last time. "I'm sorry it never worked out . . ."

His eyes are low and he speaks, "I'm sorry, too."

I turn my body around and let out a deep breath. I walk across the quad to Building B, the Self-Expression Word Wall. I set my things down and with a small, fine pointed brush I start to paint the words of my poem on the wall, letting the tears flow. I pick the color gold because that's what I want to be worth—gold. As I'm painting the words, I feel peoples' eyes on me. It's Allison, Nicolette, Tim and Chase. They start painting different colored chameleons around the poem. I smile at them as we work in silence. I hope to God some day a lost soul will find my words comforting. I sign it proudly Sadie MacPhearson and draw a small gold chameleon next to it. I slip the letters J, S and O in its tail to remind me who my real friends are.

Chapter 36

FRIDGE MANUALS, ENCOURAGEMENT AND GOLD

That afternoon, I go to see Gracie for the last time. I'm sad to leave her but I know she'll be in my life. I already told her Mama Chantel and her can come stay with Orange and I in the NYC.

"Hi." I sit next to her on the lawn on a flannel blanket. They are having an end of the year picnic and games.

"Hi." She put her hand on mine, which is unheard of for her level on the autism spectrum.

I slide my sunglasses down and close my eyes, hiding the tears. "Gracie, you never like to touch people. Do you like me today?"

"Miss Sadie, I love you all the days." She looks me in the eye for a second and then she's glaring at a boy who kicked his soccer ball towards us.

I put my hand over hers and smile. "I will miss you, my Gracie."

"Me too." Her toothy smile is plastered ear to ear. "I can do it now . . ."

"What's that?"

"Work with Miss Nancy?" I ask, perplexed. "Good." I clap.

She laughs. "Don't clap!"

I giggle.

"And, Miss Sadie, you should not do makeup. Miss Sadie, you can help more people like me and you." She claws at my arm, which may be a sign of affection.

I stop in my tracks taking the soft bullets as they hit me. She is right. Be still my heart. My journey can help others.

I give her my gift, which is all the refrigerator manuals I stole from the refrigerator department at Home Depot. I literally had to have each member of my family, Jay and Orange go in and steal them.

"Miss Sadie!" She pats my hand. "Oh man, I'm gonna be so good. Daddy won't know what hit him."

And, there you have it, a refrigerator lover at ease.

I stand, rubbing my fingers together outside of Concha's small office, waiting for my review. I feel transformed. Concha tends to other things on her walkie talkie while Officer Sob looks over my hours.

Mama Chantel walks by and hugs me. "Sadie, I cannot begin to express my love for you," she says.

Concha turns down her walkie talkie to listen from her office. "My daughter is absolutely a different person this year because of you. You . . ." she points at me, "have taught her more about herself than I could have in so many ways. She has learned a whole new style of reading comprehension, written expression and math because of you." My eyes fill with tears as I thank her.

"So the big apple with Ariana?" she says. "I'm so thrilled."

"Me too," I concur.

"I heard your parents are moving, too."

"They are putting the house on the market and making a few bids on some houses back east. I think they intend to follow me."

"Us parents always do," she smiles and leaves the office.

Concha and Officer Sob motion for me to come in her office, handing me my review and a letter of recommendation.

She has rated me excellent on all accounts and states: Sadie has become a little girl's hero. She has created an environment that has allowed for this girl to be safe, educated and cared for. Sadie has a really strong career ahead of her in special education.

I reach for a hug as I feel her resistance. "Concha, I'm trying to give you a hug and thank you."

Officer Sob grins.

"I know. I don't want to cry . . ." she says as she accepts my embrace. She pulls away. "I'll see you again someday."

I step back, "hope so."

"And, Sadie, you're going to be fine." She smiles.

My heart fills with hope and love. Hope that there's more to life than being mediocre. And, love . . . well love conquers all.

"Thank you," I say to them. I walk out, looking at the building I crashed into, get on my beach cruiser and ride to my house.

That evening, Jane leaves after dinner. My dad, mom and I are sitting in the Jacuzzi.

"I saw your review. Mom shared it with me," my dad says.

"Hard work pays off," my mom says.

"Yes, it does, Sadie. You have proven that to me." My dad's eyes water slightly. "If you want to go to Brooklyn."

More tears . . . I think I'm up to 1,001. I'm passing them to my mom and now my dad. We are filling up the Jacuzzi with more water. We stand in the middle of the hot tub embracing each other.

"Well." My mom breaks away from the hug. "Aren't we pathetic?"

We all go back to our respective sides of the Jacuzzi.

"I want you guys to come to New York with me," I verbally vomit, "I know you have the house to sell and dad's job, but...it would make the move easier."

Then I would need Jay to come to New York.

"We were hoping you'd say that. We plan to sell this house.

And put a down payment on a small condo in the Hamptons," my dad says, "I put in my retirement papers a year ago."

I start clapping. "Hey, don't look at me that way. I'm clapping because I'm impressed."

"Maybe open up a little SUP boarding company."

My mom giggles, grabbing her towel. "Good plan!" She pulls out a gold box hanging off the pocket of my jeans, "What's this?"

"It's from Jay . . ." He wanted me to wait until he was on the airplane. I look at the outdoor plastic clock hanging on the wall. It's 7:30 p.m.

I pull the box open. Inside is a thin gold necklace with a precious chameleon charm.

"That's solid gold." My dad brings it closer to his eyes.

I smile, opening up the box. "Here, it's a poem."

"Dad and I will leave you to it. Mel and Josh have some extra moving boxes they left out for us. We'll be back," my mom says.

I hold the necklace in my hand and walk to my room plopping on my bed. His writing is in all caps and intense.

Dear Sadie,
Cheesy Poem
By: Jay Felix
I know you love rock and roll
But here's a poem instead
You know who you are
So there's no need to fear
Cause girl you are the reason the sun shines
And why the waves crash
One day, I wouldn't mind if you're mine
But I have to earn some cash
Cause the first time I saw you
I knew it was something at first sight
Come on I know you feel it too
So one day it will take flight
You will always be my Hottie Blonde
And we will live our separate days
Until then I'll be Covert Bond
And take you on a proper date I promise . . .

I love you, Sades.
Jay Felix

"SOLID GOLD," I say. "Grams, I know you're here and you would be so proud of me." I blow a kiss to her picture.

I guess I had to go through all the colors of the rainbow in order to get the pot of gold.

Thank you Jesus for helping me through this year. Nothing could ruin this moment.

A text chimes through. My heart drops. I'm hoping it's Jay in Fort Benning, Georgia making his last call to me.

Tim: Hey! I need help.

I want to ignore. I do.

I throw the phone mumbling, "lost soul…"

There's a slight knock at my slider. I open it. I have to help him. There he stands with the darkness of the night. His black eyes zero in on Jay's poem and he says,

"SOLID GOLD! At least he has that part right. But, he's gone now and he won't be back," he pulls me in, "And, I'm sorry for everything."

Tribute

To my sweet husband, Gregory Galvez, for believing in me when I didn't believe in myself and encouraging me in the right direction when I steered off path daily. Greg, thank you for giving me time to write by watching the kids after long shifts at the fire station.

To my three children Joey, Jordyn and Kyle who gave me encouragement.

To my parents for investing, believing in me and babysitting my kids.

To my sister Kellie for listening to my story ideas.

To the rest of my family and friends, thank you for supporting me with positive talk.

To K.B. Jensen, my wonderful editor, for helping me dig down and find some good descriptive writing and meaning.

Beta Readers friend Darci Barrett and cousin Jennie Ontiveros for taking the time to read it. Also, to my beta readers: Lisa Brecker and Kristin Ketring.

And, to Gatekeepers Press for your efforts with the book cover illustration and help with publishing.

And, mostly, to God for shutting a door and opening this one.

About the Author

Cindy McElroy is a young adult novel writer. The *Teenager with a Chameleon Soul* is her first book. She's the wife of a firefighter, and the mother of three children and a Rhodesian Ridgeback, but she's also been a special education teacher, a camp counselor and police decoy. She does her best writing when she's beach camping, or her kids are asleep or at school. If she's not writing or with her family, she's reading, doing yoga, water skiing, snowboarding or SUP boarding near her home in Ventura County, California. Cindy loves to write humorous yet emotional novels about young adults experiencing young adult things.

The Teenager with a Chameleon Soul should appeal to readers who appreciate the wonderful characters with addictions and disabilities championed by Jay Asher, Colleen Hoover, Raquel J. Palacio, Robyn Schneider and Holly Goldberg Sloan.